T0284250
3
GOBLIN SLAYER
SIDE STORY: YEAR ONE

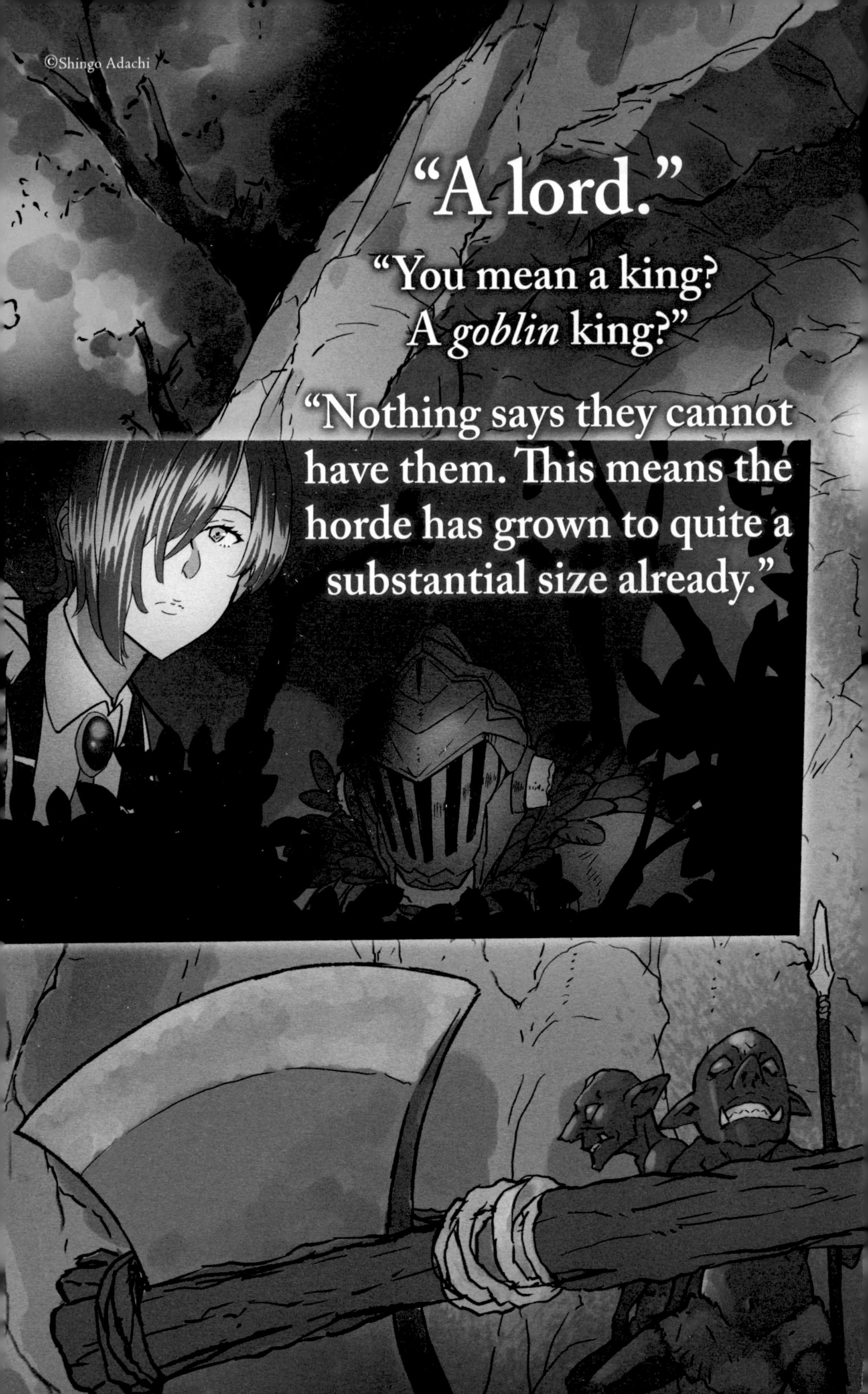
©Shingo Adachi
"A lord."
"You mean a king?
A *goblin* king?"
"Nothing says they cannot
have them. This means the
horde has grown to quite a
substantial size already."

"Yaaah...!"

©Shingo Adachi
Only much later would he learn that the weapon was an old standby called a spiked chain.

"C'mon, eat up. It'll go cold."
©Shingo Adachi

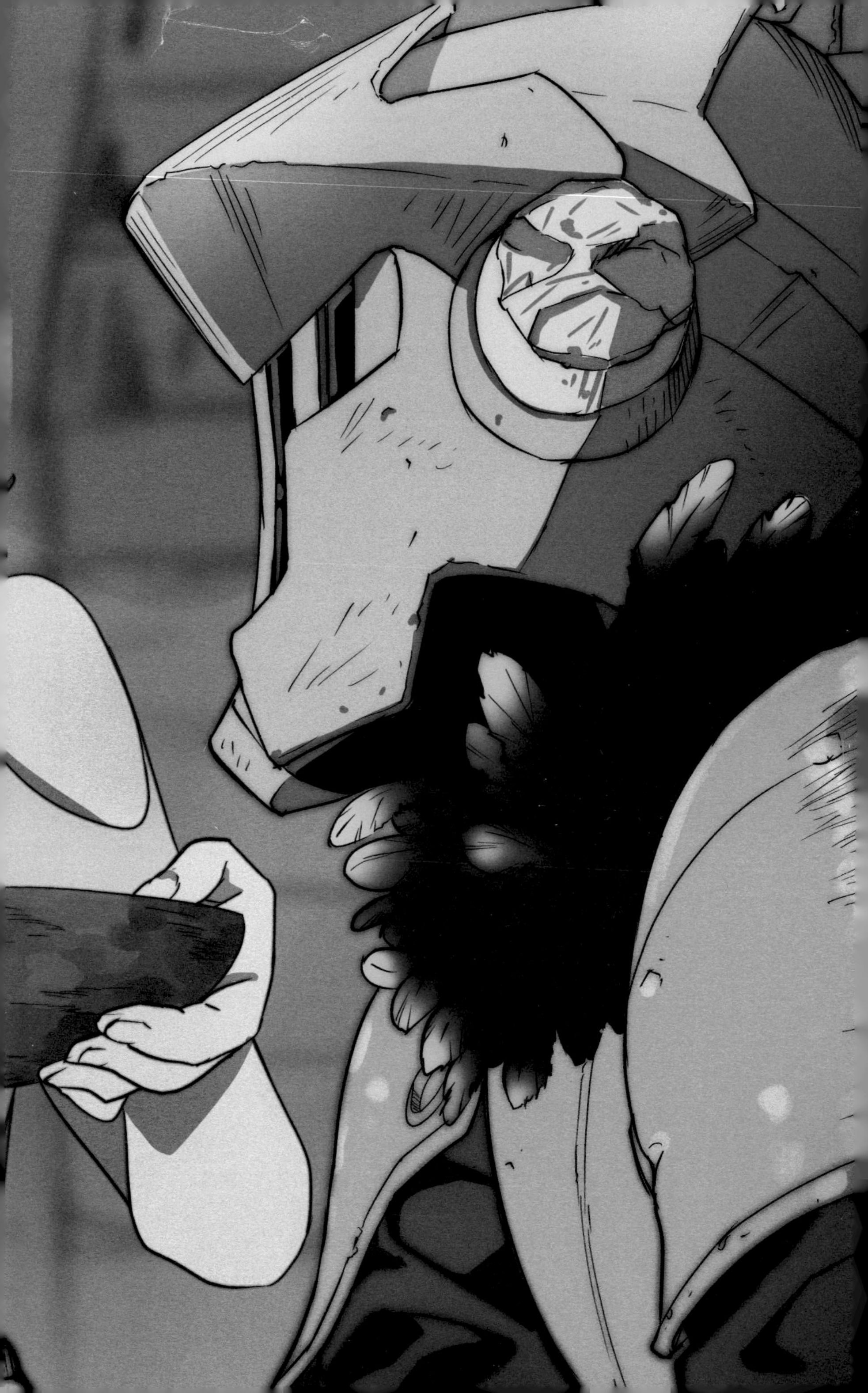

Contents

GOBLIN SLAYER

SIDE STORY: YEAR ONE

VOLUME 3

KUMO KAGYU

Illustration by
SHINGO ADACHI

NEW YORK

VOLUME 3

KUMO KAGYU

Translation by Kevin Steinbach ✻ Cover art by Shingo Adachi

Yen On
150 West 30th Street, 19th Floor
New York, NY 10001

Visit us at yenpress.com ✻ facebook.com/yenpress ✻ twitter.com/yenpress ✻ yenpress.tumblr.com ✻ instagram.com/yenpress

First Yen On Edition: April 2024
Edited by Yen On Editorial: Rachel Mimms
Designed by Yen Press Design: Wendy Chan

Yen On is an imprint of Yen Press, LLC.
The Yen On name and logo are trademarks of Yen Press, LLC.

The publisher is not responsible for websites (or their content) that are not owned by the publisher.

Library of Congress Cataloging-in-Publication Data
Names: Kagyū, Kumo, author. | Adachi, Shingo, illustrator. | Steinbach, Kevin, translator.
Title: Goblin Slayer side story year one / Kagyu Kumo ; illustration by Shingo Adachi ; translation by Kevin Steinbach.
Other titles: Goblin Slayer gaiden year one. English
Description: First Yen On edition. | New York : Yen On, 2018–
Identifiers: LCCN 2018027845 | ISBN 9781975302849 (v. 1 : pbk.) | ISBN 9781975357634 (v. 2 : pbk.) | ISBN 9781975306274 (v. 3 : pbk.)
Subjects: LCSH: Goblins—Fiction. | GSAFD: Fantasy fiction.
Classification: LCC PL872.5.A367 G5613 2018 | DDC 895.63/6—dc23
LC record available at https://lccn.loc.gov/2018027845

ISBNs: 978-1-9753-0627-4 (paperback)
978-1-9753-0628-1 (ebook)

10 9 8 7 6 5 4 3 2 1

LSC-C

Printed in the United States of America

GOBLIN SLAYER

SIDE STORY: YEAR ONE

VOLUME 3

PROLOGUE
A Morning's Events

She felt like she was shaking as she awoke. She gazed up at the familiar ceiling of her room and wondered where she was.

She wanted to go home. *This is home.* Her home. Had been for five years now. This was it.

The light that filtered through the window was the thin, blue stuff of early morning; her room was chilly, raising a few goose bumps on her skin. Despite shivering, she marshaled herself and crawled out of bed, then gave a great stretch.

"Mmmn…there!"

She changed into her day clothes and brushed her hair away from her collar. She gave another small stretch.

It's shorter than before, but…

She peered at her reflection in the water bucket, turning right, then left. She held a few strands of hair between her fingers. Hmm. *Hmmmm.*

Now—it had been worth the effort to take that step and more—she thought she could ask, if she wanted to. But really, that was all the change the days had wrought.

She simply had to go outside and do the same things she always did. Clean the barn, milk the cows. Go back to the house and make breakfast. Deliver the products to town, come home, and let the cows out.

It was a lot of work for just her and her uncle, and she saw with chagrin how much he must have labored to make things easy for her.

Maybe the fact that I feel bad about it shows that something has changed…at least a little?

She wasn't very confident. She felt like if she let herself slip the slightest bit, she would go back to the way she had been. So she reached into the bucket, almost like she was slapping her reflection in the face, and scooped up some water, splashing her own face with it. The cold was piercing; it almost made it hard to breathe.

Twice, then three times, she splashed herself—she should have done this before she got dressed, she thought. Another thing she'd learned now.

Walking as quietly as she could—not that there was anyone to disturb—she opened the door and went out.

It was true: There was no one there to hear her.

He wasn't there today.

That, too, was the way things were now.

He would go out, not come back for days at a time, and when he finally did return, it would be for only a day or so.

She was sure this wasn't a bad thing.

After all, change didn't always portend good.

The persistent routine meant the days would pass no matter what she did or didn't do. Therefore, it must be a good thing to work with her uncle each and every day, to make meals and wait for him.

She felt so sure, and yet…

Sometimes I can't help but wonder if this is really enough.

Why? She twisted herself into knots trying to answer, but she could never quite figure it out.

Was she just being selfish, wanting more and more?

That would certainly be no good.

Especially when she was about to clean up cow poop. She tied a cloth over her mouth as she entered the barn and took a cleaning tool in hand.

She shook her head and focused herself entirely on the task. That was the best thing she could do at this moment.

She breathed in and out: *hoo, fwoo*; she wiped her forehead with a sleeve. She was going to be soaked with sweat before the morning was even over!

She was so focused that it took her a moment to notice the cows lowing and shifting.

"Huh…? What's wrong?"

Cows were timid animals, insensitive—but for all that, they were also strong. If one carelessly let them get overexcited, there could be trouble. And anyway, keeping the cows in a good mood was crucial to the farm's income.

More than anything else, though, she was simply disturbed somehow by the idea of leaving the animals afraid. So she patted the cows—gently, to avoid startling them—and spoke to them in a soothing tone. It was important to show them that it was just her who had come in and that she didn't mean to scare them.

Uncle said cows are good at remembering people…

Did they remember her? She wasn't very confident.

Then there it was again. The ground shook; she went "Eep!" and stumbled. Quick as she could, she curled into a ball and covered her head. She was almost convinced the barn was going to come down on top of her. The force from below was so hard that it threw her into the air. She squeezed her eyes shut.

I'm scared!

Yes—it was frightening. Of course. And if it was this scary to her, how much more so for the animals?

She wondered what her uncle was doing, whether he was safe. He wasn't nearby. He was doing some other farmwork.

In spite of the shaking, she managed to get an unsteady grip on the pen and pulled herself to her feet. She reached out to one of the cows. At that moment, she wanted to feel the warmth of someone, something alive.

"All right… It's all right… It's okay," she repeated as she felt the cow's modest warmth on her hand.

Thankfully, the shaking soon—much sooner than it felt to her, no doubt—subsided. Much to her relief, the endangered building did not, in fact, fall down.

She gave the cow another pat, then worked her way outside.

The house is still in one piece. Let's see—what else?

"Oh...!"

The stone wall *he* had built had several new gaps. That seemed to be the extent of the damage, though.

Or is it?

She hoped it was no worse than that.

Even if she went on doing what she always did, things like this could happen, and each time they did, she grew uneasy. Afraid.

Maybe I need to do something else. Something more.

That nebulous fear always seemed to be just by her shoulder, ready to creep into her mind.

"Hulloooo! Young lady! You all right over there?" called a gravelly voice.

Her head whipped up—at some point, she'd started looking at the ground—and she saw someone on the road that went past the farm. Not very much of him, though: Only his head peeked over the fence. It was a bearded dwarf.

She hurried over, and soon she could see the rest of him. He wore battered armor, and on his back, he carried...a hand gaff? Was that what it was called?

For all that, she saw no rank tag at his chest. She stopped a short distance away from him.

"Yes?" she asked, her voice going up a register. She swallowed hard. "Can we... Can I help you?"

"I should think. I'd like to buy provisions, but it's a lot of trouble trying to get back to town on these legs!" The dwarf warrior flipped the girl a golden coin. She somehow managed to catch it, although only just. It wasn't her fault. It had been a bad throw on the dwarf's part. Not at all like *him*. "Think you could give me whatever that's worth to yeh? Anything that'll keep."

"Er, y-yes, sir!" the girl said, trying her best to sound suitably polite. "Give me a moment!" Then she spun around and ran off.

In the distance, just at the limits of her vision, she saw her uncle come running. He must have been worried by the earthquake.

"Oh..."

Suddenly, he disappeared. It was because of the way her

©Shingo Adachi

no-longer-quite-short hair clung to her forehead, cheeks, and neck on account of the sweat.

She kept running, brushing the hair out of her eyes so she could see again. Bangs were all well and good, but it was annoying—this hair around her face. She slowed down, searching her pocket for rope or a tie or something. She found one and tied her hair back, her fingers stumbling over the unfamiliar act.

The earthquake, the cows' behavior, her hair, the fact that *he* wasn't there: each of them a slight difference from the usual unchanging days.

Slight. Nothing more.

CHAPTER 1

An Examination, Suddenly One Morning

It was a perfect morning.

The sky was mostly clear and blue, the sunlight piercing through the handful of drifting white clouds, naturally inviting her to open her eyes.

Judging by the temple bell, whose ringing could be heard all around the capital, she was one or two chimes earlier than usual. That was a plus.

The egg she'd fried up for her lunch didn't burn, didn't even stick to the pan—it came out beautifully. Well! If this wasn't her greatest triumph in the last two weeks. Truly a good feeling.

She hummed as she made herself ready for the day, combing her hair, putting on just a bit of makeup. Today, it looked perfect on her first try. It was the same way she always put on her makeup, but sometimes it seemed so awful. Very nice.

The cool morning breeze was refreshing. The walk to work was quieter than usual, maybe because she was just a bit early.

Sometimes the dice, whether by Fate or by Chance, were good.

There was a lacuna in the footsteps. A moment when the tide of people ebbed away. She had the space between the tall buildings to herself.

For a second, she thought maybe it was a holiday, but even then, it would have been unusual to find *no one* at her workplace. She opened the door, nodding and offering a friendly "good morning" as she came in. Everyone greeted her back.

On the wall, she placed a placard with her name on it to indicate she was present, and her back straightened almost by itself.

Maybe it was because she had woken up so promptly this morning. This feeling of alertness was pleasant.

The preparations for the day had gone off without a hitch. It was truly the perfect morning.

"I've found a mistake in one of the Adventurers Guild's examinations!"

"I see. You wish to submit a comment regarding the Guild's management. Please go ahead."

...Until that moment.

Before her stood a young man who had charged up to the reception desk—not an adventurer. His face—indeed, his whole person—was wreathed in the aura of a man on a mission. He had nice clothes, although not quite nice enough to be nobility. Instead, he was what one might call a dilettante. Judging by his age, one still finding his way in the world.

"It's about this adventurer here—one given Gold rank in the past."

"Yes, sir."

"I've looked into the records for myself, and I can tell you for a fact: There is *no way* he could have had the adventure described. He says he defeated a monster like that? All alone? Flatly impossible!"

"Yes, sir."

"The vast underground ruins of an ancient kingdom? Ruins no one else had even heard about? And the monster destroyed said ruins in a single night? It's got to be bunk!"

"Yes, sir."

"Now, look—I'm not saying it's *all* fabrications, but who knows how much of it is really true? And this thing about the dark sect this adventurer supposedly battled!"

"Yes, sir."

"The report claims they'd taken over the entire area and were massacring people. That has to be an exaggeration."

"Yes, sir."

"Why would you kill *so many people* for no reason? You wouldn't! It's just common sense."

"Yes, sir."

"What we have here is a clear case of the victor spinning the story to their own advantage."

"Yes, sir."

"Um, excuse me? I'd like to file a quest..."

"Yes, sir."

This last statement came from an elderly man standing behind the peevish-looking youth at whom the receptionist was currently nodding. He looked like he might have been a manservant from some merchant concern. His hands, clearly those of a laborer, were clasped firmly in front of him, and he wore a grim expression.

"I am sorry, but you will need to go over to window number five," the receptionist said.

"O' course, yes, o' course. And window number five would be...?"

"Over there, sir," she replied, gesturing with her right hand and bowing to him as he left. Then she took a breath. "Pardon the interruption. You were saying?"

"I was *saying* that I want you to correct this oversight immediately!"

"Unfortunately, I am not in a position to make such judgments on my own. Furthermore, we would need more than your conjecture..."

"Conjecture? Just look at the records! Everything I've said is blindingly obvious!"

"Unfortunately, I am not in a position to make such judgments on my own." With a quill, she took down the dilettante's complaint, word for word, on a piece of paper. He looked awfully smug about that, but he seemed to have misunderstood what she was doing. Whether to write down what he said, whether to submit his allegations to her superiors—those were not her decisions to make. She wasn't doing any of this to make him feel better. This was her job, and she was simply doing it.

"Hey! *Hey!* What's a guy gotta do to get a freakin' quest around here?!" demanded an irate adventurer who burst up from the back of the line.

She answered him—because that, too, was her job. It was the sort of moment when the world seemed to breathe in and forget to breathe out. The adventurer completely ignored the dilettante, who looked decidedly less than pleased.

"I am very sorry, but perhaps you could ask at another window, sir," the receptionist said.

"I ain't got the time for another window! I'm trying to get a damn quest goin' here!"

"My sincere apologies, sir."

"Um, uh, excuse me," said another new voice. "Are there any quests that a Porcelain warrior could maybe do by themselves?" She couldn't identify the owner of the voice, who was concealed by the line. They were probably over by the bulletin board—were they even speaking to her?

"Excuse meeee! Uh, um, are there any quests that a Porcelain warrior could—?"

"I am very sorry. Everything we have is posted on the board." Except, of course, for items they hadn't yet finished the paperwork for, but she shouldn't have had to explain that.

She looked forward once more and coughed discreetly so as not to appear rude. "Pardon the interruption. You were say—?"

"Have you listened to a word I've said?!"

"A'right, I've had a-freakin'-nough'a this! I've taken dumps that moved faster than you!" said the irate adventurer. He grabbed the dilettante (still glaring at the woman) by the shoulder from behind.

The receptionist was used to not letting her expression slip, but who could blame her if she let out a sigh at this moment? Under the counter, hidden by her sleeve, she clenched her fist. A safety measure. She felt something dull and cold, heard it scrape.

She didn't care about herself, but if they were going to endanger her colleagues—

"Pardon me, but I must ask you not to inconvenience our other visitors," she said.

I have to avoid trouble here. It is my job.

She tried to sound soothing, but in her experience, that rarely got very far. So she wasn't surprised when the adventurer got in the dilettante's face, shouting, "Time's up, buddy!"

"Who do you think you are? You dare threaten violence against my person?! Hmph! *Adventurers!*"

"Look, pal, I'm here to do a job, and I'm not lettin' *you* stop me!"

"Excuse meeee! I looked, but I don't see anything!"

The dilettantc hit right back at the adventurer, at least metaphorically. This was never going to end. And the other voice was back, too.

"I am very sorry. Everything we have is posted on the board," she repeated. Even as she spoke, she was asking herself: Should she intervene? Should she call someone? An instant's hesitation.

"Listen, ya dogs." The decision was made for her by a short, forceful, and decisive interruption. "You wanna yap, do it in an alley! Where I don't have to hear ya."

A man stood there, looking like he had been carved from stone or like a bundle of muscles given human shape. The dilettante and the Obsidian adventurer looked ready to respond, but this paragon of strength was not about to hear any objections. He picked them both up by the neck like two large logs and dragged them away, shoving past the rookie adventurer, who stood dumbfounded by the bulletin board. Then he summarily flung them out the door as if he was tossing out the trash.

"Problem solved," he said, turning back and grinning like a wild animal.

She doubted the man had done what he did for anyone's particular benefit. He'd simply seen two noisy dogs nipping at each other and kicked them out. For himself and no one else—that was the truth of it.

"All right, I'm after a job," the man said, thrusting a paper at her. "This one."

"Yes, sir. *Ahem...*"

His behavior hadn't exactly been civilized, but then again, civilization could lack a certain imagination. It sometimes stopped people from thinking about what might happen if they upset others. To that extent, in the matter of decorum, perhaps this "barbarian" was the most civilized person here.

I cannot spend my time on such frivolous thoughts unless I am also able to focus on my work and process quests at the same time.

As long as she dealt calmly and fairly with him, he would take the job and go on the adventure. That was how the world was supposed to work.

"Well, look who's Miss Popular," said a colleague in the next seat, spying a break in the conversation.

"Is that what you call this?" The receptionist sighed. "People simply feel special when someone pays attention to them. It does not have to be me."

"Sure, I guess." Her colleague chuckled, then slid a bundle of parchment toward her.

The woman scowled at it for a second, but she didn't make waves. She allowed herself one more sigh, then directed her eyes at the papers and her words at the other woman. "What's this?"

"Promotion exams. They just want us to look them over."

Ah. She scanned the documents—they were all records relating to adventurers from the frontier. The recommendations for promotion had come this far. Assuming there were no egregious irregularities, there was no reason for them to be rejected at this stage. They could trust the judgment of the Guild employees who worked directly with these adventurers and could speak to their achievements and community relations.

Her face softened into a smile before she knew it. This was part of her job, yes. But getting to read more adventure logs than anyone was one of the perks.

Some of the reports were about monsters slain, others about dungeons delved or treasure discovered. Not many urban adventures, though.

"All right, good." She read one of the reports, then moved on to the next one. She read that one, then went to the next. She took down the tag by her window before she forgot, to show it was closed. There would always be a few people who tried to speak to her despite the fact that she was obviously doing paperwork, but it was always best to preempt those you could.

She read another report and flipped the page. The party that had made its name dealing with the Rock Eater was continuing to build its reputation. *We seem to have a particularly rich crop of new adventurers on the western frontier this year.*

That was a good thing. Through battle, one could grow and be more ready for the next fight. That was what made an adventurer.

It was the same with the next candidate she read about. His first quest had been in a goblin nest. Excellent.

The next quest had involved slaying goblins. And the one after that, hunting goblins. After that, destroying goblins. Then eliminating goblins…

"…Hrm?"

She stopped flipping the pages. She went back through these particular reports from the beginning, sure she must have misread something.

No problems at all.

There were no problems, and that was the problem. Goblins, goblins, goblins, goblins, goblins.

Who was this person's handler? She recognized the signature—a young woman who had been a junior colleague of hers. She'd finished her training several years ago.

The woman frowned without quite meaning to. It wasn't because something had come up that would require her to go all the way from the capital of the western frontier to investigate.

It was because she suddenly realized she'd forgotten her lunch at home.

And anyway, she liked rainy days better than clear ones.

§

"GOROOGBB!!"

"GOOBBG! GGBG!!"

The goblins cackled their awful cackles. They laughed and pointed at one of their number who was stumbling around with an iron pot on his head, holding the lid in one hand and a broken stick in the other. He swiped at the grass growing in the bog with broad, comical strokes.

The goblins stood in front of a lonely hut, apparently killing time.

He watched them, all but buried in the mud. The sun was still new in the sky, the world still cold, and the thick, sticking mud wasn't enough to keep him warm.

Peat. I believe that's what this is called.

The quest was downright formulaic: Goblins had appeared near a village. The villagers had chased them off, but they were worried. Would someone please get rid of them?

When he investigated, he found that the goblins lived in a bog near the village, in an abandoned work shed. The village headman explained that it had been used for digging peat. Peat didn't sell for much, and it wasn't an excellent fuel. It only mattered when a harvest went bad or when there wasn't enough firewood.

I would consider setting fire to the entire place.

He could cut down the grass around the area, then strike a flint and smoke the creatures out or burn them. The idea had merit, and he would have to try it sometime. But perhaps not here. Not now. He didn't know how enthusiastically the peat would burn, and he wasn't sure how the wind would behave. It was unlikely to kill all the goblins anyway—and he couldn't have that.

The goblin continued to clown around in his silly costume, putting on his ridiculous show. *He* didn't know how many of them were inside the shed. This was probably the night watch outside. Not particularly effective guards. But he wasn't surprised. There was no such thing as a goblin who took his work seriously.

As for himself, he thought he took his own work quite seriously—but whether that was true was for others to decide.

Which leaves the question: Are there any shamans or hobs in there?

It was too early to say—or was it? He didn't yet have enough experience to know.

"GOORGGB!"

"GBBRG! GOOBGGGRB!"

The goblin in the ridiculous getup seemed to be doing a cruel little parody of *him*. The goblins pointed and laughed their ugly laughs. He could hear their voices clearly.

Voices… Yes, voices. Not just animalistic cries.

Goblins had a culture of humor. He had learned that already. They knew how to joke, if only on the most vulgar level.

Maybe they had seen him arriving at the village. *I got there just about at dawn.* That had been a mistake. But it was in the past now. If he survived this, there would be a next time. If he died, it would end here.

No point wallowing in regret.

The goblin nest inspired revulsion in him, matched only by his disgust that they had seen him. If he had to try to put those feelings into more precise words, he would describe them as an intention to kill. It wasn't rage or hatred but something calmer: the knowledge that he would murder them. It wasn't cold; in fact, it practically boiled, and yet at the same time, it felt almost utterly indifferent.

He would not make the same mistake he had as he cowered under the floorboards of his house. He would do what he had to do. That was all.

The goblins never imagined such feelings were directed at them. As far as they were concerned, they were the center of the Four-Cornered World. They knew people mocked and belittled them—or maybe they didn't even realize that. At the very least, they believed they were smarter, quicker, sharper, and all around better than anybody else.

It would never cross their minds that someone would have tracked their footprints, followed them, and discovered their hideout.

No, wait…

Was it possible he had it backward? That *he* was the one with delusions of grandeur that would leave him open to attack? He was suddenly put in mind of an ancient saying he had heard—something about those who stared into the abyss.

Was it his master who had taught him those words? Or his older sister? Or could it have been the wizard he'd worked with or even a scroll somewhere?

This is ridiculous.

The words of others always had value—except at this exact moment. It was he who stared, and they who were stared at. It was clear who held the upper hand here.

It was the goblins who would be killed—and Goblin Slayer who would kill them.

"——!!"

With a great exhalation, he moved, shedding peat as he ran low to the ground, almost crawling.

There were four of them: the costumed one, a club, a sword, and a sword. He could do this.

The sneaking left him in not quite the right stance to open with a surprise throwing attack. It was too late now. So be it.

Needs some practice.

"GBBO?! GOOROGB!!"

"GROORGB!!"

The goblins noticed him. But what did he care? He didn't even slow down as he pulled the sword from his hip and all but slammed into the costumed monster.

"GOROGB?!"

"That's o—"

No. Not yet. He hadn't killed the creature. He wasn't yet used to tearing out goblin hearts.

"GRGBB?! GOBBBGGRB?!?!"

The goblin, flung backward by the blow, tossed and kicked in the mud, clutching his chest. The young man reversed his grip on his sword, intending to throw it at his next target, but then instead, he brought it down on the fallen goblin's neck.

"GGB?!"

"That's one!"

"GOOGB!!"

"GOB! GGOGB!"

Of course, the other goblins weren't going to just sit on their little green hands as he hunched over the corpse of their nestmate. They came at him with their club, with their swords, and he met each with his round shield, deflecting them away.

There was a dull *thump*. He felt a tingle race through his left arm, the one with the shield on it, and without thinking, he thrust out his right to help push him to his feet.

"——……Hff!"

He inhaled, tried to steady his breathing. He had to be careful not to trip in the mud. Keep the door of the shed in sight. He didn't want to be taken by surprise.

There were so many things to think about. His ability to process them was at its limit. But there remained always and only one thing he had to do.

"That's two!"

This time there was no hesitation; he thrust out with his sword, stabbing straight through the goblin in front of him. The monster was making to swing its club at him, and its own momentum proved fatal.

The goblin, a sword suddenly growing from its neck, foamed blood and died without a sound, toppling toward Goblin Slayer. He let go of the sword, casting aside weapon and corpse at the same time. He grabbed the club instead.

"GOORGB!!"

"…!"

But he was still too slow. A rusty sword made an opportunistic stab from behind him, and he only just managed to stop it with the club.

"GGBBBB…!"

"…Yaaah…!"

In a simple contest of strength, he obviously held the upper hand, but his positioning was far from ideal. Was it because he was holding his weapon one-handed?

There was a *crunch* as the blade bit into the wood, and his wrist was twisted backward… No.

"GOROGB?!"

"Three…!"

The sword simply cracked in half, as easily as a dry branch breaking. The goblin stopped and stared at his wasted weapon—and Goblin Slayer ruthlessly crushed his skull in.

Then he kicked the body back, almost carelessly, as liquefied brains seeped from the heavily dented head. Mud and blood jumped into the air as the corpse landed.

"One more…!"

He turned his head—right, left—to allow himself to scan the entire bog with the confined strip of vision allowed to him by his visor. The sunlight drifting down from the gray sky formed a bright line that seemed out of place here.

Then his vision was wiped out with something the color of ash.

"Hrn?!"

"GOOROGBB!!"

It took him an instant to realize the goblin had thrown mud at his face. He wiped it away and looked, the last of the goop still dripping from his helmet, to find that the final goblin was already fleeing.

So he had a runner. The monster had thrown down its weapon, abandoned the corpses of its comrades, and was making for the far side of the bog.

That's fine.

He swept his club through the air and flung it; it whistled as it went. It spun twice, then three times, then impacted the goblin's skull.

"GOROGB?!"

A muffled cry and a dull *thump*, and a second later, a *splash* as the body hit the water.

Goblin Slayer let out a breath.

He strode to where the goblin had fallen, paying no heed to delicacy as he swept across the undergrowth that covered the bog. The goblin lay there, its head caved in, twitching its limbs like a half-crushed bug.

I'm lucky that wasn't a dagger or something.

One thought he did not have was to be grateful that the goblin was a coward. There was nothing about this creature to which he owed any gratitude.

He took the knife at his hip and stabbed it through the goblin's throat with a motion as merciless as it was emotionless, and that was the end of the monster.

"Four."

He stood up and looked around, his helmet turning, focusing on the shed. No sign of movement.

Hmm.

He braced his foot against the goblin's corpse and retrieved his club, which trailed threads of sticky goo. He didn't quite feel right without some sort of blade at the ready, but a blunt instrument like this was versatile. Most of all, he could use it as roughly or carelessly as he liked, and it wouldn't matter.

He strode boldly back the way he had come, then kicked down the door of the goblins' shed. It fell in with a crash, and he jumped inside to find…

"…Nothing."

Inside, the shed was in complete disarray, but he didn't see any goblins anywhere. Once he was sure, he nodded to himself. He assumed the shovels lying around—presumably once used for digging peat—hadn't appealed to the goblins.

He really had been lucky. The shovels could have been much more threatening than some rusty swords and a club. They were certainly sturdier.

Just to be completely sure, he looked beneath the bed (stripped of its sheets) and even under the floorboards.

Still no goblins. It really had been just the four.

"Wanderers?"

He assumed that their nest had been destroyed and they had wound up here somehow. It was a common story—downright formulaic.

Even the villagers could have killed these four goblins. They hadn't needed to hire him.

No.

He *tsk*'ed angrily and shook his head. He pictured the girl and the farm owner nervously facing down goblins, pitchforks in hand. The thought showed him immediately that he had no right to say who needed to hire him.

"…"

Just to be sure:

He went outside, then carried the bodies of the goblins he had slain into the shed, one by one. Then he went around the area, turning over the mud to hide the blood—he borrowed one of the shovels, which was perfect for the task.

Once he was sure he had erased every trace of the combat, he hid in the weeds once more, concealing himself in the mud.

It was too soon to assume this was over. He didn't intend to leave any survivors.

"……"

He would keep watch here until nightfall. Whatever might happen.

"——…?"

Abruptly, he felt a great shaking. At first, his body quivered, and he thought perhaps it was an attack of dizziness, but he soon realized that was not the case.

The ground itself was quaking.

For two or maybe three seconds, he rocked as if he was on a ship—and then, as suddenly as it had started, it stopped.

A flock of whip-poor-wills rose screeching from the bog. He glanced at them, dark shapes against an ashen sky, then returned his focus to the shed.

There was nothing that warranted his attention more than goblins.

§

"Hmm…? Did you feel shaking just now?"

"I sort of feel like my head's spinning…" As the young warrior watched, long silver hair—which looked longer for being in disarray—quivered like a squirrel's tail.

The lobby of the Adventurers Guild was neither a play area nor a classroom—and yet somehow there they were, practicing their letters in chalk on small chalkboards that seem to be the personal possessions of the dogheaded man they called Teacher.

I wonder if this is what it's like being an apprentice in the God of Knowledge's temple, the young warrior found himself thinking. Not that he'd ever set foot in such a place.

He glanced at their teacher, but the dog-man was smiling placidly behind his spectacles, evidently enjoying the sight of them. He didn't seem inclined to rebuke them for chatting while they were working on these simplest of characters. Not that he looked the least ready to let them get away without working, either.

"Look, I know we're the ones who asked for some lessons…," the silver-haired girl said with a sigh. She squeezed the chalkboard between her legs and her chest and looked positively miserable. "But I can't help thinking, I'm not really cut out for this. I'm more the, you know, work-on-focusing-my-qi type."

"What's qi?" the young warrior asked, mystified. "Is it like magical power?"

"I don't really know!" the young woman proclaimed. "But then I don't really get magic, either."

"I guess that makes two of us…"

"Qi is, like… You breathe in, and you hold it at the bottom of your abdomen, then let it flow allll around your body!"

"Huuuppp," Young Warrior said, trying it for himself.

"Huuuppp! That's exactly right!" the girl responded, full of confidence. She spread her hands. "And then your hands start to sparkle, just like the sun!"

"They…sparkle?" That sounded weird to him, but it was probably true. "I guess they could…"

"Then you slam a fist straight into your opponent's solar plexus, then follow it up with a shot to the jaw, then an elbow, and finally you finish them off with a flying kick!"

This had suddenly gotten very physical.

The young woman was flailing her arms and legs—*this and this and one'a these!*—but whatever else was going on, the technique was obviously designed to be very deadly.

Young Warrior was noticing more how he couldn't look away from those arms and legs, which the girl swung with such abandon.

While he sat and squirmed, their teacher laughed, baring his fangs. "The body is a heavier thing than one expects. If you could really be lifted off the ground with a single punch, why, it would be strong enough to take off your opponent's head."

"Hrm! I'm telling the truth, you know. My master was able to do it," the silver-haired girl insisted.

"Now, now, I'm not saying you're lying."

Hrmmm… The girl pursed her lips and puffed out her cheeks, and the canid wizard waved a padded paw at her.

"It would be to my discredit as a scholar if I were to pronounce on the truth or falsity of things I do not know."

"Hee-hee-hee!" The girl's expression did an abrupt shift and became a bright smile instead; she scratched one flushing cheek shyly. It might have sounded rude to call her *simple* but perhaps *innocent.* Direct. It was one of her strengths.

Young Warrior was gazing at the girl's ever-changing expression

when Teacher rapped his chalkboard. "Now, chat is all well and good but not when it stops the hands. Keep writing!"

"Yes, sir!" The silver-haired martial artist, apparently mollified by the brief diversion, obediently sat back down and resumed her work.

Well, Young Warrior could hardly slack off, then, could he? Although not totally refocused, he adjusted his grip on his chalkboard and went back to work, scribbling letter after letter from their teacher's examples. Whatever else, he'd never remember how to read or write these things without plenty of repetition.

"As with anything, some people are more adept readers than others. Think of it like any other kind of training—the more you put into it, the more you'll get out of it." The dog-man wizard certainly *sounded* like a teacher. He slid his spectacles up the bridge of his nose. "And as to your actual question: Yes, I believe it did shake."

"There's been a lot of those quakes lately, haven't there?" Young Warrior hadn't exactly been counting, but they came quite frequently, or so it seemed to him. "You think it's the beginning of the end of the world?" That was about the only explanation a bumpkin like him could come up with for why the ground might be shaking.

Their teacher crossed his arms, his silver-furred tail bobbing up and down as he looked thoughtfully at the ceiling. "There could be many reasons. A fish or perhaps a dragon stirring in the depths of the earth. Some disturbance in the veins leading to the fiery mountain. Or perhaps the gods have upended the board."

"None of those sound like especially good news."

"I'm told that the wizards of old used red magic to cause rifts in the ground that would swallow their enemies as easily as we might throw a pebble into a well." He sounded calm, although his story was as unsettling as the silver-haired girl's. But the wizard snorted. "These quakes might have multiple causes—and the fact is, no one has yet investigated what they might be."

Even their teacher couldn't say with confidence what was going on—and what could someone like Young Warrior say to that but "oh"? His teacher was far smarter than him; he was a man of much more learning. No point in Young Warrior debating with him.

"I agree wholeheartedly. It's nothing to panic over, my dear mortal."

This new voice was the very picture—well, the very sound—of pride, of haughty arrogance.

"These things are not yet for the likes of you to know. It's as simple as that," the voice continued.

"Huh! You're a real good bullshitter, I'll give you that!" said yet another new voice.

"You only think of it that way because you are yet inexperienced."

Young Warrior looked over. Their elf cleric was looking very smug, while their dwarf scout was looking very peeved. Young Warrior looked up at the mountain of cargo they had with them, although he was careful not to let himself stop writing. "Thanks. Appreciate you taking care of the shopping," he said.

"Hey, it's all good. Real pain trying to keep this clown from blowing all our money on worthless crap, though," the dwarf replied.

"To whom do you think you are speaking, Dwarf?!"

"You! I'm speaking to you!" The young dwarf woman, small but muscular, elbowed the elf in the side, earning a voiceless squirm from him.

Young Warrior told them both to tone it down, ignoring the elf's exclamation of "Do you see the way she treats me?!"

You know, I'm almost starting to get used to this, he thought. The group was much more boisterous than his last party—which was to say, his first party. Perhaps a little *too* boisterous, if you weren't feeling so generous. But all the gabbing, laughing, and chiding that took place while they went about their business was something he never got tired of.

"All right, let's treat ourselves to a little change of pace. Try calculating how much we spent on the shopping and how much we have left," their teacher said.

"Ugh."

"Eep!"

I wonder about this…

As their teacher happily tossed problem after problem at them, Young Warrior couldn't help but feel a twinge of regret: Academic study had never been his strong suit and indeed remained a weakness.

"Well, lively bunch we've got here," came a rumbling voice, accompanied by thumping footsteps and a shadow that loomed over them. Young Warrior looked up to discover a towering heavy warrior.

Young Warrior felt distinctly embarrassed but decided to simply give him the truth. "We're, uh, studying," he said. He owed this heavy warrior a lot and didn't want to waste his time quibbling. Still, though, Young Warrior wasn't self-possessed enough to walk his own path unawares. "Just thought it might be good to learn how to read and write and stuff."

"I gotcha." Heavy Warrior nodded, but his brow creased. "Maybe my group should be doing some of that."

"You've got those kids, right?"

"Yeah. A couple of real young ones and one a little older. Although," he added with a sigh, "*someone* learned to read, write, and do sums, and it hasn't improved his character any."

Young Warrior thought he had an idea who Heavy Warrior was alluding to. He gave a wan smile.

"You know him?" asked the silver-haired girl in surprise.

Young Warrior nodded. "Pretty much. We were on the Rock Eater together."

"Oh!" she exclaimed. "Olgoi-Khorkhoi!" She sounded deeply impressed, although Young Warrior wasn't sure about what.

Doing his studying in the lobby like this meant people who knew him were going to spot him sometimes. He'd tried to tell Teacher that he'd prefer to avoid being noticed, but the canid had replied that "Study is nothing to be ashamed of!"

I mean, he's not wrong about that.

"...Hmm?" Young Warrior was just about to turn his attention back to his chalkboard when he noticed something. "Hey, you okay? You don't look so good."

"Aw, I'm fine. Just been busy." Heavy Warrior's rugged face relaxed ever so slightly, and he shook his head to show that it was nothing. "Turns out it ain't so easy being party leader."

"I hear you."

I sympathize. But still...

Young Warrior had certainly never thought of himself as his

current party's leader. If anyone was the glue that held them together, he thought, it was the wizard who was their teacher. As for who was likely to give the orders on the front line in battle, though—well, that was probably him. Neither of those roles was superior or inferior to the other; they were equal participants in the party.

Man, it is tough. He couldn't shake the thought. He had to manage their remaining magic spells, the state of their equipment, the relative positions of both allies and enemies and what each of them was going to do, plus lots more. The simple fact that Teacher helped them with the shopping and planning their strategies—

It takes a lot of the load off my shoulders.

And so it did.

The classic adventuring party was six people—like the group that had delved into the Dungeon of the Dead—or at least not more than ten. Any larger than that and it would be impossible for a single person to hold it all in their head.

Cases like the Rock Eater, where many parties gathered to work together, were rare. *That noble, he was something else,* Young Warrior thought. When he considered how hard that upper-ranked adventurer must have worked to coordinate them all together, he could only feel gratitude.

After some thought, Young Warrior found he didn't have any practical advice he could offer Heavy Warrior. Instead he said simply, "All right, well, take it easy, okay? You don't have to handle everything for all your party members by yourself."

"Hoh," said Elf Cleric, sounding as amused as he did dismissive. "You almost make it sound as if the rest of us were a burden upon you!"

"Hey, don't drag *me* into this!" snapped the dwarf, glaring at him. "*You're* a burden. He wasn't talking about me!"

"You only say that because dwarves are such shallow thinkers. Or should I say *short*-sighted?"

"Well, believe me, we get pretty pissed when people look *down* on us!"

"Come, now," Teacher said to the two jabbering party members. He wanted them to quit arguing and take out the fruits of their shopping trip, as well as the change. It was nice for things to be lively, but when they got too exciting, that could be a problem.

The martial artist probably didn't see that thought on Young Warrior's face, but nonetheless, her silver hair rippled slightly. "Um… Am I a burden?" she squeaked, looking at him for any sign of reassurance.

Young Warrior was too embarrassed to say *Hey, of course not* or even *If you're a burden, so am I*, so instead he replied teasingly, "I dunno. Could be!"

"Nooo!" the martial artist wailed, and Young Warrior laughed. She smacked him with her fists in frustration, which was both adorable and threatening.

Young Warrior quickly apologized, admitting his defeat, and then he looked at Heavy Warrior. "Hey, share and share alike, right? Burdens, too."

"Share and share alike, huh? Still, the buck stops with me…" Heavy Warrior still looked troubled. Just like every party had its own story, every party leader had their own worries.

At that moment, Heavy Warrior looked away and his eyes narrowed, suspicious. The adventurers dotting the lobby likewise frowned or *tsk*'ed.

"Whazzat?" Young Warrior followed their collective gaze and saw a black carriage pulling up outside the Guild.

The only sound as the carriage stopped was the clack of the horse's hooves. "Huh!" said the young dwarf woman. "Pretty good work for human construction."

Ironically, the human warrior with her couldn't have told her what was so good about it to save his life. He just hoped this meant there would be a quest from a noble, not that the hope was worth much.

"Doubt it'd be something we could ever handle," Heavy Warrior mumbled.

"You said it," Young Warrior agreed.

The Guild door opened.

A woman appeared in it like a gust of wind. She had short-cropped black hair—no, it only looked like that on the left side. Her head moved, and Young Warrior could see that the hair on the right was much longer, covering that side of her face. Her expression was cool and composed but not tense; she looked decidedly in control.

Even with all the adventurers watching her, she seemed confident that she belonged here. She was slim, clad in the uniform of an Adventurers Guild employee, albeit one that was uncommonly well fitted. It appeared to be a man's uniform, but the gentle curves of her figure showed immediately that she was no man.

Ah, so this was what they meant when they spoke of a beautiful woman in men's clothing…

He'd heard the expression in a street play he'd seen. He'd never met such a woman up close before. Young Warrior was hardly an expert, obviously. *Still, I guess she's not necessarily disguising herself as a man.*

He had the sense that this wasn't about gender—she'd simply picked what looked good on her, what looked *right.* That seemed clear from the way her walk emphasized her long, lovely legs. She headed directly to the reception desk, spoke briefly with the clerk, and soon disappeared behind the curtain into the back.

"Wow… She's beautiful," breathed the silver-haired girl beside him, her hands on her cheeks.

"Uh-huh," Young Warrior replied almost indifferently, although he had studied the woman's every move until she was out of sight. It wasn't as if he'd been immediately smitten—and if the girl thought he had been…well, that wasn't a problem. Still, somehow he wanted to avoid giving her that impression.

"It seems we were right about the noble stature of our visitor," the canid teacher said, squinting behind his glasses. "Most guilds are associations of craftspeople or merchants, but the Adventurers Guild is a special case. Effectively a government organ."

"Oh yeah," Young Warrior said. "The employees are public servants, right?"

"You need a sense of responsibility to move the country, and you need to be smart to move the country—and you can't get smart without money." In short, you had to be nobility.

Back in his village, they'd said nobles were only good for being beat up by adventurers or maybe having their daughters kidnapped by dragons…

But no. When he thought about it, Young Warrior remembered that it had been the local governor who had kept the village's waterwheel running, its windmill turning, and its bread ovens in good repair. He didn't know how many villages the governor was responsible for, but he guessed it was more than just one or two. He could barely puzzle out how much his party had spent doing the shopping—he couldn't imagine juggling the numbers a governor must be faced with.

"You know the stories: So the princess was saved, they got married, and they lived happily ever after. The end. Never gonna happen to an adventurer," he said.

"Probably not," Heavy Warrior replied with a laugh. Although Young Warrior wasn't sure what the laugh meant.

"All right, come on." *Whoops!* Teacher was clapping his padded paws together noiselessly, and Young Warrior promptly went back to scribbling. "If you want to be able to take quests from nobles like her, you'll need to study. Also, I need my change from the shopping."

"Heh-heh. Now is not yet the time to speak of such th—"

"Yes it is! Right now!" the dwarf girl snapped, and soon they were arguing again.

Heavy Warrior waved at the lively crew, then started away, his footsteps as heavy as his armor. Young Warrior had tried to warn him to watch out—for his health, for anything that might happen on an adventure—but he wasn't sure he'd gotten through to him.

Beside him, the silver-haired girl was staring so hard at her chalkboard that it looked like she might bore a hole through it as she confronted the rows of chalked letters.

It's not easy being a party leader, and it can't be a lot easier being the guild that has to look after all the parties. It was a subject that concerned him but not one in which he ever expected to be involved.

Soon, all thoughts of the newly arrived Guild woman were gone, submerged in a sea of letters.

§

"Here you are! Thank you for your hard work!"

"Sure. Thank *you*!"

She bowed energetically as the adventurer walked away, clutching their reward. She waved and smiled. Beside her, another employee, a cleric of the Supreme God with the symbol of the sword and scales at her chest, sighed.

I wish all the rookie adventurers were so easy to work with.

"All right, my dear receptionist, I'm on my way. But don't worry—I'll be back!"

"Certainly. Please be careful. And do your best!"

Her friend beside her was encouraging a spear-wielding adventurer. She smiled that pasted-on smile as the spearman set off. He jogged a few steps, then turned and waved before he ran again to catch up with his companion, a witch who looked for all the world like she was pouting.

Hmm?

Her friend was still smiling as she checked some paperwork, made a note on one she was holding, and then moved on to the next thing. There were no more adventurers waiting in line for her; she shouldn't need her business smile at that moment. Which could only mean…

"You look like you're having fun."

"Do I?" her friend replied with a show of surprise. Did she really not realize this, or was it feigned?

Her friend had been so apt to seem a little panicked until just recently—in fact, sometimes she still did—yet now she seemed almost relaxed. Who wouldn't want to find out what was going on?

"I think I'll just take a look at that!"

"Oh! Stop! You can't just grab a person's papers!" her friend exclaimed, but it didn't save her from the ambush. The young lady was no spy or scout, but if the target didn't have her armor on, it was just this simple. She reached out and snatched the document from her friend's hand. When she looked at it, she discovered a perfectly ordinary, unremarkable quest submission: a request for someone to slay some goblins.

Ahhh, I get it…

"Come on—give it back!"

The young lady was so busy smirking to herself that her friend was able to snatch the paper back. She'd already learned what she wanted to know, though. Judging by the village named in the request and its distance from their town—

"Betting today's the day, huh?"

"I don't know what you're talking about." Her friend puffed out her cheeks—she was still such a little girl. Then again so was the young lady, who was quite enjoying the sight. She still didn't know if her friend was aware of how she was behaving or not, which took some of the fun out of needling her about it. It was all too easy to assume every little thing betrayed love or romance…

But life's not that simple. Makes things a bit more complicated.

Well, so it went. It was easier to entertain yourself if you assumed everything was simple.

Everyone was always, "Oh, I'm evil, but I've got a sad-sack backstory!"

Oh! Might be okay if he's totally hot, though, she thought, remembering some of the stage plays she'd seen. How often was there a beautiful young man with a terrible secret or a tragic young lady in love with the enemy?

It was nice not to know how it ended.

"I'm sorry, but do you think you could stop treating people as if they are here for your personal entertainment?"

"Oops. Was it that obvious?" She laughed out loud, provoking a "hrm!" and an angry glare from her friend. The young lady shook a finger at her friend. "The Supreme God teaches that we are all but shadows walking upon life's stage, merely actors in the great drama of—"

"The Supreme God never said that."

"Ha-ha! Saw through me again, huh?"

"Believe me, I'm *going* to saw through you at this rate…"

"That guy passed his promotion exam, didn't he?"

"The first part," her friend said, nodding. "I haven't heard about the rest yet."

"Maybe they'll want an interview or something."

It didn't happen all the time, but once in a while, a local guild had to ask the capital for guidance on what to do in a particular case—but that didn't mean they would get a timely answer. If getting a message safely down the road and back was as easy as that, adventurers would have substantially less work to do. There were endless seeds of adventure in the world. A world where nothing happened might be nice in theory, but a world full of drama was more fun.

At least as long as I'm not the one getting eaten by the monsters!

Well, that was how it always went. The Supreme God could wink at that, right?

She and her friend were both untested children still. There was no one in this world who was perfect anyway. She just needed to be careful that she didn't go from "she's got a few flaws, but she's a good person" to "she's a good person, but she's got a few flaws."

That's the kind of thing that ends friendships!

"Maybe exclusively doing goblin hunts is going to make things harder, you think?" her friend asked.

"Yeah, it might be tricky for them to pass him on that alone," she said. "It's a tough call, though."

"Yeah, true," her friend said with another nod. It was worth a lot to get plenty of experience doing one particular thing—but for some reason, it could be hard to get people to recognize the value in that. Wasn't that what it meant to be an adventurer? To grow by gathering experience? If this guy just kept hunting goblins, then one day he might be as strong as any hero…or not. More likely not.

"Anyway, not our call. All we can do is the job in front of us."

"Good point," her friend said. "Yeah, I'd better do everything I can before lunch."

"Sure. And the harder you work, the quicker the time passes, and the sooner he comes home—right?"

"I told you, that's not what this is about!"

She savored her friend's annoyance but knew she had to get back to work herself. She had lots to do, after all. She was one of the functionaries whose work kept the country running. If she slacked off, the nation would grind to a halt.

She had to keep her quill working, her mind turning, and be ready to greet any visitors with a smile. Then be ready to do it all over again. That would keep the world turning.

Whereupon…

"Ooh? Whazzat?"

Perhaps it was a gift of her devout faith that allowed her to react when the door opened quite unexpectedly. Namely, that she was able to squelch the "Ugh!" that almost popped out of her mouth and instead straighten up and look very much the proper bureaucrat.

Her friend obviously lacked faith, because she continued to study her paperwork, failing to notice the approaching footsteps. A second later, she exhaled, evidently satisfied with her work, and looked up.

"Phew! All done," she said.

"Oh? That's good to know."

"Yes, thank you! I mean… Yes?" When she finally spotted the person standing in front of her, a composed expression on their face, she made a sound that defied description and went stiff.

A woman with black hair and wearing an Adventurers Guild uniform stood at the counter. There was no mistaking her—or forgetting her.

While her friend sat frozen, the young lady behind the desk could only fervently (though silently) recite a charm of lightning deflection and wait with a smile for the storm to pass.

"It has been a while. If you are done with your work, then perhaps I could have a few minutes of your time?"

"Er, uh, ah—ah, y-y-yes, of course…"

"Very good!" The black-haired employee smiled, her eyes narrowing, and she nodded, satisfied. Then her sharp gaze turned toward the other receptionist. "We will borrow one of the rooms in back, then, if you do not mind?"

The friend gave the receptionist a pleading look. It provoked a flood of emotion in the latter woman, all of which she poured into her response: an enthusiastic nod and a "please, make yourself at home!"

The Supreme God said two drowning people couldn't cling to one piece of driftwood. *When you're talking emergency evacuation, there's a colder logic than friendship at work.* She didn't even hear her friend's anguished cry. How could she since it was silent?

"Off we go, then. I would not wish to take too much time on this, even if it is work related," the newcomer said.

"Yes, ma'am," the young lady's friend said, hanging her head like a condemned woman.

The young lady watched them go, then let out a breath.

As I lift this blade, I pray for life eternal for this offender. I cast this in the name of God.

"You have no sin."

Having recited this prayer for her friend, there was nothing for it but to get back to work. If she was caught slacking when the two of them reemerged, it would be her turn next.

I definitely don't want to have to face her *inspection.*

Still, she could take a pretty good guess as to why her friend had been dragged back there.

Oh, look. Here comes the reason now.

The Guild door opened with a *creak*, and a nose-prickling odor drifted to her on the breeze. Adventurers hanging out in the building looked in his direction with frowns and glares, and the young lady wasn't too thrilled herself.

It was the adventurer with the very strange outfit.

A metal helmet with broken horns. Grimy leather armor. A small, round shield strapped to one arm and a club hanging from his hand. Also, notably, mud *everywhere.* The adventurer made a beeline for the bulletin board and tore off several quests. Someone who saw him muttered, "He's gonna try to keep all the goblin hunts to himself again."

He should let some of the other rookies—no, he'd been here for months now; he was no longer one of the rookies—have a crack at them.

The adventurer paid absolutely no heed to the venomous murmur. He already had a nickname, one he earned early and that stuck fast. People used it partly in jest, with a bit of a smirk on their faces.

They called him Goblin Slayer.

§

"And when people started calling him that, did you not think something might be…wrong?"

"N-no, ma'am…"

The woman had given Guild Girl a stern rebuke (it had been so long, it almost brought back fond memories), and she had shrunk down like a squirrel squeezing into its nest.

They were behind a curtain in one of the back rooms at the Adventurers Guild, not one of the reception rooms upstairs. Unlike a squirrel, Guild Girl had no nest to run to; she could only sit on the sofa, trying to make herself smaller and smaller.

The female employee—a senior colleague of hers—sat across from her, looking impeccable. "This is technically a formal inspection, so I would appreciate your full and complete answers." The examiner smiled.

Guild Girl swallowed hard, then finally managed something close enough to "no, ma'am, I didn't" for the woman's satisfaction.

Guild Girl had asked if the woman wanted tea but had been gently rebuffed with a "that will not be necessary," so the tabletop was empty. Unfortunately, that left Guild Girl with no way to insert a beat to the conversation. Instead, she looked uneasily at her colleague and said, "Um, *ahem*. You arrived quite s-suddenly. May I take it this has to do with his…his promotion exam?"

"Are you suggesting there might be another reason?"

"N-no!" Guild Girl shook her head furiously under her colleague's probing gaze. She felt like she was being watched by a snake. No need to poke the nest and provoke another snake to appear. "It's just… This was so abrupt…"

"If I had given you prior notice of my arrival, it would defeat the purpose of a surprise inspection."

Guild Girl sighed. Then she looked at the floor.

"I see you have not changed since the capital," the examiner said. Her words pierced deep into Guild Girl's heart. They were as good as saying that she hadn't grown at all.

We can't all be like you, she thought—but of course couldn't say that.

The woman conducting this examination was a senior colleague of Guild Girl's from the time when she had been training in the capital. Though Guild Girl had studied diligently, she had still been the sheltered daughter of a noble family, and there had been much to learn.

To be quite honest, during her training, there had been moments when she had seriously considered giving up her aspiration to be a Guild employee. It wasn't that the work was inhumanly brutal, and she wasn't placed under unreasonable demands. What she had to do and why were all perfectly fine. And her colleague who had been in charge of her instruction had been just, upright, dedicated, impeccable…

…and just so cool.

That was what Guild Girl had thought of her. If she hadn't had this woman to give her on-the-job training, she believed she would be a less competent Guild employee today. Or maybe she would have quit and gone home, where she would pass the days imagining that if she had only worked harder, things might have gone differently.

It wasn't that she was convinced that she was fully formed now. Just look at her. She knew her colleague didn't say mean things just to be vindictive. She wasn't the type to simply humiliate others.

Which is exactly why it hurts so much…

Guild Girl almost found it hard to breathe, but she forced herself to appear unmoved as she summoned everything she had and replied, "I…I understand your point, but there are no notable issues with his character or his results…!"

"That is correct. Nor am I suggesting there are."

"You… What?" Guild Girl blinked. Her colleague's wan smile never slipped.

"I have never met him, so I am not in a position to pass judgment on those subjects," the examiner began. Then she looked at a sheaf of adventure logs in her hands. "I have no particular objection to your evaluation of him, notwithstanding its admixture of personal opinion."

The words seemed to come so easily to her. Guild Girl blinked again but not for the same reason she had a moment ago. Then it had been incomprehension. Now it was disbelief.

Does this mean they do *accept him?*

Was that so? Could that be? Maybe what her colleague had said to her a moment ago wasn't intended to be humiliating at all. Was it possible her opinion had improved ever so slightly? Her opinion of Guild Girl?

"However," the examiner continued, dashing all Guild Girl's inflated hopes with her utterly unchanged tone, "I do take issue with his technique."

"I'm sorry, you mean…?"

"Goblin hunting is all this man has done, is it not?"

And always solo at that.

As much as Guild Girl hated to admit it, the answer to her colleague's question was clear. She found she couldn't manage even a squeak.

An adventurer's rank was not decided based on combat prowess alone. Of course not. There were such things as scouts. Clerics. Sages and scholars and cartographers and porters.

No one could earn a good reputation just by being burly and fighty. Nobody wanted someone so fixated on killing monsters that they ignored the people and things that needed protecting. (Granted, the vast majority of such people would claim that what they were doing was right, and the people and things that suffered as a consequence were collateral damage, necessary sacrifices.)

What about in this case, however? Goblin slaying was a legitimate pursuit. No one would question that. In fact, the Guild had a high regard for people who took such quests that involved helping others.

Nor did this young man do anything that made him difficult for Guild employees to deal with, even if there was an "admixture" of her personal feelings in that evaluation. At least when he was asked a question, he answered properly.

Well, then.

"My questions are these: Can he do anything but hunt goblins? And can he work with a party?"

"Yes, ma'am..."

That was what it came down to. Rank wasn't based on combat prowess alone, but that factor couldn't be overlooked, either. Goblins were not the only threat in the Four-Cornered World. If someone couldn't go toe to toe with creatures more powerful than goblins, was it really appropriate to promote them? Especially if that person was so focused on goblins that they neglected to ever work with other adventurers...

"W-well, but consider this," Guild Girl said, desperately trying to organize a counterargument in her head. "Not long ago, he engaged in exploration while acting as a wizard's bodyguard...!"

"But they were not a party, correct?"

"No, ma'am…"

Pretty pathetic as counterattacks went. And promptly rebuffed.

"But, um, he was able to rescue a captured woman. He also protected a village from attack single-handedly…"

Pathetic or not—he had other accomplishments. Things like this. Yes, they all involved goblins, but he had still achieved laudable things. Quests that others sneered at because of the paltry rewards, he took without comment. Was all that not helping others?

He had even helped her. He'd helped the people of the village. He'd helped that wizard. He simply, silently went about his business. It would be wrong not to give that proper credit, wouldn't it?

He was diligent. He always did what he was supposed to do. There was nothing to complain about or criticize.

Each time Guild Girl repeated these arguments to herself, she became more convinced.

A thought flitted through her mind: Why was she so bent on defending him? When they talked about a quest, they were simply conversing, no more and no less. Just day after day of that kind of conversation—and yet…

"As I said, I am not questioning the validity of those achievements."

Her thought, her doubt had been inspired by the slightest softening of the examiner's expression. Or—well, her smile never changed nor her gaze. It just somehow seemed the faintest bit gentler, or so Guild Girl imagined.

"P-pardon me. I didn't mean to get ahead of myself…" Guild Girl realized she had been talking too fast; she blushed and looked down. Her cheeks were hot. If there had been tea, she might have taken a sip to collect herself, but she didn't have that choice.

"Please do not misunderstand me," the examiner said. Her voice was the same as ever—although perhaps the edge was just a shade gentler than before. "I have not come here to deny his promotion nor to undermine your opinion of him."

"You wish to redo the promotion interview, then?"

"Not exactly. Perhaps we could call it…hmm… A test."

So that was it. Guild Girl was flooded with relief. This was about determining whether promotion was appropriate. Removing all cause for doubt. A test, just to be sure.

Any of the regional guilds could, in principle, be subject to this, and to Guild Girl's chagrin, this time the capital's eye had fallen upon hers. A surprise inspection, sudden and without warning.

She actually found it somewhat reassuring to know that was what was going on. It meant they weren't questioning her judgment in the promotion interview.

At least...I don't think so...

They were interrupted by a hesitant voice.

"*Ahem*, um..."

Guild Girl turned toward the door to see the friend who had so ruthlessly abandoned her, standing there with a smile. Guild Girl gave her a withering look (although she tried not to let the examiner notice), but the other woman let it roll right off her back.

Guild Girl couldn't believe her.

"If I may say so, I think I know who you're talking about," the friend announced. "And he just walked in."

I can't believe her!

"Well," said the examiner. "What fortuitous timing."

Guild Girl's mind was already working. She had to speak before the examiner could say anything further. "Ma'am? If he's just returned from an adventure, perhaps we could give him a few minutes?"

"Mm. A perfectly reasonable suggestion." The examiner nodded.

Excellent. Under the table, Guild Girl clenched her fist in triumph. This way, at the very least, she could get him to wash off the mud and goblin blood before he met the examiner.

"In that case, maybe he can go home—," Guild Girl began, but then she stopped. *That's not right, is it?* He was staying at a farm, as she recalled. It was where that red-haired girl lived, wasn't it? She wondered what the relationship was between the two of them. "Er, back to where he's staying and clean up. Could you tell him to come here tomorrow, please? Would that be all right?"

"Tomorrow," her friend said with a nod. "Is that all?"

"Let him know it's about his promotion," Guild Girl replied. That would ensure that he'd come looking his best.

"Sure thing," her friend said, sounding like she was distinctly enjoying this. She turned and left, her hair bobbing behind her like a cat's tail. Guild Girl privately swore she would get the other girl back later. She had to, in order to preserve their friendship! She wouldn't want to leave any festering resentment.

"Well, then. Since it seems we have some time, perhaps I could sample that tea of yours," said the examiner, looking quite relaxed. "I worked so hard to teach you how to make it. I want to see if you still remember."

"Yes, ma'am!"

Ah, the perfect chance: She could offer her colleague the snacks from her friend's secret stash…

§

They had told him to come back, so he had to do exactly that.

For Goblin Slayer, it was simple. His decision was made without hesitation.

He felt no compunction as he returned the quests he'd torn off the board to the reception desk.

Finish a goblin hunt, come back to the Guild, make his report, take a new quest, go back to the farm, get ready, and leave. An extra day had simply been inserted into that cycle. That was all.

He strode boldly into the Guild, spoke to the clerk, and strode boldly out again. He paused only to nod at a young warrior, someone he recognized, who gave him a friendly greeting. Then he opened the door and went out. It was much brighter than he had expected.

The sunlight poured down, piercing, and the sky seemed so terribly clear and blue. A second later, he began to catch the sounds of people milling around, along with their footsteps and voices.

"Hrm…" He grunted softly, gave the people the barest glance, and then went on his way.

Only very recently had he begun to feel that he was what one might call used to walking this road. Had he ever walked it at this particular time of day?

Surely I have. Surely.

It hadn't left much of an impression. Perhaps simply because it hadn't needed to. The thought made him realize how rarely he had consciously looked at the faraway sky or the shimmering moons.

"You're no goddamn poet, that's for sure!" he remembered his master saying, the old rhea jabbing him in the head as he spoke. He knew the man was right. Although he understood words, what was beyond the words never made much sense to him. He never had and probably never would stop and pause specifically to take in the sky or the moon or the stars or the town. If he had time for that, it would be better spent looking for any goblins who might be lurking about. At least for him, it would.

He turned his helmet right, then left, scanning the shadows and never slowing his pace. Looking for enemies without slowing down was an important form of training for him.

That barrel, the roadside, in the shadow of the trunk there, behind those trees, in the ditch leading to the sewers—all places a goblin might hide.

By now, he didn't have to think about what would happen should a goblin suddenly appear in the town. It was no different as he left the gate, walking the byway toward the farm until he arrived.

"Hrm…"

There, just look. The stone wall—which, humble as it was, he had built himself—was broken in places.

Did a goblin do that?

That was his first thought. He squatted down, inspecting the scene. The wall could break if a storm came through—in fact, simply being out here in the elements could do it. But there had been no rain for several days. So first he looked around for any footprints.

I don't see footprints.

That was a good start, then. Few if any goblins were smart enough to cover their tracks. Few was not none, however, so one always had to be careful.

He picked up a tumbled stone and put it back in place, making sure it fit neatly and was held fast. He would have to reinforce the wall at some point and extend it, make it longer. To begin working on those things only once he had everything ready, however, would be much too late.

"...Hoh," someone said. "You're back."

"I am," he replied. He stopped and looked up to find the farm owner standing over him. He had a handkerchief tucked at his neck and looked mildly tired. He was between jobs probably. Trying to think of something to say, Goblin Slayer ended up just crouching there silently. He could thank the man for his hard work, but that would make them sound like strangers, wouldn't it?

"I'm glad you're so enthusiastic, but the least you could do is poke your head in and say hello when you get back," the farm owner said.

"Yes, sir. I'm sorry." Because he had nothing else to say, he simply nodded at what was said to him. After all, he knew the man was right. As such, what followed that was not an excuse nor did he intend it to be. "It's simply that if I don't do something when I notice it, I soon forget."

The farm owner sighed, but all he said was, "I see." He took his handkerchief and wiped at the sweat on his brow, then looked up at the piercing sunlight and slowly shook his head. "About time for lunch. Come on in. Whatever you have to do, better to do it after you've had a bite to eat."

"Understood, sir."

That was excellent advice. Goblin Slayer placed one more stone back on the wall, then nodded. The farm owner set off toward the main house, a farm implement in hand, and Goblin Slayer silently followed him.

The smoke drifting from the house's chimney was a clear sign that lunch would soon be on the table. He couldn't see her from here, but he knew that young woman must be working in the kitchen. It seemed certain.

What was she making? He didn't know. He thought it would be good if it was stew. He wasn't sure why, though. Just somehow that was what he felt like having.

§

"Welcome home!" she called. She was finally getting used to giving that greeting.

Her uncle lived a highly regulated life; she even knew what time she would hear his footsteps each day. If they were even a little late, she knew what it meant—and anyway, *his* footsteps were very distinctive.

Stride, stride. Stride, stride. Unhesitating, wild. Maybe it was because of his boots. An adventurer's boots.

She wasn't sure where adventurers went on their business—she could think of places like old ruins and caverns and dungeons but not much more. Even the way she pictured those places probably didn't have much to do with reality. So when she heard those long boots smacking against the ground, she knew right away. She would call out and scuttle from the kitchen to the dining area—that is, to the door.

"Thanks. We just got here," her uncle said.

There was a pause, and then a few beats later, she heard a simple "I'm here."

Her uncle spared him a dubious look—only now, as they stood next to each other, did she realize he was shorter than her uncle. She suspected that under that helmet, he was at a loss for what to say, and she giggled.

He always does go quiet when he wasn't sure what to do.

He'd been that way ever since they were small—or so she thought. The memories were hazy and getting hazier.

That was why the bundle of long hair tied behind her head felt so unfamiliar. It wasn't as long as a pony's tail yet, but it was tied up high and tugged at her scalp.

I wonder if a braid might have been easier, she thought, but that was simply too childish. If she was going to do anything with her hair, she should grow it out, like the receptionist at the Guild did. That looked more grown-up…

"…"

"I'll have lunch ready in a second!" Cow Girl said and then pattered back into the kitchen. The way her hair bounced against her neck was oddly ticklish, and she couldn't help smiling a little.

Behind her, she heard a chair creak as something heavy settled into it. Her uncle couldn't do that—it had to be *him*, with his armor and his helmet.

It must be awfully heavy.

It was also, not to put too fine a point on it, a bit filthy.

Then again, even she and her uncle got dirty working in the fields and with the animals. Maybe it was a bit late to worry about cleanliness.

"Thanks for your patience!" she said, bringing out the meal: stew. With some trial and error, she'd developed a pretty tasty recipe, she thought.

There he was at the table, in his armor, as she'd suspected. Her uncle sat beside him, looking less than pleased about it. "You could at least take that stuff off at mealtimes," he said.

"No," came the clear response. "I need it."

"...Do you now?" Even Cow Girl could hear the note of resignation in her uncle's voice.

He spends all his time hunting goblins.

He woke up in the mornings, went out on a goblin hunt, then came home only to go out on another one. That cycle seemed to describe his entire life, with breaks only to fix the farm's fence or the stone wall.

Oh, but then again...

These days he also helped her, if she asked him to. That was a step forward, and so she didn't find the current situation as trying as her uncle did.

One step at a time. Much better than standing paralyzed with indecision.

"C'mon, eat up. It'll go cold," she urged.

"Er, yes. Of course. Let's eat," said her uncle, and after a brief prayer to the Earth Mother, that was exactly what they did. *He* remained silent, but he didn't start eating in the middle of the prayer or anything, so that was fine.

Plus, he is *eating.*

When she considered how things had been even just a little while ago, it was clear that he was making slow but steady progress—or anyway, she thought so.

Cow Girl stole a glance at him. He was silently sticking the spoon between the slats of his visor and eating. She found she couldn't keep her hand from wandering to her hair, playing with the ponytail.

Was he looking at her? Under that helmet, she couldn't tell what he was looking at.

"Tomorrow," he said.

"Hrk?!" Distracted by her thoughts, she was caught so off guard by his utterance that she nearly dropped her spoon.

"Tomorrow, I will go out again."

"Um..." She worked her brain as hard as she could, trying to squeeze out some words. "On another goblin hunt?"

But he wouldn't have to specifically mention that to us.

So when he answered no and shook his helmeted head, she almost expected it. She did not, however, expect what he said after that. "I'm told the Adventurers Guild wants to discuss my promotion."

"They what?!" her uncle exclaimed, his chair scraping loudly as he jumped to his feet.

Cow Girl was almost beyond surprise; she just blinked and looked from her uncle to the young man and back. Her uncle stood there, bracing himself against the table; he didn't make any move to sit back down but looked at the young man's helmet. "You're going to be Obsidian?" her uncle asked.

"No," Goblin Slayer said. "I'm already Obsidian."

"First I'm hearing of it," the man grumbled, although he seemed somewhat calmer. He let out a long sigh, then slowly lowered himself into his seat, his chair clattering again as he pulled himself forward. Nonetheless, he was obviously still treating the moment very seriously. He didn't pick up his spoon but rested his hands on the table with his fingers steepled.

The young man went quiet—at a loss again—and then, after a moment, he asked slowly, "Should I have told you?"

"Of course you should have!" her uncle snapped. She wasn't sure if he was lecturing or just plain unhappy. "That's the sort of thing you tell people!"

"...I'm sorry." The young man's helmeted head bowed humbly,

and it was then that Cow Girl's brain finally caught up with what was going on.

She blinked again, then exclaimed, "Oh!" and clapped her hands. "Th-this… That's… That's incredible! Wonderful!"

She was no expert when it came to adventurers' ranks, but she knew that Porcelain was the lowest and Obsidian was higher than that and that Platinum was the highest of all. So he'd taken a step—or was that two steps now?—closer to being one of those Platinum heroes.

"That's amazing…!" she said.

A feast—that was what they needed! She would cook up a feast. It was too late to do it tonight. But tomorrow. She would make it tomorrow.

She was excited! Her heart was pounding! Cow Girl could hardly sit still. She just kept exclaiming, "Wow! Wow!" as if she were the one being promoted. What should she do? Where should she start? Her hand went to her cheek, and she shifted in her chair.

He was watching her fidget and shimmy from behind his helmet with what she took to be an expression of hesitation. "It isn't yet confirmed…"

"Y-yeah, but still! But they *might* confirm it! You might get promoted!"

This was all new to her. Maybe he would need to prepare. Probably? Maybe there was some way she could help. How could she help?

Cow Girl hemmed and hawed, then finally made up her mind and decided to take her own step forward. "What happened last time?" she asked.

Start by asking. That's the first thing.

It was an important thing. Much better than just standing paralyzed, as she had learned.

"Last time, the Guild told me I'd been accepted for promotion. Then I exchanged my rank tag for a new one."

"…That's all?"

"Yes."

He nodded, and it seemed from that simple gesture that he wasn't hiding anything.

I mean, I don't think he's the type to hide anything or lie...

He wasn't the type to play such silly little games.

So Cow Girl decided to push a little further. "What about this time?" she asked.

"They told me to come looking decent," he replied, his tone as clipped as ever. Then he looked at his leather armor and the shield attached to his arm and grunted. "I believe this will do."

This time it was Cow Girl's turn to jump to her feet and smack the table. "No, it won't! We have to clean you up!" She barely even registered the clattering of plates as she pointed an accusing finger at her childhood friend. Her courage at this moment was powered by sheer momentum. "You need to clean off that helmet and polish that armor... You *have* to!"

"Hrk..."

"Then there's your shirt and all the rest! I'll do some laundry!"

"I see..." The words were like a rumble in his throat, but they signified that he was accepting her demands.

Perfect...! Cow Girl clenched her fist in victory and nodded vigorously to seal the deal.

"Whatever you're going to do," her uncle said, finally contributing to the conversation with a bit of a smile, "it can wait until after we've finished lunch."

"Right," Cow Girl replied, her voice vanishingly small. She looked at the ground to hide the flush in her cheeks.

When she took another bite of stew, it was stone-cold, but it didn't bother her. She hoped it wouldn't bother *him*, either, but she couldn't say. Whether it did or not, the stew vanished from his bowl in a matter of moments.

§

I just can't get used to it.

Goblin Slayer ran a hand through his increasingly bushy hair and paged through a book that lay open on his lap. Things looked brighter, his head felt lighter, but it was like the visor of his helmet was burned into his vision. He was accustomed to the gloom of his shed and the light of the lantern burning within, but tonight both of them seemed inordinately bright.

What was worse, the sudden reduction in his body's weight and heft made all his movements feel...off. He would extend his hand in what he thought was a normal way, only to find the motion crude and exaggerated.

Even as he struggled with this subtle sense of dislocation, he tried to prepare for the next day.

To prepare, that is, for goblin hunting.

"Hrm..."

The stuff he had received as a reward for an earlier quest packed the shed and made it pretty cramped. Several books were stuffed onto the bookshelf, and then there were all the things he couldn't bring himself to think of as junk, lying wherever they would fit. Goblin Slayer didn't understand what most of them were for, but that didn't especially bother him. If he knew how to use something, he would use it, and if he didn't, he would try to learn.

He could sit here at his desk and open the book, but there were often many things inside it that he still didn't comprehend. He tried to absorb what he could.

For example—here was a concoction that irritated the eyes and nose. Naturally, it wasn't listed under a convenient heading like "a powder to induce weeping and snot." But by looking at the pictures and the index and understanding the effects of specific plants and bugs, the recipe was there, in its way.

Most of the ingredients were things Goblin Slayer had never seen or even heard of.

But these... These, I know.

He recognized some of the poisonous bugs and plants. He picked the ones he could identify and forced himself to remember them. Then he got up, went to the shelf, and picked out several small bottles, reading the labels as he went.

He came back to his desk and put on a pair of gloves before pouring out the bottles' contents. To an uninformed observer, they would have looked like unidentifiable plant roots and bug corpses—maybe herbal medicines of some kind. Goblin Slayer transferred them delicately to a mortar, then began to crush them with the pestle.

After a moment's work, he *tsk*'ed, then pulled out a handkerchief and wrapped it around his nose and mouth.

It was unfamiliar to him, frustratingly so. Now that he thought about it, all his older sister had taught him when he was younger was their father's hunting techniques. If he had asked, would she have also taught him their mother's knack for gathering medicinal herbs?

No, that's not right.

She had *tried* to teach him; he just hadn't listened. He hadn't been interested; he was convinced a bunch of plants would never be any use to him. He'd probably assumed he could ask any time. That she would always be able to teach him.

Could he have been more foolish?

"What else…? I have to polish the edge of my shield."

The words left his mouth at the same moment that he briefly stopped working because it had become hard to breathe.

Several times now on his adventures, when he had lost his weapon, it was his shield that had saved him. A small, round shield strapped to his arm. He'd become accustomed to wielding it, to the point that it now served him as a sort of sidearm. Above all, the goblins never expected a shield to double as a weapon.

But tomorrow…

At the moment, he did not have his shield with him. His childhood friend had taken it, along with his armor and helmet. It made him realize that eventually he should prepare a backup set of equipment for times like this. He didn't have much extra money for such things, and until now, he had never felt the need for them, but now he realized…

It's quite possible that I'll escape unscathed at some point because my equipment got destroyed instead.

That was the whole point of armor—and he wouldn't want to have to sit around and wait until he could go out again. He knew it was dangerous to trust everything to just one weapon—it was the same to have just one suit of armor.

He carved it into his mind as something he would have to take care of, and then his hands went back to work. Shortly thereafter, a considerable quantity of red-black powder filled the mortar.

Is this enough?

As carefully as he was able, at least with gloves on, he pinched some of the powder and rubbed it between his fingers. How fine or how gritty would it have to be to scatter effectively? He had no idea. He suspected the finer the better, but it might also be possible that there was such a thing as grinding it too fine. He had a suspicion that if it went in every direction, that might defeat the point.

"…I guess the only way to be sure is to test it."

He shouldn't think of it as something special to be held in reserve—the best thing to do would be to try it in a real battle.

Goblin Slayer sat and looked at the powder, then crossed his arms and grunted. *The question is how to transport it.* At first, he thought he might put it in a small bottle, but that would make it difficult to use in a hurry. He would have to take out the bottle, pop open the stopper, and scatter the powder. Three whole moves.

If he could throw the bottle and hope it shattered—that would be better, but bottles could be surprisingly sturdy. If it didn't break, then it would be no more than a standard projectile. Not to mention that it seemed like a waste of space and effort to have a bunch of bottles clacking around in his item pouch. Worst of all, though, would be if he ever confused one of the bottles with a potion; that would be disastrous.

I know it's in my nature to fail, he thought. If he acted based on that assumption, it would actually make mistakes less likely.

"All of which means…"

He gazed at the wick of the candle in the lantern, watching the flame dance, as he tried to put it all together in his head. He needed a container that was easy to use, suited to throwing, and which would break easily. Something smaller than a bottle and shaped differently, something he couldn't confuse at a touch.

"An egg," he muttered.

Sometimes inspiration meant tying together seemingly disparate bits of information.

As a child, he had once thrown eggs as a sort of naughty game. His sister had scolded him roundly for it.

She would never scold him again.

He stood up, made to leave the shed—then stopped. He removed the handkerchief over his mouth and instead placed it on the mortar in lieu of a lid. Then he resumed walking.

"_____"

As he stepped outside, the night breeze swept past him, carrying away the stuffiness and heat of the shed. Goblin Slayer stood and looked vacantly at the sky. It was black; it was blue; it was dark—the sky of night.

He saw clouds roiling low in the heavens, scudding along on the wind. When he was young, he would stare at the layers—clouds, sky, stars—and think how strange they seemed. Now, though, they simply looked to him like clouds, sky, and stars. Nothing mysterious about them.

"Hrm." Goblin Slayer let out a grunt, then went to the main house and opened the door. No lights burned in the house, and he crept through the halls silently, more carefully than if he were in a goblin nest. He was heading for the kitchen, for the eggshells that had been set aside but not yet thrown away. They supposedly made good fertilizer or something—he realized he didn't know much more than that.

I wonder how many I can take before it becomes an inconvenience.

After some thought, he decided to borrow two or three of them, and then he withdrew as silently as he had come.

He returned to his shed, sat down at his desk, and took a breath. He would pack the powder into the eggs, seal them, and then throw them. That would work, he thought. Whether or not it had the intended effect.

Besides the question of how fine to grind the powder, there was also the matter of how much to put in each egg. He would have to go by trial and error. One thing he didn't expect to have trouble with was carrying the eggs around; after his earlier failure with the bottles, he now kept them padded with cotton in his item pouch. The real issue was how to close the shells up.

"...Maybe I can stick papyrus on them," he said. It wasn't very durable, but then he needed it to break or there would be no point. Next time he made these weapons, he would poke a hole in the egg, extract the contents, and then pour the powder in the same way.

After considering the construction and committing several possible improvements to memory, he resumed his work…almost.

"……"

How effective will these actually be?

The handkerchief he had used to cover the mortar had trace amounts of the powder on it. He didn't intend to assume that he could treat the tear gas bombs as his ace in the hole, but he was uncomfortable at the idea of using them without having any clue of what they would do.

"…Hrm."

He took a deep breath, then pressed the handkerchief to his face.

It was a decision he immediately and deeply regretted.

§

Now, who exactly are we dealing with here?

The examiner seemed all but oblivious to the tension that swirled around her as she stood at the reception desk of the Adventurers Guild. The usual friendly burble was replaced this morning by a predominant quiet, everyone constraining themselves to only absolutely necessary talk. Just by having her sharp gaze there, the Guild employees walked a little straighter and spoke a little more properly.

Adventurers—at least those who survive—are extremely sensitive to tension. When you stand at the entrance to some old ruins or when you're about to put your hand on a treasure chest, you have to be able to feel it if there's something there. Sometimes that can mean the difference between life and death.

Right now, the men and women who stepped up to the Guild door sensed danger emanating from it every bit as much as from a dungeon chamber. And if they didn't pay it much heed at the door, it would slap them in the face when they stepped inside.

If they ignored both these signs and started chatting away, the collective stares of those around them would pierce them through. If someone ignored even that and really raised their voice—well, they were either a big deal or someone stupid enough to pretend that they were. In most cases, it was the latter.

When you think they are destined to die or be broken, it somehow makes them… endearing, the examiner thought with a sigh. She didn't actually pay that much mind to the adventurer running his mouth and promptly being told off by his friends.

This Guild on the western frontier was home to many adventurers, wearing a mélange of armor. There were adventurers of different races with many different kinds of gear. Each one had their own areas of expertise—and their own ideals. Elves stood shoulder to shoulder with dwarves, lizardmen bowed to rheas as their teachers, and among them all were the humans.

Some percentage of them would quit adventuring, or they would die. How many of them would survive to rise through the ranks?

It was a good thing, the examiner thought. A very good thing. It was as simple as this: An organization that could accept a certain amount of excess was strong; one that felt compelled to eliminate such excess was weak. There were always some people who clamored to get rid of the flab, but they never considered the possibility that they might fall into that category.

At this moment, this nation was weak as it began to regain its footing after the disaster of five years earlier. But behold: In front of her was a chaotic, miscellaneous gathering of hoodlums and ruffians.

Who knew where they were from or where they would go? That was part of what was so good. Didn't the dwarves have a saying? Something to the effect of one who picks only gems that are already polished is a fool?

It was because there were so many stones here that they would be able to find the gems. Even the All Stars, had they not begun as anonymous adventurers? Out of all those gathered at the Golden Knight, those six were the ones who reached the Death. No one—not even they themselves—would have predicted that at the beginning.

They had to be sifted—that was different from deciding whom to cut loose—and sifted they would be.

Before her now were the adventurers who had emerged from that process. Around her, Guild employees were pointedly going about their business. Each of them was, in their own way, working toward a single goal: adventure. Together, they were like an instrument, perfectly tuned. The examiner watched them as they made the music of the Guild together.

Still…

It will not do to upset these ladies' "country" too much.

It was important for superiors to keep an eye on what was going on below them, but outsiders shouldn't interfere unduly. Self-discipline, that was the thing. Restraint.

"U-um…," said Guild Girl, who was standing next to the examiner and only just managing to keep the worry out of her voice. The examiner's silent observation seemed to have given her the wrong impression. "Is…is everything all right?"

"Yes," the examiner said, giving her adorable junior colleague a bit of a smile to relieve her anxiety. "I was just thinking, look how far we have come in the five years since the Death's dungeon."

"…Yes, ma'am. I heard things were no easier in the capital. Something about a vampire…"

Guild Girl seemed to be thinking of all the chaos and confusion that battle had caused. She couldn't have been very old at the time, but fear knew no age and remained long in the memory. Nor should it have been surprising that the daughter of a noble family would be aware of a situation that had engulfed her parents and those around them in consternation.

She was not really mistaken, so the examiner saw no reason to disabuse her of her misimpression. In the last five years, the number of those who knew what it had been like at the Golden Knight had become fewer and fewer.

Commotion. Reports of battles fought. Negotiations over the purse. Planning for the next delve. Deciding where to go from here…

Just for an instant, the examiner merely had to close her one eye and it was all there before her, though it was so far away now.

"So?" she said sharply, to shake herself out of her reverie. She felt bad for her junior colleague who flinched, but then again, it was just as well—she couldn't have her getting too relaxed on the job. "He will come, will he not?"

"On a normal day, I would expect him anytime now…"

"Goblin Slayer? Is that what he's called?"

There are some strange characters among adventurers.

She questioned someone who would gladly—had it been gladly?—accept such a nickname. To give *yourself* a heroic sobriquet was the mark of a second- or even a third-rate adventurer. Instead, those ruffians—that is to say, adventurers—who had made a name for themselves among the rivers and lakes were given nicknames by the people around them. Consider the old cases of the burglar, Strider, the red-haired adventurer, the knight-errant, or the wild woman of the Supreme God…

Even in that light, however, *this* name seemed like a poor choice, no matter how you looked at it. No one denied that goblins were evil and terrible creatures, but that was only natural. They were monsters. There was no monster in the world that wasn't terrible and evil. Compared to becoming a vampire's snack, a BEM's little toy, or having your brain sucked out while you still lived by a mind flayer, goblins seemed a minor nuisance. "Goblin Slayer" didn't even sound like much of a compliment.

Ah! There it was again—the examiner was letting herself get lost in thought. She snapped back to reality.

As she did so, just for a second, the entire Guild seemed to go quiet except for the tinkling of the bell over the door, which opened with a gust of warm air from outside. It brought with it a new visitor. Not just the employees but even the other adventurers came to a halt, taking furtive glances at this newcomer.

He entered the Guild with a bold stride—but look at him. He wore a metal helmet crowned with broken horns and cheap-looking leather armor. He carried a sword of a strange length, and there was a small, round shield strapped to his arm.

I see. A scruffy man, indeed.

His armor and helmet had been polished just enough to keep him from looking like a suit of Living Armor, but not by much. At the door, he spoke to a young woman with red hair—if circumstances had been different, someone might have challenged them, demanded to know who they were. Instead, once the adventurers and the clerks had ascertained the identity of this intruder, they all went back to their business.

He was no stone along the roadside to be ignored, yet he was a blasphemer whom it was impossible not to look at.

One could say only that this was without a doubt a very strange adventurer.

"Um… *Ahem.* That's, er… That's him," Guild Girl whispered to the examiner.

"I can see," she replied. She meant only what she said, yet her colleague's shoulders hunched, and the girl shrank into herself.

No, no. Must be careful. She knew how she could come across and tried to be careful, but the niceties of spoken language were sometimes still hard for her. This was why she hadn't become a wizard.

Then Guild Girl let out a quiet "oh…" She glanced to one side, then slapped a hand over her mouth. The source of the unintended exclamation seemed to be the fact that this Goblin Slayer was striding directly toward them. Practically charging, in fact. The examiner almost thought she could see an eye glowing behind the slats of his visor.

"You asked me to come, so I've come. What now?" he said. He wielded his words with the subtlety—and efficiency—of a hatchet. His voice was brusque and terribly cold.

Now, here's a real menace.

"Oh yes! Well, *ahem*, we wanted to speak to you about your promotion…"

"I heard." The gaze from behind the visor shifted for a second, acknowledging the examiner, then returned to Guild Girl in front of him.

He is observing closely, the examiner noted, although she took it all in without so much as arching an eyebrow herself. There was no hesitation in his walk, in his words—but it was different from the reckless courage of an adventurer who failed to consider who or what he might be facing. *Novice adventurers have a right to recklessness, of course. The possibility of their own defeat never enters their minds.*

He was assessing the situation, then proceeding with determination. He was treating this exactly like it was a dungeon chamber.

Or, I suppose, a goblin nest.

She had no doubt that if someone attacked him at that moment, this man would respond instantaneously. Whether he could do anything about it or not was not the issue. This was not about level, about strength. There was every chance that he would be sent sprawling, humiliated—and yet she could tell this young man would make the attempt. The examiner let a smile creep over her face and clenched her hand gently.

"So, you see, uh, in order to complete your promotion, you'll need to take an examination..."

"I don't care if I don't advance."

"Maybe not, but I'm afraid we do. So, uh..."

Guild Girl was struggling to keep up with the man's terse pronouncements; she desperately looked for some way to explain. There was a certain cuteness to it, like a puppy, but the Adventurers Guild didn't need puppies.

The examiner decided to throw her junior colleague a lifeline. "What she is saying is that we would like you to take a further test."

"I see," Goblin Slayer said, low and deep in his throat. He nodded, almost sullen, and then he asked, "Does it involve goblins?"

The examiner clenched her fist a little harder.

§

Goblin Slayer hadn't known that there was a reception room on the second floor of the Guild. It was a sumptuous space adorned with trophies brought home by past adventurers—monster horns, weapons and armor, and more. It turned out that it was not only adventurers and the heads of poor villages who visited the Guild. Royalty, nobility, and important merchants sometimes came as well, and it was crucial that they be received in fitting style.

In any case, this discussion wasn't one to have in public.

"...Hrm," said Goblin Slayer. There were so many things that were obvious when you thought about them but which would never enter your mind if you didn't.

This carpet, for example. He had never before walked on a carpet so thick that his boots sank into it. Did it really need to be that thick? It must have, or it wouldn't be, he supposed. Although what reason there could possibly be for that, the knowledge and experience gained in a short fifteen years of life couldn't tell him.

When he stepped in, he was delighted to discover the footing was far better than that in a cave or cavern. It made it easy to stride into the room, where he took a seat as far as possible from both the entrance and the window. Guild Girl and the examiner (this was how she had identified herself) stared straight at him.

"...Sure you don't need a chaperone in here with you?" whispered the woman who had gotten the room ready for them.

"I'm sure," said Guild Girl with a nod, while the examiner replied evenly, "It will not be a problem."

The woman glanced at Goblin Slayer, then again at her coworkers, and then she bowed and left the room. Then, at last, Guild Girl and the examiner sat down across from Goblin Slayer.

"...I see he gets failing marks for etiquette," the examiner murmured. Goblin Slayer paid her no mind, but Guild Girl flinched. The examiner spared her a brief glance, then looked back at Goblin Slayer. "Do not worry. I do not intend to make an issue of that today. Etiquette is not expected of Porcelains and Obsidians."

Well, no. Goblin Slayer nodded. There was no need for etiquette when hunting goblins.

"I will, however, take this opportunity to advise you that if you are to proceed up the ranks, it is a skill you will need to master."

"I'm not interested in it."

"N-now, that's not right! Etiquette is very important!" Guild Girl babbled. The tea in the cups on the table swished quietly. "We don't want people to go around thinking adventurers are uncouth bullies, plus you have to leave the right impression on villagers..."

She continued to multiply reasons and explanations. Goblin Slayer listened silently.

It came down to this: To adventure and adventure and eventually become someone people called a hero, one must earn the trust of all and sundry. Porcelains and Obsidians were hardly more than toughs fresh off the streets, but once one reached the middle ranks, people started to look at them differently. These were the ones people looked to as examples of what an adventurer was and should be. Evidently, it was necessary to act the part.

Honor. Glory. The great deeds adventurers do. It wasn't that he had no regard for such things. But…

The trust of villagers.

In his mind, that seemed far more important. When he thought back to his own childhood, he realized that the adults had been on edge whenever adventurers came to the village. His sister had always told him to stay out of their way—maybe she had wanted to keep him away from them.

They were strangers, fighters, members of an uncivilized clan. Some of them shadowy spell casters with strange magics. The clerics were another matter, but still. Even he himself, who now had some experience of the world, however modest, continued on some level to view magic as a fae and awful thing.

When he thought of how he had been back before he had ever left his village, he saw how small the world he knew had been.

He was constantly reminded that he was just a human who knew little or nothing.

He remembered that once he had broken his promise and gone to spy on the adventurers.

What kind of adventurers are they? he'd wondered. He had only a hazy image in his memory, although he was sure at least that they were different from how he was now. True adventurers were not like him.

After a lengthy silence, he grunted, then said only, "I will attempt to improve myself."

He noticed Guild Girl sigh in relief, although he wasn't sure why. He didn't believe he could do the sorts of things she was hoping for. Still, he understood that it would be useful for getting information about goblin hunting.

It wasn't so difficult. He might not know how to behave like a heroic adventurer, but he knew how things were done in the villages. That was all he needed to know.

"I applaud your drive for self-improvement," said the examiner. She didn't know what he was thinking… Did she? She fixed him with her one eye, her gaze seeming to peer straight past the slats of his visor.

Goblin Slayer found himself just slightly uncomfortable. It was an unusual feeling. It was the same way he had felt under the gaze of his master and of his older sister—as if they could see everything about him.

In the event, the only thing the examiner did was pick up some papers on the table and tap them into order. She made it look very natural. Not the least theatrical or performative. Yet even Goblin Slayer could understand what she was saying.

"As far as it goes, none of the villages you have worked for have reported any problems with you," she said.

She wants me to see that she knows everything about me.

The bundle of papers was probably his collection of adventure logs. It would be full of the details of all the goblin hunts he had gone on.

There shouldn't have been any issue with that.

Some goblin captives he had been able to rescue, while others he had failed to save. He'd been wounded himself on occasion. But he had killed the goblins. He hadn't let them touch the villages. He felt, in his own opinion, that he had done a rather good job…

No. That thought in itself is arrogance.

"To reiterate, I do not intend to make an issue of your failures of etiquette," the examiner said.

For now. That part was clearly implied as she gave him another sweeping glance with her single eye. Her gaze was like that of a creature lurking in a dark cavern, staring out from the entrance at him.

Goblin Slayer had a thought: If he leaped at her at this moment, what would happen?

He had no intention of doing any such thing, of course, but for some reason he also had the distinct sense that he would come off the worst if he tried it.

"For me, the real question is whether you are capable of any kind of adventure besides hunting goblins," the examiner continued.

"I don't need to be," he replied immediately. A speed prompted by how the examiner's words and actions felt to him like his master's riddles—fast, sharp, precise. If he fell one step behind, all that waited for him would be a beating. "I slay goblins. I'm not interested in anything else."

"I am not asking what you are interested in. I am telling you: It is a problem."

"If you're saying that's what stands between me and promotion, I don't care."

"Oh! Um, uh, ah…" Guild Girl looked like she would have been flinging her hands around in a panic if she hadn't been so dedicated to sitting stock-still.

"Sadly, what you care about is also not germane." Beside her, the examiner's expression shifted for the first time. She let out the smallest of sighs. "Your experience points— Pardon me." That was a slang term encompassing one's combat results, total reward, and reputation within the Guild, and she pushed it away with a cough. "Your examination shows that you are qualified for promotion. If we did not promote you, it would be to our discredit."

"That sounds like your problem," Goblin Slayer said without any particular malice. "Maybe you should change how you do your examinations."

"Why? For your personal benefit? Amazing. I did not realize I was dealing with a Platinum-ranked adventurer here!"

"Hmm."

It was precisely his lack of malice that caused Goblin Slayer to stop and cross his arms when confronted with the examiner's blunt riposte. He had never once in his life thought of himself in such superlative terms. Yes, he might have dreamed of attaining such status one day, but the adults around him had simply laughed and shaken their heads.

Don't make stupid suggestions—is that what she means?

Maybe that was the real answer. It was stupid. He would never reach such heights.

Therefore, he instead turned his full attention to the situation he was in at this moment. He could see that, caught between the two of them, Guild Girl was in a pitiful state of panic. Was his promotion really that important to her? If nothing else, he could tell that she had expended a considerable amount of her own time to make this meeting possible. For example, she was the one who'd written out all those adventure logs the examiner was holding.

Goblin Slayer let out a breath. He was not the kind of adventurer they thought he was. But he knew how to be grateful.

"I stand by what I said," he began, "but if a test is necessary for promotion, then I am willing to take it." He was cautious, choosing his words carefully; his tongue felt slow, like he was chewing over every syllable before it could come out. "However, it's also true that I have no intention of doing anything but hunting goblins."

"Hoh," breathed the examiner, and the eye gazing at him narrowed slightly. To Goblin Slayer, it almost looked as if she had smiled. "But you are willing to submit to a promotion exam?"

"I believe that's what I just said."

"Ma'am…?" Guild Girl urged. *Is this really all right?* she asked with her eyes.

The examiner's unflappable demeanor never wavered. "There are exceptions to every rule," she said. She uncrossed and recrossed her legs, appearing fully aware of how lovely and attractive they were. "The great heroes who conquered the labyrinth of the Death never did anything but delve that dungeon."

"Oh…!"

"That being the case, if a person can demonstrate their abilities by hunting only goblins, it may still be acceptable to promote them."

Guild Girl blinked, seemingly in spite of herself, and the examiner's lips softened, turning up in a graceful arch. It was as sharp as the expression she had leveled at Goblin Slayer but many times warmer. Of course it was. She had no reason at all to offer *him* any human affection.

"There are three reasons I am choosing to test you," the examiner stated, raising three fingers, and when she turned back to him, the smile on her face was once again the pasted-on kind.

"Mm," grunted Goblin Slayer. "Tell me."

"First, I wish to know: Are you capable of doing anything other than hunting goblins, and can you work with a party?"

The former condition in this case was not to say that he was not *allowed* to hunt goblins. As long as he demonstrated the adaptability, a goblin hunt would be sufficient.

"So it's goblins," he said.

"Yes. It would be goblins," the examiner replied. She sounded like a teacher affirming a quick student. "My second reason is motivated by the fact that you have only solo experience."

Goblin Slayer thought for a second, then shook his head. "Not true." The rural village. The dwarf warrior. A bold monk. A half-elf girl holding a lamb. And a young warrior. "I did once work alongside another party."

"Stumbling onto another group is not the same thing as working with them. I believe you also then traumatized them by subsequently dissecting the…" As the examiner scanned the paper, she trailed off. There was a beat. Guild Girl held her breath. "Dissecting?" the examiner repeated.

"It was necessary."

Guild Girl let out the breath, almost like a sigh. In fact, she sounded quite resigned.

"Hence my second reason," the examiner said, nodding to herself and scribbling something in a notebook. "In that case, let us decide who will go with you. What are your plans today?"

"This interview. When it's over, I was intending to go on a goblin hunt."

"Very good!" The examiner beamed at him, the papers fluttering as she set them down on the table. He had no idea what that meant, but she seemed to have come to some kind of conclusion. "Go downstairs and choose a quest. Wait before you leave. I will be with you shortly."

"Understood." Goblin Slayer nodded his metal helmet, and then after a second's thought, he asked, "So I may go?"

"Yes, go ahead."

I don't know much about this "etiquette."

When it came to things he didn't understand, he thought it was both faster and better to ask about them than to do them half-assed.

He got to his feet almost as if jumping out of his chair, then headed for the door with the same stride as he had entered. Now that he got another look at it, he saw what a fine room this was, carefully maintained, with thick walls that he suspected were for soundproofing.

He had just opened the door when a question occurred to him. He turned back to the women. Guild Girl, who had just been relaxing, said "Eep!" and straightened up again. The examiner beside her looked exactly as she had earlier.

"What was the third reason?" asked Goblin Slayer.

The examiner brought her cup of tea to her lips with an elegant motion and gave him a small smile. "A woman's intuition."

Goblin Slayer nodded and closed the door.

§

"Hey, man! What's the good word on that promotion?"

The moment Guild Girl got downstairs, her colleague—the woman who had showed them upstairs earlier—handed her a quest paper, which she took. The voice, however, belonged to a young warrior speaking to Goblin Slayer, who was waiting for his quest to be processed.

The metal helmet turned. He discovered that the young warrior was not wearing armor and only had a sword at his waist. He didn't look like he was here to take on a quest, yet he also didn't appear to be coming back from an adventure.

Goblin Slayer grunted, then asked the first question that came into his head. "You know about that?"

"The, uh, receptionist filled me in after you went upstairs."

In this case, the receptionist did not mean Guild Girl but one of the other guild employees.

Goblin Slayer could not fathom why someone would have a genuine interest in his progress; this must be just a way of making conversation. This man, Goblin Slayer, was not important enough for anything more.

Goblin Slayer was what people called him, but it evoked no special emotion in him. Now he nodded.

"I don't know yet. I was told I must take on a quest with a companion."

"Ahh, they wanna know if you can work with a party. Sure thing." The young warrior scratched his cheek, his expression suggesting that he understood exactly what Goblin Slayer was talking about.

At that moment, Goblin Slayer noticed the color of the tag hanging at the young man's neck. It was no longer Porcelain, so he was evidently making his way steadily up the ranks himself. Goblin Slayer had never previously taken much note of other people's statuses or their rank tags, and he had missed this one as well. The closest he had come to noticing such things was in some goblin nests, where he had picked up a Porcelain or Obsidian rank tag on one or two occasions.

"Were you also tested?" he asked.

"Nah." The young warrior shook his head, looking a tad embarrassed. "I've worked with a couple different parties now, so they didn't give me a hard time about that."

"I see."

This young man was a far more accomplished adventurer than Goblin Slayer—beyond compare. He should have known better than to ask such a question. It didn't specifically bother him, but he fell quiet for a moment.

Is there some subject of conversation that I should bring up in my turn?

He doubted the young warrior actually had any business with him. It would be safe to end the conversation at this juncture. However, Goblin Slayer had been told to wait here for a while, so perhaps it would be just as well to continue to talk.

"What about you?" he said.

"Aw, y'know. Slow and steady."

The question Goblin Slayer ultimately came up with was a common and unremarkable one, and the answer he received was similar.

"The big thing is we're learning to read and write right now."

"I see."

Goblin Slayer knew the rudiments of reading, writing, and arithmetic. His sister and the rest of the village had taught him. Which was another way of saying that if they hadn't taught him, he wouldn't be able to do those things. Logically.

I am very lucky.

This had nothing to do with his promotion or whatever. Being able to read meant he could obtain far more information. If there was one thing that these months of adventuring had taught him, it was the value of knowledge.

A question presented itself to him: *Can goblins read and write?* As quickly as the thought arose, he reached his conclusion. *No reason to think they can't.*

He would have to be careful. Always. He would have to go out of his way to avoid the foolish mistake of giving the enemy any information. He should not assume that he wouldn't fail or make a mistake.

"You have a thing for just falling quiet, don't you?" the young warrior said.

"Is that so?" Goblin Slayer replied. The young warrior gave him a look that Goblin Slayer found unreadable. He could only go so far in guessing what someone was thinking when that someone was simply a person he occasionally traded greetings with. They knew only the slightest fragment of each other's situations, but that was all that was necessary to hold their conversations.

"We tangled with this necromancer the other day, and we've got money to spare. Seems like a good time to do some training, I figured," the young warrior said.

"Necromancer?" Goblin Slayer remembered the spearman bragging about some monster he had killed. Called a…something or other. The thought led most naturally to Goblin Slayer's next question: "Is that amazing?"

"Well, it's not like we beat him. We managed to escape with our lives—that's about all I can say for us." The young warrior shrugged and smiled grimly. He wasn't being self-deprecating or prideful or even humble: It had been a simple difference in level. "Not very amazing."

"I see."

The young warrior muttered that the opponent was probably just a pitiful spell himself. Goblin Slayer didn't know what that meant. When the young warrior realized as much, he smiled again. "And how are things with you?"

"Hunting goblins."

"I might've guessed," the young warrior said, not sounding the least bit surprised.

With that, the conversation ended. The two adventurers were not friends or anything else, just two people with some time on their hands who happened to be standing near each other.

At that moment, they heard a young woman shouting incredulously from the reception desk, "What do you mean I have to join the Adventurers Guild here?!" The scandalized speaker, talking loudly enough to be heard all over the building, was a young woman who looked to be a warlock. Her sodden robes suggested the long and tiring road she'd had to travel.

The scabbard of a sword peeked out from under the hem of her robe; she probably had some idea how to use it. That constituted Goblin Slayer's entire impression of her as she started filling out the registration forms, grumbling about it the whole time.

Like Goblin Slayer, whose eyes moved behind his helmet, the young warrior also glanced at her. "Guess we'll be seeing more and more novices," he said.

"Is that so?"

"You ever think maybe it's time you left behind newbie work yourself?"

"Hrm?"

"I mean goblin hunting!" The young warrior grinned at Goblin Slayer's obvious incomprehension, then said, "Catch you later." Some distance away, a young woman with her silver hair tied up in a way that reminded Goblin Slayer of a pony's tail was bouncing up and down and waving energetically, her tresses bouncing with her. Was that the warrior's party? Goblin Slayer watched the warrior go, but in the end, he never quite remembered who the young man was with.

Then once again, he was alone.

"——……"

Should he just continue to wait here? He took a few steps toward the reception area, looking for somewhere to put himself where he would be out of the way.

If he'd had his druthers, he would have gone into action immediately. He didn't want to wait any longer than he had to.

He wasn't used to not *doing* anything.

Pausing in the middle of a battle, in the middle of a goblin hunt—that was different. But here, he couldn't shake the sense that he was missing something he should be doing, something he should be thinking about, some action he should be taking. He scuffed at the floor with his toe, restless and uneasy.

I should polish the edge of my shield.

Could he do that by himself? It was possible, but for just a few coins, he could have a master craftsman do it, and that seemed better. It was faster and the result was more reliable. Of course, if he was the only one around, then he would have to do it himself.

Should he go to the workshop right now, then?

No.

He didn't know how long the work would take, and it would be unconscionable if having been told specifically to wait, he was not waiting when the examiner arrived.

Because they had told him to come to the reception area first thing in the morning, it hadn't occurred to him to drop off his shield at the workshop before coming—that was the source of this mistake. He could go to the workshop before they left and hand over his shield. But he still didn't know how long it would take.

If worst came to worst, he could try to get his hands on another shield or otherwise go off on the goblin hunt without a shield. But…

I don't have a system.

He *tsk*'ed at his own disgusting lack of preparedness. He would get nowhere this way. Any adventurer worthy of being promoted, he was sure, would have handled things much, much better. Far more skillfully.

Nor would they find themselves fretting over such things. He was nothing like skilled enough to be considered—

"Have you finished your preparations?" asked a cold, sharp voice that cut straight through his gloomy ruminations. It was accompanied by the *click* of shoes on wood.

The question was perfectly simple, perfectly ordinary, and yet the voice was so clear; it carried so well. He raised his metal helmet to see the woman whose hair covered one of her eyes—the examiner he'd been sitting across from until a few moments ago. Guild Girl was with her. They looked no different than they had in the room upstairs.

Well, perhaps there was one difference: The examiner had a sack over her shoulder, its mouth cinched shut with a string.

"Well, boy? Shall we go?" she asked.

"______"

Goblin Slayer hesitated over what to say—even where to start. He supposed he should begin by asking the most important question, but he wasn't even sure which questions were more important than the rest.

Under his helmet, he tried to scan the area, but he couldn't even do that, for the examiner's gaze pierced straight through his visor and held him fast. It reminded him both of his master's eyes and of his sister's. It wasn't identical, but the resemblance struck him.

"Boy," he repeated. Did that refer to him?

With all the considerations in his head, with the memory of those other eyes on him, that modest question was the most he could muster.

The examiner responded in a brusque tone, as if she couldn't believe he was asking something so obvious: "I saw your papers. You are fifteen, only just reached the age of majority. Which means that you are still a child—in other words, a boy."

If age alone were enough to make one an adult, the Four-Cornered World would be overflowing with them, she went on. Well, he reflected, she was right. He had never once thought he was an adult.

In which case, the next question was simple. When the words thankfully came to him, his voice followed. "You said someone would be accompanying me."

"I believe I said I would be right with you, did I not?" the examiner replied, once again as if this should have been obvious.

Goblin Slayer worked his mind furiously, trying to understand what she meant. He could come to only one conclusion.

Does this mean that she will be accompanying me?

He felt uncharacteristically shaken, although he didn't really register it; instead, he turned his helmet, asking Guild Girl the question with his gaze.

She looked puzzled, but after a second's thought, she said, "Oh!" and seemed to understand. "*Ahem,* yes. My senior colleague—erm, I mean, an employee of the Guild will be accompanying you as your proctor."

Her expression was ambiguous, and he wasn't sure what it meant, but the words themselves were clear enough. Goblin Slayer grunted quietly. If the two women said there was no problem with this, then there was no problem.

"In that case," said Goblin Slayer, "I will go to the workshop to prepare and then leave directly from there."

"Of course. Do as you see fit," the examiner replied. "I will not be telling you what to do from this point on."

That appeared to mean that the promotion exam had already begun. Still, he had no idea what would actually be the "right answer," the right thing to do. Would she be taking note of details as minor as whether he polished the edge of his shield? Even if attending to his shield counted against him, he had no other bright ideas for what to do. Then again, maybe it was such a minor point that it wouldn't be factored into his evaluation?

Then there was the whole question of whether he wanted to be promoted at all. In his own mind, he had no answer. His childhood friend as well as Guild Girl, standing before him now, both seemed eager that he should be promoted.

All it means is that I'll do what I always do.

That, in the end, was the only conclusion he could come to.

He set off at his customary bold stride, his boots smacking against the floor; the examiner raised an eyebrow but then followed him. The distance at which she followed him, neither very close nor very far, made Goblin Slayer feel oddly uncomfortable. That, however, was not why he came to a halt.

"Um… So…"

It was Guild Girl's voice that stopped him.

She wasn't quite sure what to say, but nevertheless, the metal helmet turned slowly toward her.

"D-do your best, okay?"

His best at what? He wasn't really sure.

§

The pounding sunlight had gone from bright and clear to a dark orange almost before she knew it. Cow Girl, huffing and puffing, took a break from her farmwork exactly long enough to wipe the sweat from her brow with the back of her hand.

Maybe I need a hat...

If she wasn't careful in this heat, she could easily be caught by the god of sunstroke, and even if not, the body could overheat. At the very least, she might get tanned—and she would be lying if she said she didn't care about that.

At the same time, her body could work much more than it had been able to when she had first started helping her uncle. Back then, she'd sometimes found herself overtaken by sudden dizzy spells.

"Mm. Good. All that's left is to bring the cows home, and then we're—"

She was about to say *done for the day*, but she abruptly froze in place and stared into the distance. She could see a figure approaching down the road from town, coming toward the farm. It moved with a bold, unconcerned stride. *Huh?* She was just giving the figure a quizzical look when the metal helmet with the tassel came into view. *That thing is really getting beat-up*, she thought. She had washed it, polished it, and carefully combed the tassel the night before, but she could see how much good it had done.

More to the point, she wondered if he wasn't hot in that thing. That was what worried her the most. Plus, a suit of armor was so heavy.

I guess it doesn't seem to bother him...

The thought brought a wan smile to Cow Girl's face, and she jogged up to the fence. His pace slowed—he must have noticed her. She felt a little thrill at that.

"......"

He came over and stopped, then stood silent, staring at her intently.

"So... Um..." What were the eyes behind his visor looking at? She suspected it was...

My hair?

Still not entirely sure, Cow Girl played unconsciously with the bundle of hair that bobbed at the back of her neck. "Does it look, uh, weird?"

"No," he said and shook his head, then resumed his silence once more.

Cow Girl shifted uncomfortably, but she was no longer the young woman who would have scared herself off at this moment (if not by much). Instead, she took a deep breath and a step forward and said, "Your, uh, promotion! Did it go well?"

"No," he said again, another laconic answer accompanied this time by a quiet groan. Cow Girl waited anxiously, and then, as if it were just occurring to him, he added, "I don't know."

"You don't know?"

"I'm supposed to take a test."

A test? Cow Girl cocked her head. A test… Like, a *test*? An examination? It took a moment for the idea to come together in her mind—and then she noticed the woman trotting up behind him.

Oh! Cow Girl instinctively straightened up, not so much because of the woman's uniform but because of her bearing. She looked completely cool in spite of the sun; she exuded something that made you feel like you needed to be on your best behavior.

"A pleasure," the woman said with a gentle smile.

"Oh! Uh, the—the pleasure's mine!" Cow Girl said with a hurried bow. When she raised her head again, she couldn't keep her eyes from flitting back and forth between the woman and *him*. She'd been deeply shaken by his association with the eccentric wizard before, but this time…

Um, uh…

This time, today, she didn't feel shaken so much as nervous. She had the distinct sense that she should try to do everything by the book. It was a test, after all. Not that she was sure what was being tested. Him evidently.

The woman from the Guild seemed to sense exactly how Cow Girl was feeling. Her lips arched in a smile, and she made a small motion of her head. "Would you be his younger sister?"

"N-no, ma'am…" Cow Girl gave several quick, hard shakes of her head. Granted, she *was* younger than him.

"His spouse, then?"

"No, I'm not!" she said louder than she'd meant to. Her face was beet red. She didn't regret saying it, though; this, of all things, she needed to be clear on.

"Ah! Please, pardon me."

"Er, I'm sorry, *ahem*… We're not…related. Technically. We're…"

What? What are we?

Cow Girl felt the words swirling around in her head; her brain seemed so full of them that she could only go quiet. She looked to him for help, but he simply stayed silent behind his visor.

What, in the end, were they to each other? Childhood friends? Regular friends? Just living in the same house?

"Let me rephrase, then," the woman said, her sharp voice cutting through the chaos of Cow Girl's thoughts. She jerked and looked at the woman, meeting her eyes—the Guild employee still wore that same slight smile. Cow Girl straightened up again, feeling like she had been pierced to the core. "Were you the one who polished his armor?"

"Oh y-yes, ma'am!" Cow Girl nodded before she knew what she was doing, then clapped her hands over her mouth, aghast. Should she have let the woman think he prepared his own equipment? If this was a test, wouldn't it be better if they believed he was attentive to every detail?

"I see," the other woman said, and quite contrary to Cow Girl's fretful ruminations, she nodded, cool and calm. "Very good. I think it is a very good thing, indeed, that he has family like you to support him."

"Oh…" Cow Girl blinked several times.

I see… So that's it. Family. Was that what they were? She'd be happy if that was how they seemed to others. *But is it true?*

"Er, um…" She looked toward him, even though she didn't even have a handle on her own feelings at that moment. She couldn't begin to guess what expression must be on his face under that silent helmet. Instead she bowed as respectfully as she could and, mustering every bit of her conviction, said, "Take good care of him!"

"But of course," replied the older woman as if it were the most natural thing in the world. The gentle smile was still on her face.

INTERLUDE

Of How an Adventure Is Something You Should Seek Out but Is Not Enough to Destroy You

"Hey, did you hear *he's* getting promoted, too?"

"Who?" Heavy Warrior asked, surprised by the annoyance in his own voice as he looked up from his sand tray.

"That guy! You know, the one who only hunts goblins. Ooh, the last thing I want is for the likes of him to get promoted ahead of us!"

Maybe it was the fact that they were in the Guild tavern that caused the female knight's voice to sound less emphatic than her words. It was still enough to cause the young boy and girl across from them to shrink back, so he slapped a hand over her mouth just the same.

It was heart-wrenching, the way the kids looked fixedly at the ground. He gave them a reassuring wave. He and his group had been promoted several times before it officially became clear that the children had lied about their ages. The truth had come out only recently. They were lucky—he supposed—that their established record of results got them off with no more than a very stern warning.

But it's gonna come back to haunt us on our next exam, he thought. He let out a sigh, small enough that no one would notice.

Nonetheless, in his mind, chasing the kids out of the party was never an option. It would have been easy enough to come up with a reason to justify it had he wanted to. Efficiency, just cause, karma.

But that wouldn't have been…cool.

I'd be no better than a guy who hogs all the novice quests for himself.

If that was what it took to get himself promoted—well, then he was no adventurer at all. Anyway, no one who was only concerned with efficiency would ever go adventuring.

Not to say that Heavy Warrior had sat down and thought this through. It was sort of a hazy collection of ideas in his head. He was more concerned with what was right in front of his face. Taking quests and completing them—or rather, no. Getting everyone home alive. That was true success.

To do that, they needed to prepare. They had to think about how they would act. Whether they would need provisions or supplies.

That was what led to him bending over this sand tray, scratching in it with a quill and working his brain as hard as he could.

"Perhaps I could help?" Half-Elf Light Warrior asked quietly. Heavy Warrior glanced at him and discovered he had succeeded in comforting the two young children. He was always so attentive to those things. Heavy Warrior didn't know if it was the elven blood that flowed in his veins or just a talent he happened to possess. Then again, maybe it wasn't possible to make fine distinctions among blood, talent, and simple effort.

"Nah. It's fine," Heavy Warrior said with a shake of his head. "If I don't do it myself, I won't have the big picture."

He trusted his party members, but this was still something he preferred to do on his own. He was frightened by the idea of their being out of step. However well people might communicate, they were still separate individuals. As long as he took care of all the finances himself, there might be unpleasant surprises, but there should never be anything unexpected at the planning stage. Above all, if there was a mistake, he would be best able to accept it if it was something he had done.

He never wanted to have to blame anyone else.

Let's see here: We've got this much gold left, and we'll be in transit for this many days… So how many provisions does that come to?

He wanted to make sure the kids could have good square meals if at all possible. They would need to be able to train, too. There were so many things they had to do, so many things he had to think about. The questions could go on forever.

Tackle one thing, then move on to the next. When that was done, move on to the one after that. They kept increasing. And if he didn't attend to them, it would all be over.

Problems only seem to grow… Guess I can't complain, though.

In fact, he was glad he'd come out here with his friend to make money as mercenaries. The captain leading the big mercenary band they'd joined up with had been unpredictable and full of himself, and Heavy Warrior hadn't liked him at all. But at least the way he carried himself had been something Heavy Warrior could learn from.

He thought his friend had been more suited to the mercenary life than he was, though.

If only he hadn't gotten hurt.

If only he hadn't gotten hurt, gone back to their hometown, and left Heavy Warrior wondering what in the world to do. His answer had been to become an adventurer—and now here he was. He needed to do something he could be proud of…

"Hey, you okay?" This time it was Female Knight asking. She watched him across the table over the beer she was swiggi— No, actually, that she was sipping at, worried. That wasn't how the brave—or perhaps overbold—or perhaps devil-may-care knight normally treated alcohol. "You don't look so good," she said. "And you haven't been eating…or sleeping, am I right?"

"No, you're *not* right. I've been eating *and* sleeping. I just haven't been very hungry."

It was true, although not quite in the way he was implying. Having an empty stomach and being hungry weren't the same thing; neither was being tired and sleepy. For Heavy Warrior, it was simple: He just didn't want to waste time on things that didn't matter. If he didn't feel like eating, then getting food moved down the priorities list, and if he wasn't sleepy, then he might as well stay awake.

He didn't see himself as struggling, not really. It wasn't like he was unhappy this way. He wanted to go adventuring. And this looked likely to be a very big one.

If we pull this off, it might just give us a boost on our next exam, he thought.

Out loud, he didn't say anything, just continued working the quill through the sand tray. Female Knight gave him a highly annoyed "hrm!"

"What? What?"

"You haven't eaten a bite of your meal. You haven't even had a drink!"

"Oh…"

Female Knight was openly angry now. She didn't have to say anything more: She exuded a commanding aura. *Order something!* it said. *Drink! Eat!*

Heavy Warrior saw it would be no use arguing. Maybe he could get them to put some ground meat between a couple slices of bread for him or something. He sighed and braced himself against the table and stood up.

"Hey, 'scuse me! Could I get a—?"

No, he *tried* to stand up.

"Whoa?!"

His vision went dark, as if someone had put out the lights, and his head swam like he was being shaken. Up and down seemed to change places, swinging like a giant pendulum, and Heavy Warrior discovered he couldn't stay on his feet. He simply collapsed.

"Hey, what the hell?!" Female Knight shouted.

"Well, this won't do," remarked Half-Elf Light Warrior.

Heavy Warrior didn't hear them, though, nor did he hear their rhea druid cry out. His ears were full of an insistent buzzing that muted all other sounds, and everything seemed so far away from him.

"I b-b-brought someone!" their scout boy spluttered. He'd grabbed the arm of the nearest member of another party and dragged them over.

"Whoa, hey! Hey! Are you all right?!"

Heavy Warrior could tell that the anxious exclamation came from that young warrior.

He thought he said, *Yeah, I'm fine*, but he wasn't sure if the sounds made it out of his mouth.

"I think you'd better take him to his room… Wait, no. Do you think it's safe to move him, Teach?"

"Ah, let me see here… Hmm."

A canid padfoot hunched over Heavy Warrior, whose breath was coming in hard rasps, and peered into his face. He made a thoughtful noise, then rose back up, asked Female Knight several questions, and nodded as if it made sense to him. "I suspect he's overworked," the padfoot said. "Although I must say that medicine is not my specialty, so I can't be certain."

Whatever the case, the teacher concluded, Heavy Warrior clearly needed some rest.

Almost before the words were out of his mouth, Female Knight had grabbed Heavy Warrior's arm and was hefting him up on her shoulder. "What in the gods' names am I going to do with you?!" she groused. "I swear, you're no end of trouble..."

She was much stronger than she looked; her slender frame belied toned, powerful muscles. The two of them were about the same height, though, so Heavy Warrior's feet ended up dragging along the floor.

"I'll help!" said Druid Girl, rushing over. She was small and delicate compared to the knight and the warrior and wasn't going to be able to do any heavy lifting, so to speak. But as a druid, she knew something about medicine.

"Um, uh, um..." Scout Boy, desperate to help but with nothing really to do, looked anxiously up at the half elf. "What about our quest?"

"I guess we'll have to tell them it's off," he said.

The buzz of the tavern quickly returned to normal. This wasn't the first person the patrons had seen falling-down drunk.

Over the chatter, Half-Elf Light Warrior could be heard saying easily, "I don't think this is something we should tackle without our front-row warrior-cum-leader, nor do I wish to attempt it. Do you?"

"No, uh...no," the boy said.

"The reality seems to be that he's taken too much upon himself. He'll need time to recover."

"Right..." That much even Scout Boy could see.

He was painfully aware that he himself was the source of most of Heavy Warrior's problems. He also grasped, though, that if that caused him to do something stupid, it would only make Heavy Warrior's burden weightier. He'd been rash to run away from his indigent household—but if he hadn't, he might not be alive right now.

"Um!" A clear voice sounded, belonging to a girl with tied-back

©Shingo Adachi

silver hair who flung her hands into the air. "If you'll let us… Maybe we could do that quest!" It was unlikely she knew what Scout Boy was thinking, yet still she said it. "Th-they say a-adventurers have to help one another, right?"

The martial artist speaking was among the young warrior's party. Unlike their leader, she and Heavy Warrior didn't have any history; this might have been the first time she had talked to them.

Half-Elf Light Warrior and Scout Boy looked at each other.

"*Do* they say that?" asked a dwarf woman standing on the fringe of the party.

"Perhaps they do, and perhaps they don't," replied an elf cleric with a knowing nod. "But now is not yet the time to speak of such matters."

"Oh, I'll show *you* the time to—"

They began quarreling loudly, drawing a reprimand from the canid spell caster.

Ignoring the bustle behind her, the silver-haired martial artist leaned toward the young warrior. "H-how about it?!" she said, eager but uncertain. Evidently, she had a habit of speaking before her anxieties caught up to her.

The young warrior smiled. Well, why not? Studying was getting a little old. And hey, since they were of similar rank, it probably wasn't a quest that would get them into *too* much trouble.

Always best to repay a debt just as soon as you can, too.

People died. They died so easily. He knew that as well as anyone. Best to make good on favors you owed while you and the other guy were both still around.

"If we can just take expenses out of the reward, it's good by me," he said.

"—!"

The silver-haired girl's face lit up; she half spun so she was facing Half-Elf Light Warrior, her long silver locks following her. "Y-you heard him! We're g-good with it if you are…!"

"Well, uh…" Scout Boy was going to say something, but then he looked at Half-Elf Light Warrior for help. He couldn't get the words out all by himself. Half-Elf Light Warrior smiled and nodded.

"Many thanks for your suggestion," he said. "I'll make sure our knight is all right with the idea, and we'll have to inform the Guild, but assuming they both agree…"

He bowed to the martial artist, who exclaimed, "Right!"

Young Warrior couldn't keep a smile off his face, his expression softening more and more. The canid spell caster stepped up beside him and nodded. "All right, then. First, we must examine the details of this quest."

"Yeah, good call. If this is about finishing off the warlock of the willow vale or something, we might be in over our heads."

"R-right. Good point!" said the martial artist, who didn't seem to have thought that far ahead. Laughter came easily in her panicked state. It provoked an annoyed "hmph!" from her, and the young warrior had to talk her down even as he took the quest paper from Scout Boy.

He was hoping it wouldn't be too difficult…

"Hrm," he said.

"What is it?" asked the martial artist, her spirits repaired as quickly as they had come undone. She stretched to get a look at the paper, her hair bouncing as she moved.

Young Warrior picked out the letters he'd just been studying, then nodded. "It says… They want us to find out what's causing those earthquakes."

Well! That sounded like an adventure.

CHAPTER 2
Tool Grid

"Wanderers, then."

Goblin Slayer's assessment was decisive; Examiner responded with only a modest raise of her eyebrow.

They stood in an open field, the wind rustling the dull brown grass. The adventurer in the grimy armor was on all fours, searching for tracks in the dirt. He rose up again, and as he did so, he looked less like a warrior than a tracker or perhaps a dead man heaving himself out of the earth.

"What are wanderers?" Examiner asked.

"Goblins who have lost their nest or been chased out and now roam at large. They are not a threat." Goblin Slayer didn't even bother to brush the dirt off his armor but gave her an inquisitive tilt of the head. "You don't know about them?"

"I cannot say I condone your attitude at this moment," Examiner replied, sharp and brusque. She was still dressed in her Guild uniform, which didn't seem very appropriate for adventuring. It left her exposed to the biting wind. Her tone of voice, almost as chilly as the breeze, suggested she didn't care. "There are far more people in the world who know things that you do not than the other way around."

"That's logical," Goblin Slayer said, nodding. She was right. He didn't think of himself as someone with any special knowledge. His sister—she had been wise, as had his teacher. Also that wizard who had arrived at a plane he could not even conceive of.

What of the young woman on the farm, or the farm's owner, or Guild Girl, or those adventurers who every once in a while spoke to him in town?

They're smarter than me, no question. They know more than I do.

So also, he was sure, did the woman who was now giving him this warning.

"You are also mistaken to think they are not a threat," she continued.

"At the Adventurers Guild," Goblin Slayer said, never lapsing in his study of the footprints, "I've heard that goblins aren't considered very dangerous."

"*Every* kind of monster is dangerous."

Yes. That was logical, too.

"There is no monster that is not terrible—even if there may be a hierarchy to such terror." Examiner spoke rhythmically, as if she hardly noticed what Goblin Slayer was doing. "Do you believe that the creatures you meet on the first floor of a dungeon are not threatening?"

"I've never been in a dungeon," Goblin Slayer replied.

At least, he didn't think he had. He didn't spare much thought for the nature of the ruins he entered in order to hunt goblins. To him, they were not primarily ruins—they were goblin nests. Just like this field at this moment.

"What, then, do you think of villagers and other people who cannot eliminate even these unthreatening creatures?"

"Hrm...," Goblin Slayer grunted softly. He saw well what she was trying to say. Consider the young woman on the farm or the farm's owner. Or his own older sister and the people of his home. Consider the black-haired girl in that village and all the victims he had met in the course of his goblin hunts. Was he so superior that he could look down on them? No, no—in fact, he might well be below them.

With that thought, the answer came clearly to him.

"The wanderers are a threat. But a minimal one."

"How can you be sure?"

"The footprints."

She sounded almost like a teacher, this woman. What made him think that when her voice was so different from that of either his sister or his master?

Goblin Slayer felt he didn't cope well with her. He didn't find her unpleasant, but he found himself shrinking away from her. He didn't think he would learn to be comfortable in her presence.

"There are a lot of footprints, but their numbers are minimal," he said. "The prints are small and shallow, and the strides are not uniform. The goblins must be thin—"

"—and starving," Examiner concluded. "Very good." She nodded at Goblin Slayer's answer. She was pleased—or was she? No. Goblin Slayer rejected the idea. Earning her approval was something to work toward, but it was not his main priority.

Much as it pained him to admit it, she was right: There was a hierarchy. And killing goblins was at the top of it. If he let himself become more interested in pleasing Examiner than killing goblins, it would upend everything.

"You seem to at least understand that a solo adventurer cannot achieve everything by force alone. Where did you learn your techniques?"

"...The basics from my older sister. Our father was a hunter." Despite his frustration, Goblin Slayer found that he couldn't maintain a sullen silence. He could have just grunted to sidestep the question, but instead he found himself delivering a full answer in steady words. And he hated himself for it.

It wasn't about the woman. What he hated was what he felt inside, like a child frightened by a lightning strike. He thought he could still taste the dirt under the floorboards.

"After that...I taught myself," he said.

"Oh, you did?" Examiner sounded like she was scrutinizing a book open in front of her. She gave a slight tilt of her head. "But it is also possible that a horde has sent a small unit of scouts in advance. What do you think about that?"

That caused Goblin Slayer to fall quiet. He couldn't immediately articulate what made him sure that these were wanderers. The words fluttered up to his throat, but he swallowed them back down before they quite took shape.

Examiner's gaze seemed able to pin him in place through his visor. Finally, he squeezed out: "A horde would have to have a nest somewhere. But this field—"

"There are no forests around nor copses of trees. And of course, no caves. Hmm. Good enough." Very good. She seemed to approve of his answer. "So your enemies are wanderers. What now?"

What would he do next?

The answer was obvious.

"I'll kill them."

With that pronouncement, Goblin Slayer strode ahead across the field. Goblins couldn't move very far or very fast, and the tracks didn't look that old. Wherever they were, they would be close.

"...Hmm." Examiner snorted softly, then followed him, moving readily through the grass.

The quest was veritably formulaic. Goblins had appeared on the outskirts of a village, just wandering around. Some of the local youngsters had succeeded in driving them off—but everyone was scared. They wanted someone to get rid of the goblins before anyone was hurt.

It's strange, Goblin Slayer thought, not because of anything in the content of the quest. He crushed grass and snapped branches underfoot as he blazed a path across the field, never looking back. He tried to move as quietly as he could, but silence was impossible, especially for one so inexperienced.

Yet he couldn't help noticing that *she* made no footsteps. From behind him, he heard only the sound of her regular, steady breathing. Even though she wasn't dressed for the outdoors, Examiner sounded the same as she had in the Guild's halls...

No.

She was moving even faster than she had there, keeping up with him. The way she moved—her footwork, perhaps you would call it—was different somehow.

It's strange, he thought for the second time. Before he could pursue the thought, he pushed all extraneous chatter out of his mind.

Examiner wasn't what he should be focusing on at that moment. Nor was the promotion exam. Killing goblins: That was all.

I will chase them down.

He had no proof of that, yet somehow he didn't doubt it. Call it intuition of a sort. His master would have said there was no such thing, that it was only subconscious experience at work. Did that mean, then, that he had accumulated enough experience to draw such conclusions? Or was it simply a foolish delusion to think he had done so?

What do I care?

Whichever it was, the answer lay ahead.

An ashen sky hung above him, and he couldn't shake the sense that the field seemed to go on forever.

§

"GOOROGGGB…?!"

"One…!"

Goblin Slayer flung his dagger, which neatly pierced through the goblin's throat, choking it to death. There was some modest pleasure in seeing his morning practice pay off, but it was subsumed by more important things.

The reeds crackled as he burst out of them. He saw a small group of goblins.

Three. No, four.

"GORGGB!!"

"GOORRG! GBBB!!"

The goblins, who had been dozing on guard in the midafternoon sun, scrambled to pick up their weapons, a mismatched collection of clubs and rusty swords that came from who knew where.

Goblin Slayer, covered in grass and leaves and mud, barked a mocking laugh. Were they not even smart enough to keep off the night dew? Or didn't goblins care about such things?

It's possible.

The group seemed to lead a fairly pleasant existence in this cave, despite the lack of much to sleep on. Then again, for these goblins in particular, the days might have seemed frustrating and irritating.

"...Yah!" Goblin Slayer exhaled sharply, setting his thoughts aside as he carried his momentum into a kick that shattered a goblin's jaw.

"GOROGGB?!"

His master had forever told him that he should always wear good shoes. That he, not being a rhea, would need them.

He was right.

Satisfied by the feeling of his toes digging into the monster's flesh, he pressed his boot down on the goblin's face, snapping its neck. "That's two...!"

Two goblin corpses beneath the leaden sky. Two more to come.

"GOROOG!!"

"Hrm...!"

A goblin club came swinging in from the left, and he caught it on his shield. There was a dull shock; he knew he wouldn't be able to defend with his left arm alone for very long.

Is that because I've worn down the edge of my shield?

He would have to find the feel for this. Without hesitation, however, he grabbed the knife from the goblin's corpse with his right hand.

"Hff!"

"GRRGBB?!"

His opponent was short. Just by thrusting out with his sword from under his shield, he could easily stab through the creature's guts.

The goblin dropped his club and fell writhing on the ground. Without a pause, Goblin Slayer jumped on him. "This makes three!"

He pinned the flailing creature with his shield, then stabbed it once in the neck. Not from any compassionate desire to put it out of its misery—this was simply the quickest way to kill goblins.

There's one left.

"GOROOGGBB!!"

That was not to say, of course, that he had let his guard down or that he wasn't paying attention to what was behind him. The fact that the goblin slipped right past him just the same spoke to his inexperience. He'd already fought battles where he had to protect someone but always in confined spaces, and although the experience had been intense, he still hadn't fought so many of those fights.

There was a slim woman at his back row. The goblin would drag her down, beat her with his club, and take her hostage. Goblin Slayer assumed, at least, that was the sum total of what the creature had in mind, and it was a most unpleasant thing to imagine.

"...Pfah." Goblin Slayer *tsk*'ed at himself, annoyed, and then he turned to throw his dagger—

"_____"

But he was interrupted by a gust of iron wind blowing past.

"GOOR?!"

Only much later would he learn that the weapon was an old standby called a spiked chain.

"Yaaah...!"

"GOROOGBB?!?!"

It had flown forth from Examiner's sleeve—a long length of chain studded with sharp spikes. She controlled it with a ring on the end, making it leap and dance like a snake and wrapping it around the goblin. The spikes bit like fangs, and the moment the enemy was within range, she swept his feet out from under him. It was an extremely sophisticated technique; no doubt more than a goblin could comprehend.

"Sshhaaa!" she cried, leaping toward the goblin with a lightness Goblin Slayer would never have expected. He thought he heard a single long *whack*, although it was probably two hits. No more than that. But then:

"G...BB...ORG...B...?!"

The monster began bleeding profusely from its eyes, ears, nose, and mouth, and then it crumpled to the ground.

It all took barely an instant. To Goblin Slayer it looked like—yes, it looked like magic. As any advanced enough technique would to the uninitiated.

He simply stood there; to his ears came a clear ringing of steel scraping on steel. He blinked and discovered the chain had disappeared from Examiner's hand. Hidden back in her sleeve, he suspected.

She gave the slightest of sighs. "It is over, then."

"..." Goblin Slayer was quiet for a long moment, then nodded. "Yes."

He put the rusty dagger at his hip, then pulled his own sword with its abbreviated length out of the throat of the first goblin he'd killed.

There were many lessons he would have to learn from this encounter, even though he hadn't panicked or made any serious lapses.

I wish I had tried my tear bombs.

He grunted softly when he realized he had failed to even consider his newest equipment.

He had never felt accomplished after hunting goblins. Not once.

§

"You forgot to bear in mind that you are now part of a party."

"Hrm..."

Goblin Slayer was crouching in the bushes, examining the bodies, when this undeniably accurate assessment came from overhead. He looked up at his examiner, his hands still grimy with goblin blood. The Guild uniform she wore, which bordered on formal clothing, was an outfit he was familiar with, but seeing it out here in the field never ceased to seem strange to him. The way she stood there, prim and proper with her arms crossed, only reinforced the feeling that he was right back at the Guild.

Goblin Slayer, however, did not forget that he was squatting over a goblin corpse at that moment. He always had one eye on their surroundings, watching everything vigilantly. He considered her comment for such a long time that it bordered on rude. His tone was grave as he finally said, "What do you mean?"

"You did not give me so much as a single instruction, did you?" she replied, paying no mind to the lengthy pause, her answer as sharp and as fast as her chain.

Her tone was no different from usual, but Goblin Slayer had the distinct sense that he was being rebuked, and he fell silent. For it was a fact, wasn't it? He couldn't deny it. Moreover, to have allowed an enemy to go straight for her on the back row was a critical mistake.

Suppose he was more of a talker. Imagine he was the loquacious kind. It wouldn't change the facts one single bit. And he was, at the very least, not shameless enough to try to deny facts.

Instead, he asked, "What should I do?"

Examiner sighed—partly, it seemed, in resignation and partly to hide her pleasure at being asked the question. It could have been either. Goblin Slayer wasn't good enough at guessing how people felt to say one way or the other. He only crouched there, waiting for her words, covered in leaves and mud and goblin blood.

"Seek opinions," she answered, her one eye narrowing. She sounded like she was simply putting one and one together. "There is always another way of thinking, something that you would never come up with on your own."

"But," he said, his mind working, "there may be times when there isn't."

"Then that is when *you* must give the alternate perspective. Or you must find companions who will give it to you."

"Even if I don't believe that perspective is correct?"

"Especially then." The woman nodded, then gave him an elegant wave of her finger, the same one that had killed a goblin moments before. "A leader must make decisions only after considering all possible viewpoints. If you are a leader, that is what you must do."

"Hrm..."

"Mercenaries may be happy so long as they alone survive, but adventurers stand and fall together."

A damp wind rustled the undergrowth. Intermingled with the stench of goblin blood, he could smell something faintly sweet. The fragrance of a woman, something Goblin Slayer had never smelled before.

Was it perfume? he wondered. He had never noticed such a thing in the past.

"To join a party brings particular responsibilities, and to lead one brings others," Examiner said. At least, that was the ideal. She smiled ever so slightly, then cleared her throat to cover herself. "So?"

"Hrm...," Goblin Slayer grunted softly. Had he understood her words completely? He would have to say no. But he thought they made some kind of sense to him. Even a modest goblin hunt like this one had shown him how many things there were in the world that he did not or could not think of on his own.

...No.

He'd already learned that lesson in spades as a young boy, hiding under the floorboards as goblins ransacked his village. If someone had gone to take word that day, if someone had hired adventurers, it might have been different. But no one had. *He* hadn't. He'd done nothing—not one thing.

He couldn't pin the blame on anyone else. It was his own fault things had turned out the way they had.

It would be sheer hubris to imagine that he could deal with everything that might happen. Which meant that now, at this moment, it was obvious what he should do.

"What...do you think of the situation?" he asked.

Well! Examiner's eyes widened slightly; she seemed surprised to find him so pliant. With a calm stride of her long legs, she stepped up beside Goblin Slayer. He shuffled aside to make room for her—and she pointed to something beside the dead goblin's corpse. Something imprinted in the soft earth.

"Are those footprints?" she asked.

"Yes. From some kind of wolf," replied Goblin Slayer. "I suspect."

"Probably wargs, more specifically," Examiner said, and he saw with a start that she was closer to his helmet that he had realized. Behind his visor, he moved his eyes, and he had the distinct sensation that he met the gaze of the eye she kept hidden behind her hair.

He must've been imagining it. Most likely.

"Do goblins ever keep such animals?" Examiner asked.

"I know they do," Goblin Slayer answered with a nod. He had encountered them before.

What did she say again?

He seemed to recall that wizard saying that goblins had stolen the knack of riding.

"Wargs. Is that what they're called?" he said quietly.

The woman nodded, revealing her pale throat. "If you read the old texts, you will find them there."

"I see."

He thought of the piles and piles of borrowed books in his shed.

Might some of them mention these creatures? They might. He would have to read through them sometime.

If there is *a sometime.*

For now, he should focus on what was right in front of him. He would work on the assumption that he might never get to read those books.

He suspected that wizard would only have muttered, "That right?" with much the same expression as Examiner wore now.

Goblin Slayer grunted softly. He who didn't know where the finger was pointing would never find the moons. Where Goblin Slayer had to go now, however, was much closer than the moons. He could start by taking his first step.

"These w…"

"Wargs."

"…Whatever they are, I don't think a few wanderers would be able to keep them."

More importantly, Goblin Slayer saw that the footsteps were moving away from their location.

He'd gone to help pick medicinal herbs when he was young, but truth be told, it had been mostly a game for him. His sister had pointed out animal tracks to him, telling him these belong to this animal or those belong to that animal.

She probably knew I wasn't really listening.

Now he desperately wished he had paid more attention.

How many simple daily things had he ignored, never knowing their true value?

In spite of his inattention, some vestige of his sister's teaching remained with him, and now it was whispering to him which way the beasts had gone.

"What are you going to do?" Examiner asked, brusque, business-like, almost mechanical, and piercing.

Goblin Slayer's eyes moved behind his visor. She stood just as she had before, with her arms crossed casually just under her chest. As if to say that she didn't really care how he answered—it was all the same to her.

"Technically, we have completed the quest," she added.

Well. If it was all the same to her. "There's only one thing to do," Goblin Slayer said. "We pursue them and kill them."

§

"Fwaaah..."

"Gee, someone's tired."

"Look who's talking."

It was a long, languid afternoon. At the reception counter, Guild Girl stretched mightily, sparing a smile for her friend, who was slumped out on the wood.

The sunlight pouring in through the window was going from clear to golden. Motes of dust drifted through it, glinting and dancing as they went. It was warm, calm, quiet, and nearly deserted—yes, a languid Adventurers Guild, indeed. Usually, even moments like this were punctuated by the occasional adventurer passing through or a quest giver stopping in to file a quest, but not today.

I guess you get days like this, too, Guild Girl thought. Only the truly paranoid would complain that things were a little *too* quiet.

Guild Girl's relaxed mood, however, didn't actually have much to do with the afternoon torpor.

"...Just *having* her here, like, it makes everything harder, doesn't it?" Guild Girl's colleague asked, looking like she was going to melt into the counter beside Guild Girl.

"She's not a bad person," Guild Girl replied, but she couldn't deny it. Their senior colleague was as kind as she was demanding and a good person in her way, but things could still be tough around her. Well, it wasn't her personally—it was more the sense of tension that she brought with her. *That* was what was so tiring. "I have to admit, I sort of admire that poise."

"It's suffocating. I wish you would find a different idol."

"Don't worry. I don't think I could be like her if I tried," Guild Girl said with a bitter smile directed not at her friend, nor at her senior, but at herself. Her senior was so composed. She was—what could Guild Girl call it? *A mature woman*. Yes. That was it.

Guild Girl didn't feel that was something she could ever become. As a girl, she'd looked up to her elder sisters the same way, but it turned out that just getting older didn't make her one of them. Sometimes the world was that way. Sometimes it felt like it was always that way.

"...That reminds me," she said. Well, she hadn't really forgotten, but it moved her to open a drawer in the counter and take out a piece of parchment. Worked with a grid of squares, it was a map of the surrounding area.

Needless to say, such a precise diagram was not to be taken off premises. They had a map they lent out to adventurers, but it wasn't quite so detailed.

"Let's see. Today makes... How many days since they left?" she mumbled. She counted the days and did some calculations based on an average movement speed. The weather had been fine, so she had a good chance of guessing their location. She didn't need a ruler; she simply counted the squares. A simple estimate was enough. Guild Girl nodded. *They should be just about done with the quest by now.*

A goblin hunt.

As long as nothing out of the ordinary happened, they would be fine—probably. It was just a goblin hunt, after all. The quest itself had been downright formulaic, and the number of goblins the witnesses reported suggested a modestly sized group.

Goblin hunting was dangerous, but then so was all adventuring. He'd already been promoted before and was about to be promoted again—as long as nothing unusual happened, he would be fine probably. And even if something did...

My colleague is there.

She would do whatever had to be done—pull him out of danger, talk him out of doing anything crazy, drag him back. So it would be okay...or so Guild Girl kept telling herself.

"......"

She never got used to this. The way you could say hello to someone in the morning who didn't come home at night. Well, okay: One-day adventures were the exception, not the rule.

Then they didn't come home for several days. No notice of completion ever arrived. Such things happened, of course, and happened with some regularity. Sometimes you remembered who had taken those quests, and sometimes you didn't.

Sometimes all you had was a name, skills, and achievements—what were popularly called "stats" and "experience points." But in between those numbers and letters, you might catch a glimpse of a person's life. Were they waylaid by mountain bandits? Was their head crushed by a troll? Were they captured by dark elves and tortured to death?

Maybe they got lost in a dense forest, fell off the side of a mountain, or maybe they were trapped in the rock down in some dungeon…

Sometimes adventurers were simply lost. It happened.

Would there come a day when she was used to that?

Maybe this was why they taught Guild employees not to get too friendly with the adventurers. She wondered if her friend beside her felt the same way. Or her senior.

There were so many things Guild Girl didn't understand yet.

"Y-yikes?!"

Her ruminations were interrupted when she suddenly found herself being thrown upward. She felt the shock wave all the way through her body, and then the floor was shaking so hard she thought it might crack open.

"Wh-wh-whaaat?!"

While Guild Girl tried to fling herself to the ground, her receptionist friend had thrown herself toward the nearest shelf, pressing her back against it. The big, heavy piece of wooden furniture would be the last thing to fall down around here, but even it was shaking violently. Guild Girl let out another yelp as books and papers came tumbling down on her like a rainstorm.

It's another earthquake…

The shaking was so bad it felt like the whole Four-Cornered World might be overturned and thrown clear off the tabletop.

To Guild Girl, it felt like the earthquake lasted forever, but it was probably just a few seconds. The shaking ceased as suddenly as it had begun.

"I-is it…o-o-over…?" she asked. She started to get to her feet but had to grab the counter to steady herself. Her body felt like it was still rocking.

"I…I think so." Her friend, all but clinging to the bookshelf, nodded, looking just as uneasy as Guild Girl felt.

If the Guild had been quiet before, it certainly wasn't now. People rushed around, and everyone seemed to be talking at once. There were, in fact, plenty of adventurers renting rooms here, plus employees who had been doing work in the back.

The adventurers emerged, wanting to know what was going on. The other employees immediately put their work aside and went out front to make sure everything was all right.

Guild Girl recognized one of the adventurers: a young man holding a spear, who grabbed the railing of the stairway and flung himself over it, leaping straight down to the first floor. Behind him on the stairs, she spotted a witch in sheer night clothes, covering herself with a sheet. Beside her was a warlock who had just registered the other day. As was the way of these things, the warlock wore an absolute minimum of clothing. She had a fairly toned body for a spell caster, and Guild Girl had some questions about the fact that she was carrying a longsword.

But they're quite a pair to look at, she thought. Neither of them was openly afraid—but then if they let that emotion show on their faces, the men would never have been able to leave them alone. It hadn't been that long since either of them had registered. They were just a couple of novice young ladies.

Based on her experience in the capital, Guild Girl had no reason not to sympathize with the two. She glanced up at them with a look that said, *Everything's okay*. Witch nodded and quietly returned to her room. Warlock continued to survey the situation for a moment, then muttered something that didn't sound very complimentary and turned on her heel.

"What's goin' on, my dear receptionist?!"

"Oh! Um…"

She couldn't fault him for his enthusiasm—if *nothing* else.

I still don't know…quite how to handle myself with him…

The spearman slapped a hand down on the counter, eager as could be, and now she had to deal with him.

Guild Girl tried to file the sharp edges off her stiff smile and give him the vaguest answer she could muster. “Well, probably…nothing to speak of, I think, but—”

She was interrupted by her immediate superior, the chief of this branch of the Guild. “All right, everyone calm down! First, let’s see what our status is!” He gave a sharp clap of his hands like this was nothing new to him, his voice carrying all around the Guild. Throughout the room, people turned toward him. “Running around like chickens with our heads cut off can come *after* we’ve ascertained whether anyone has been hurt or any property damaged! You there—are you okay?”

“Uh, yes, sir!” said Guild Girl’s friend with a quick nod. “I’m fine, sir.”

“Then clean up these papers, make sure they’re all in order, and put them back where they belong. If we lose any of them, it’d do more harm than that earthquake!”

“I can help!” Guild Girl offered, partly out of professional responsibility and partly as an excuse to get away from Spearman. She darted over to her friend like an eager puppy. Behind her, the adventurer looked disappointed, but she would pretend she hadn’t seen it.

“If our adventurers would please keep your heads as well,” the chief went on. “If there are any serious problems, a quest will be issued. I’m sure none of you wants to miss the opportunity to make a little spending money, right? So don’t go running off in a panic or you might miss your chance.” A nice little joke thrown in there, and it got the ruffians listening to him and doing what he asked.

Adventure was what they were here for, after all, but given the choice, they were especially interested in ways to get rich quick or else great deeds that would see their names go down in history. Spearman, too, headed back up to his room, although at a distinct plod.

Come to think of it…

Guild Girl couldn’t help noticing—and worrying—that the heavy warrior and his party, the ones who had had some problems at their last promotion exam, were nowhere to be seen.

"It's nothing to be so upset about," her branch manager said with an incongruous smile when she expressed this concern to him. "Compared to what happened in the capital five years ago or to the Dungeon of the Dead, this is a walk in the park." That made her feel better.

He righted a toppled inkpot and shrugged at the ink spreading across the floor. He sounded like an accomplished warrior himself as he said, "It's not like the world is going to end over a little thing like this."

§

"More shaking."

"I see."

Their conversation was brief and to the point, with a quality not unlike the crackling of a fire. The gloom of evening was just overtaking the sky.

Goblin Slayer and his examiner sat on either side of a dancing bonfire, somewhere on the side of the road. Goblin Slayer's armor, so recently polished, was freshly splattered with mud—but the examiner's uniform still seemed practically unruffled. He couldn't imagine what her secret was, but more to the point, he didn't care. The only thing he was interested in was the tracks of the wolves—which meant the goblins.

The two of them seemed to get no closer to their quarry, yet neither were they being left behind. They were decisively on the trail.

Of course, Goblin Slayer was doing more than following the footprints as such. There would be no tracks left in hard earth—but there was always a trace. A broken branch here, trampled flowers there. Wolf or goblin excrement, scraps of food. Something.

Did the goblins not care that they might be followed, or did the possibility never occur to them?

Both probably.

Whichever it was, he was lucky. He had never once considered himself unlucky. He knew that it was not his skill alone that had allowed him to track his prey this far. It showed how much was possible with just the modest degree of tracking knowledge he had absorbed from his sister, along with a little experience.

Some shaking ground wouldn't be enough to disturb the tracks, but if rain fell, it would all be for naught. This was a rare opportunity to be able to track by the light of the moons and stars.

He was no Rainmaker; he couldn't affect the weather with his own skills. And given that he knew no spells that would restore the tracks after so much as a drop of precipitation had hit them, this was a fortunate moment indeed.

I want to catch up with them before the rain starts.

It had already been several days since they had left the pioneer village without sending word. Goblin Slayer poured some of the contents of his canteen into a small stewpot, tossed some dried meat in, and put it over the fire. He wasn't thinking much about quantity or flavor. He wouldn't die of starvation nor would it be inedible, and that was all that mattered.

One of the handful of his master's teachings that he had been unable to abide by was regarding food. Eating was a bother. He would rather be tracking. Every step forward would give him strength. He would cease to notice his empty belly—only when it got so bad that it made him feel nauseous would it be worth stopping to eat. Even then, his interest would not be in satiating his appetite but merely in forestalling the physical cramping of his stomach. If there hadn't been a biological need, he probably wouldn't have eaten even that often.

Such was how he would have been if left to his own devices, but something stopped him—or rather, someone. The presence of a companion.

"Do you need a rest?" he had asked, the question coming to him suddenly as they were marching along the evening they had killed the goblins.

"If you think one is necessary," Examiner had replied flatly.

That forced him to think. He was doing what he preferred to do, but maybe he shouldn't force others to do it as well. They could make camp, have a simple meal, catch a few moments' rest, and then resume at dawn.

If the wolves—or wargs, he wasn't sure—moved at night like the goblins, then he and his companion could make up ground during the day.

This had gone on for several days. The hours passed quietly: Examiner spoke rarely, and Goblin Slayer stayed focused on the ground. This woman was the exact opposite of his previous quest giver, who had seemed to talk almost nonstop. This was much more like Goblin Slayer's normal life, and yet he felt uneasy.

Most likely, it was because of the way Examiner was forever watching him, studying him, like a cat stalking its prey.

Thus, when she said, "I think...," at first Goblin Slayer thought it was the rustling of leaves. When he saw Examiner's lips move for certain, he corrected that misapprehension. "...that taking every goblin quest off the board for yourself is rather bad manners."

"Bad manners," he echoed. He hadn't heard that one before—at least when it came to adventures, to things that involved hunting goblins.

"You are stealing work from the novices."

"Hrm."

"Stealing jobs means stealing options, which means stealing the opportunities for them to grow."

"Grow," Goblin Slayer parroted again. Not that he knew anything about parrots, other than that they supposedly imitated human speech.

"Is there any way to attain maturity ultimately, except to accumulate your own experiences?" Examiner asked. It was very logical. Goblin Slayer's master had taught him many things, but that was a different kind of learning from what Goblin Slayer had discovered for himself. If all it took to do something well were someone telling you how to do it, his first goblin hunt would never have been so pathetic.

It was only due to a happy roll of the dice that he hadn't died that day. And one reason he had come as far as he had now was because of the experience he'd gained that time.

Even understanding that took a certain amount of experience itself.

"Those who beg someone to share their map of the first floor will be no different on the tenth," Examiner murmured, although

Goblin Slayer didn't understand exactly what she meant. "Those who demand to be *taught* how to hunt goblins will likewise demand someone teach them how to hunt dragons."

Those who want surefire, safe strategies—there was a touch of bitterness in Examiner's voice.

My teacher, Goblin Slayer thought. What would he say? What would he think of an adventurer who was angry at someone for not teaching them, when they themselves had not asked to be taught? If Goblin Slayer had raised a fuss like that, his master would have beaten him and then left him where he lay.

"In any event," Examiner said, her words a clear demarcation between one part of the conversation and the next. They were about to come to the heart of what she wished to say. "If you are to be promoted, you will have to start thinking about things like that—thinking like an established adventurer."

"But I may not be promoted," Goblin Slayer countered, matching her brusqueness with his own. The water in the pan had begun to burble; he spared it a glance and then said, "Aren't you thinking of failing me right now?"

"Heaven forfend," she said, shrugging as if to show the idea was ridiculous. "I am merely examining you, boy. There is no room for personal sentiment in that."

"Then why would you give me any advice?"

"I believe I just explained."

"..."

He didn't understand what she meant. He watched her from behind his visor. Only one of her eyes was visible; the other was still hidden behind her long hair. But the eye he could see flickered with a flame that threatened to scorch him.

"To be quite blunt, we do not need adventurers who do nothing but hunt goblins."

"But the quests are there." Although he felt himself starting to fidget, Goblin Slayer didn't back down. He didn't understand why he felt so compelled to push back, but he did. "There are always goblin hunts."

"You do realize that there are monsters besides goblins out there?"

"Hrk…"

"Goblins are not the only threat to the Four-Cornered World. In fact, they may be the smallest threat of all."

One couldn't be obsessed with them.

Examiner's words were self-evident, inescapably logical. Even Goblin Slayer couldn't say what bothered him so much about them. He was well aware of the facts she laid out and had accepted them himself. Therefore, there was no problem with the content of what she was saying.

He took the branch he was using as a poker and jabbed listlessly at the fire.

"You speak as if you've seen it," he said.

"I have." The words were stark, and although they almost sounded embarrassed, there was no change in her expression. She did, however, *tsk* softly, perhaps feeling that she had shared too much. "As far as the exam, you seem well acquainted with making camp and building a fire."

"I see."

"I must ask, however—what do you do about a watch when you are working solo?"

"It's not a problem," he said somewhat firmly. "I can sleep with one eye open."

Examiner's eye widened slightly. Breath escaped her lips—a sound of frustration perhaps. "Lack of sleep can be fatal, boy."

"…"

"Your mind dulls, and your reactions go with it—and therefore, perforce, your skills. If you think you can be victorious in such a state, you are deluding yourself."

Is that the case? Goblin Slayer wondered distantly, even as he took the pan off the fire. The water was lukewarm now; the juice it had formed could hardly be called a soup, but it had softened up at the meat, which was damp when he chewed it.

He ate, not caring about the moisture that dribbled out of his food, and he drank. The soup was not particularly good and had an odd salty flavor.

Examiner produced some hard bread from her own cargo, broke a small piece off, and nibbled on it. "Further, if you are such a bad cook, you should purchase provisions and learn how to prepare them." She spoke rhythmically, her eyes on her own hands.

"That will cost money."

"Nothing in this world comes without a price."

"What about that thing the clerics speak of? Love freely given?"

"They merely repeat what they are told," she said, popping another piece of bread into her mouth and licking her fingers. "But it brings happiness."

"To whom?"

"To the one who offers the love."

"Is that the case…?"

He didn't understand at all. But if she said so, it was probably true.

He didn't believe in the gods—anyway, not enough to dedicate his life to them. But neither did he resent them. Why should he? What had happened that night was entirely his own responsibility.

All this meant was that clerics were people who could do something he could not.

It's only natural that clerics should accept alms.

Examiner's explanation was as logical as always. Goblin Slayer, however, didn't put that feeling into words but continued to chew on his soggy meat. The only sounds were the wind bringing the night ever nearer, and a few birds, and the crackling of the fire.

Just under those things, he could hear Examiner's breathing again.

"…You seem to me to be less of a warrior and more of a scout or a tracker," she said.

"I see." Goblin Slayer thought for a moment, then swallowed what was in his mouth, which was by now reduced to a flavorless lump. "My father was a hunter, and my older sister taught me his ways."

"You said that already."

"I did?"

"You did."

"I see…"

That was all Goblin Slayer said, and then he fell into silence.

This night promised to be very long.

§

His niece had been keeping the night watches for some time now. After they had done the day's work and had their dinner, she would gaze into the purpling sky. Sometimes from just in front of the main house, sometimes from the window of her room or even from the shed.

Could she have a case of melancholy?

Such was what he'd thought at first.

He remembered telling the uncomprehending girl that she lived on this farm now, that she wouldn't be able to go home again. He remembered when she had watched them bury empty coffins for his little sister and her husband—that is, the girl's parents.

He remembered well when his niece had begun to simply drift through life.

He hadn't really known her in her early years. They didn't live near each other, and the girl and her parents rarely if ever came to his farm, so he didn't see them unless he had business that took him to them.

Nonetheless, he knew the girl to be cheerful and spunky. She reminded him of his sister when she was young. He recalled that his niece spent a lot of her time running around with one of the village boys—or really, dragging him around. His sister sent him occasional letters in which he could clearly hear of the little girl's growing up.

"It's the way of things." That was what the cleric sent from the temple of the Earth Mother had said, sounding calm and composed. They'd said that ultimately, only the gods knew the workings of a person's heart. If anything, the cleric seemed more concerned about the farm owner, offering him words of sympathy and support.

The little girl wasn't the only one who had lost her family, they pointed out. So had he.

He didn't intend to use that as an excuse—for his niece was in the same position.

Luckily, he was an adult.

He had experienced death in his time, in a life that had taken him into battle as he earned his money before finally becoming a landowner.

So he could endure. He had the resources at least to provide for his niece. He would give her what he could.

He'd tried to care for her, tried to look after her, puzzled and wondered at her, and finally…

In the end, I couldn't do anything for her. It was only after that kid showed up at our door.

From inside the house, he could clearly see his niece sitting and staring out the window. The farm owner sighed deeply.

It was the first time his niece had ever asked him for anything. A child had lost everything, then disappeared for years, then emerged again as an adventurer. Why? Why would he choose that path?

The motivation seemed clear enough. Whatever he had been doing all those years, he hadn't been leading an ordinary life, the farm owner suspected. But between his niece's heartfelt request and the young man's basically decent conduct, he hadn't hesitated to say yes. If he had reached the point where he could turn away a child who had lost his family, his life, and everything without batting an eye, then it would have been better if he'd simply died in those battles.

Then again, who else would dare take in a novice adventurer—an untested ruffian from who knows where?

He believed, however, that his decision was showing its worth. His niece had begun to work—hard, single-mindedly, and above all, of her own volition. She helped around the farm without being asked, went into town, and had even cut her hair. His niece, for whom he had been unable to do anything himself, had been transformed. He merely had to look at her to know that he had made the right choice.

If there was one thing that could still provoke a sigh from him… Well, it was how that boy looked—and how his niece looked when the boy was gone…

In the end, she just sits there and stares.

The farm owner frowned, sighed yet again, and got up, his chair groaning as he rose. His niece didn't so much as move, even though she must have heard him coming over. The owner walked to the window, calling to her where she sat outside. "Don't stay out too long in the night breeze."

His voice came out sharper than he'd intended. His niece flinched, and he felt a rush of shame.

"…It's getting colder. You'll get sick," he added.

"Oh. Right…" She sounded distracted, like someone just waking up from a dream. He had spoken to her, and the words had entered her ears, but that was all. She wasn't responding consciously, not really. After a long moment and still sounding like her mind was elsewhere, she said, "You're right."

That was it.

His niece continued to sit there, staring at the twin moons and the stars—no, he realized. She was staring at the road from town.

The owner found there was nothing more he could say. Thinking he should at least get her a blanket, he turned back into the house.

His body felt so heavy. He was getting old, he thought—and that brought another sigh.

§

He hated that feeling of falling just before he dropped off, literally falling asleep. He always felt like he might just keep falling and never make his way back. He felt like he was hanging from a cliffside.

If he fell asleep, there was no guarantee he would wake up again. He might be hit on the head and die.

Then again, when he considered the alternative—being dragged out of sleep and then murdered—he thought it might be far preferable to die without knowing it.

Was this related, he wondered, to his fear that the road would crumble away from under him while he was walking?

It was something he would never know.

For his part, he fought the awful feeling of falling, opening first one eye and then the other in turn.

Judging time by sensation alone was difficult. He should look to see how low the fire was, how light the sky was; that would be better.

Just then, he heard something: the sound of rushing air.

He saw Examiner, haloed by the gray predawn light, her toned body covered by only the lightest clothing. Her sharp gaze was not directed anywhere in particular, and her fist was punching the empty air.

Whoosh. Breath came out from her gently parted lips. Or perhaps it was going in. He wasn't sure. All he knew was that she looked more collected than he had seen before.

She stood there, her fists at the ready. No more, no less—and yet she looked as if she had been standing there for a hundred years. Her chest, describing a perfect curve, moved gently up and down, all her muscles and sinews supporting her delicate flesh.

Her foot moved, relaxed, and she took a natural step forward, almost rolling into it. Her arm, which had been as loose as a limp bowstring, snapped forward, her fist striking the air. He could hear it from where he sat.

A branch a good hundred paces away swayed.

"Hoo…"

This time, he was sure, Examiner was exhaling. There was a slight flush in her cheeks, and her breath fogged as she breathed out.

She swiped at the sweat on her brow with her arm. She appeared dissatisfied with her own technique.

Her bangs were swept aside.

Behind her hair, there was puckered skin and a pale, cloudy eye—a nonexistent gaze that nonetheless met his eyes.

His eyes, hidden under his helmet, behind his visor. She shouldn't have been able to see him. And yet he was seen. He could feel it.

Goblin Slayer felt he should say something. He somehow forced his dry, thick tongue to move.

"…Goblins?" he asked.

"Hardly," Examiner replied, brushing off the idea with a laugh. She took out a cloth and wiped the sweat away theatrically, knowing full well that she was being watched. Then in a single perfect motion, she grabbed her shirt, which was hanging from a nearby branch, and shrugged it on. "You must be very optimistic if you think every catastrophe in this world is caused by goblins…"

Her words seemed to be directed at him, yet at the same time, she appeared to be talking to herself. No matter which it was, however, Goblin Slayer could not answer in time. While he was still moving his

dull mind, trying to grasp what she had said, Examiner had already pulled on her outfit.

Regardless, he had lost forever the chance to respond. Her sharp gaze pierced him, almost pinning him in place. "Tell me you do not seriously believe that you are going to take on all the goblins of the Four-Cornered World alone."

"Of course not," he—Goblin Slayer—replied immediately. "But there is the story of a giant who drank all the water in a lake."

"We are not talking about fairy tales here." Her words were like a physical slap. Even as she spoke, Examiner straightened her collar and finished changing. There wasn't a wrinkle in her shirt, her tie was smartly tied, and there wasn't a single stain on her jacket. She looked flawless—one would never imagine that she was camping in the field and pursuing an enemy across open terrain.

Then she turned toward him and said almost as one would to a friend staying at one's house, "You intend to have breakfast?"

"I do," he replied with a nod, and she beamed at him.

"Very good!"

Granted, the expression promptly disappeared when she saw the breakfast he had prepared.

But let us pass over that in silence.

Adventures—not that he remotely thought of what he was doing in those terms—were not a case of seen one, seen all. They weren't endless processions of dramatic moments. Only country children or the especially ignorant thought of them that way.

Sometimes, an adventure simply involved proceeding. Putting one foot in front of the other.

Forward, forward. Tracking the footprints across the field. Counting the squares of this Four-Cornered World the gods had made as you went.

It was the sort of thing that might have been passed over in a short verse or two in one of the sagas. Who wants to hear about their hero crawling along in the mud, inspecting animal dung for clues?

"Some people might complain about this kind of work," Examiner said as softly as if she were letting out a breath, but Goblin Slayer never looked up. He was focused on the ground at his feet, or just ahead of him, or checking the sky, or watching for goblins. "In that respect, boy, you are at least better than them."

"I see."

Examiner, walking casually behind him, was unconcerned by his response. Had she just been making conversation? Or talking to herself? Goblin Slayer couldn't decide. Either way, it didn't matter to him.

"Insofar as you are taking risks and venturing forth, you are on an adventure. Nor do you complain that this adventure isn't safe." He heard her snort quietly, as if the idea of a "safe adventure" was ridiculous. "No one who would quail and quarrel at goblin hunting will ever destroy a demon."

"I have no intention of facing any demons," Goblin Slayer said—as he believed he'd made clear. He rose slowly to his feet, not even brushing the dirt from his hands, and looked left and right. "Not now, not ever."

"That will not do."

"Hrm."

Facing demons was perfectly respectable work, but in his mind, it was something far removed from him. Demons—and dragons, too. He knew he would never in his life battle such things.

After all, he had his hands full with a few goblins.

"You cannot reach the moon if you never look at it, boy," Examiner said, and the sense that she had seen straight through him caused him to fall into a sullen silence. The one eye glanced at him, and then she raised a slim finger and pointed. "We're there," she announced. "The village."

INTERLUDE

Raiders of the Lost Ruins

"Wah—ah—ah—ahh—ahhh?!"

Young Warrior himself didn't know what he was trying to say, if anything at all. He could only flail his arms and kick his legs. He felt like he was floating, and there was a violent rush of wind all around him—he couldn't feel anything else. He was gripped by a terror that would have claimed his sanity had it continued forever. He felt the corners of his mouth tugging upward into a smile. Maybe that was what you did when you were terrified, he thought.

All of which is another way of saying: He was falling.

"Hyaaaahhhh!" The yell he heard from overhead must be the girl, the silver-haired martial artist. The more guttural one from below him must be the dwarf scout. If she was still yelling, that meant he still had a ways to drop.

He could also hear the jabbering of an elf, but from their canid teacher—well, he was all right. Surely.

Okay, bigger things to worry about!

What to do? What should he do? He couldn't seem to think.

The only thought he could get into his head was at least they weren't on a slope. He'd heard a fairy tale when he was a boy. Something about someone at the top of a mountain who lost their footing and tumbled all the way down to the bottom and was never seen again.

Being battered to death is a thing...!

It was not a happy thought. Maybe it was actually good luck that there seemed to be no walls here and no footing.

"Waah—hagh?!"

At that moment, from far below him, he heard the dwarf's unmistakable shout. It didn't sound like she was dying, though—he was pretty sure.

"What's going—obbb?!" Young Warrior tried to call out but found something stopping his mouth.

What the hell is this?!

He was choking. He couldn't breathe. Something had jumped into his mouth—or had he fallen through it? Just for a second, he felt something cling to his body, but then he was past it and falling again. "Yarrrgh!"

And then—the bottom.

Young Warrior screamed as he slammed into what he took to be a stone floor. He would have sworn the impact should have broken all his bones, but fortunately for him, it didn't.

How? When we were falling for so long?

He was rubbing some of his sorer spots when he discovered the reason. "Y-yikes! What are these?" There was something white, pale, and sticky all over his face and hands, clinging to his armor. It stubbornly resisted his attempts to sweep it away. "Spiderwebs?"

As if in answer, the silver-haired girl came plummeting from above with an almost comically brave "hiiiyaaaaahhhh!" The shout echoed all over. She slammed a fist and one knee into the ground, landing neatly from her wild fall. *Boom!* The impact seemed like it shook the four corners of the very board, but the silver-haired girl was perfectly steady; she looked downright unconcerned.

He'd heard before that martial artists could fall safely from any height because they knew how to land, but this—

"Arrrgh! Pins and needles!" the girl exclaimed, tears leaping to her eyes. Apparently, she was still learning.

"...You okay?" Young Warrior asked wryly, to which she snapped, "I'm *so* not!" as she tried to get the goo off herself.

Sounds like she's doing fine, Young Warrior thought. "How about the rest of us?" he asked.

"I seem to have managed. If not quite as gracefully as her," said their teacher, who had landed on all fours. He got to his feet and picked up his glasses, which had tumbled to the ground.

"Even the great dragons who fly among the clouds cannot fight their own weight and may fall into the forest below, they say…"

"Spare me the classical quotations! What were you going to do if I died, eh, scout?!"

Nearby, their elf was hissing and spitting as he tried to extricate himself from a very awkward landing among the spiderwebs.

"I thought elves didn't die. Don't they just go over the sea to the west?"

"But what if I *had* died?!"

"All right, glad to see everyone's okay," Young Warrior said, pulling the last of the cobwebs off his armor.

This adventure is turning out to be bigger than I'd expected.

He didn't think they had done anything out of the ordinary. They were supposed to investigate the source of the earthquakes—and it seemed likely that the tremors were the doing of another Rock Eater.

The teacher's appraisal had been simple: *"Everything is not riding on us; we should prioritize bringing back concrete information."* That had seemed like a good idea, and so into the mines they had gone. That was several hours ago now.

Well, sometimes he'd won and sometimes he'd lost; he wasn't going to stand here and complain about it. They'd worked their way around the empty mines, following their map, investigating whatever they could…

"And then the ground gave out, am I right?"

"Yeah," the dwarf girl said, brushing the dirt off her equipment with a scowl. "I just wanna be perfectly clear: This is not my fault. I didn't miss anything."

"Thanks. I hear you. Helps fill in the little gap in my memories…"

He wasn't interested in arguing with his party members right now. There were times when it was worth hashing things out, but this wasn't one of them.

Parties were fragile things; they could fracture for any number of reasons. Young Warrior wanted to hold on to the connections his group had. With that thought in mind, he looked toward the silver-haired martial artist. "Can you stand?" he asked.

"Pins and neeeeedles!" she wept, bouncing from one foot to the other. Her silver hair bounced with her like a tail. "But! I'm okay! It's only pins and needles!"

"Great."

If she'd been hurt, they would have had to treat her, whether by conventional or miraculous means. When Young Warrior looked up, all he saw was a vast darkness overhead. There was no obvious way out. Which meant their resources were all the more precious.

"Wait..." If it was so dark down here, why could he see everyone else? His torch had gone out early in the drop. Had his eyes adjusted to the darkness already? No, that wasn't it...

"......Look there," their teacher said, providing the answer as he so often did, in a voice at once relaxed and firm. He gestured with a twitch of his nose toward a pale light glimmering in the darkness.

"Can you tell what it is?" Young Warrior asked.

"Not exactly, but there's a faint breeze from that direction," his teacher answered.

Well, how to handle this? Young Warrior tried to think through his options—not that there were that many cards in his hand.

"Think our only choice is to go check it out," Dwarf Scout said.

"Ahh yes, of course," Elf Cleric said from beside her with a knowing nod. "So that's what's going on..."

"You have *no* idea what's going on, do you?"

Young Warrior laughed out loud. Getting all grim and serious wasn't going to solve anything anyway. He was actually grateful that his companions behaved exactly the way they always did.

"Guess we'd better go have a look," he said. He drew his sword and nodded. "Watch your heads; watch your feet."

"Right!" the silver-haired girl said cheerfully, a bracing thing to hear in this hollow.

Yes—hollow. That's what it was. It wasn't a cavern, not quite. Yet Young Warrior also hesitated to think of it as a dungeon or ruins. There seemed to be packed earth or perhaps stone underfoot. It was flat, yet the featureless terrain seemed to be natural, not artificial.

There were no walls immediately to either side, and the ceiling was high above them, so far away that it didn't seem like something either nature or man would have made.

The only thing he could compare it to was a great, yawning hollow.

Young Warrior's first concern, based on rather unpleasant past experiences, was that there might be a monstrous spider down here. But other than the cobwebs, there was no sense that there were any living things in this pit.

There was no sound of breathing, there was no fur or bones, and there wasn't even any stink of dung. The pit might have been dug out of the earth this very instant. That was how new, how untouched it seemed.

Something's not right.

The air down here wasn't living and wasn't dead; Young Warrior lacked the words to put a name to it. The fine turns of phrase hummed by the bards didn't come so readily to his lips. Even that word—*hollow*—might not have come to mind if he hadn't been so busy learning lately. To be fair, he wasn't even completely sure what a *hollow* was as a place.

"...Careful. Road breaks off up ahead," the dwarf girl warned, snapping Young Warrior back to alertness.

"Wh-whoops!"

At some point, they had arrived at the edge of the cavern. Young Warrior nodded, looked at his party members, then turned his gaze across the hole...

"——"

Words failed him completely.

It was a town. No, a city.

It had walls. A highway. Close-packed houses, looming guard towers, and even a palace. It was unmistakably a metropolis, bathed in faint purple light that seemed to cascade down upon it.

The cavern was far bigger than anything Young Warrior and his party had passed through to get here. Big enough to house a city beneath the ceiling vaulting somewhere in the darkness above them. It looked alive, as if even now carriages might trundle down the streets and people might fill the avenues.

But Young Warrior could see from where he stood that this was impossible.

For the road at his feet, which should have come from somewhere in the Four-Cornered World and gone somewhere else, ended abruptly at a sheer cliffside. So, he suspected, did every other road coming from the city's gates. It was as if the metropolis had been cut out of somewhere else and pasted here wholesale.

It was strange, it was majestic, and Young Warrior found it overpowering. What could he do but stand in amazement?

"Wha—wha—wha—?"

Beside him, he saw the silver hair bounce, shimmering even in the gloom. The girl leaned out beside him to look, and she appeared absolutely flabbergasted, whether from ignorance or from naïveté, he didn't know.

"What *is* this?!" she asked.

"Now is not the time to speak of—"

"If you don't know, then keep your mouth shut, elf," the dwarf said, elbowing him. "What about you, Teacher? Do you recognize it?"

"Goodness gracious. I am still just an inexperienced student myself, and there's much I don't know." The canid wizard pushed his spectacles up the bridge of his nose, but he looked as calm as ever… almost. "Perhaps we've found an underground city of the dwarves or the far reaches of the dark elves' empire—or perhaps something no one has seen before."

To the members of his party, the glimmer of excitement in his eyes was perfectly obvious.

§

The adventurers worked their way down the cliffside, holding hands, then started toward the city. Strangely—or perhaps, on some level, not strangely at all—their progress was very easy. The flagstones of the highway were smooth and even; none were missing, and everything was well maintained. There were wheel ruts in the stones, showing that many carts and carriages had once traveled this route. Although where they had come from or where they had been going was now lost to time.

"It's been at least a century, maybe two," the dwarf girl said casually. "Can't be more precise than that."

"This doesn't appear to be dwarven architecture, but neither does it look like the doing of the dark elves," the canid wizard—their teacher—muttered in fascination. "Although I must admit, I'm outside my specialty."

Nobody else said anything. There wasn't much they could say. The elves did not build cities of stone, and apparently, this was neither dwarven nor dark elvish. So who *had* made this road? They preferred not to contemplate it.

Anyway, what better way to find out than to go and see with their own eyes? Once again, it proved remarkably easy to do. They advanced down the roadway without difficulty, and the city gates stood open to receive visitors. From this distance, they saw that the purple aura seemed to settle slowly over everything like falling snow.

Without that light, this might simply have been an ordinary, if exciting, discovery of some ancient ruins. For a moment, the adventurers could only gaze up at the imposing place in silence. There was no sign of any guards.

"...Let's go," Young Warrior said softly but not because of any bravery. Simply because he began to feel that if someone didn't say something, they might stand here for all eternity. Already, thoughts of the earthquakes and even of finding a way out of here remained in only the most remote corner of his mind.

Slowly, cautiously, they went forward. They wanted to find out what this city—these ruins, this abandoned place—really was.

Adventurers are those who take risks.

Confronted with an unknown place like this, anyone who turned tail and ran home in fear could not call themselves an adventurer. Then again, maybe it was that very caution turning them back that allowed adventurers to live to fight another day.

"I don't think anyone's here. Do you...?" asked the silver-haired martial artist, her voice quivering as she went forward one sliding step at a time. She clenched and unclenched her fists restlessly, her hair swinging left and right like a small animal's tail.

This place, surrounded by walls as tall as a giant, was a true metropolis. Neatly laid flagstone streets spread out in every direction, and the houses likewise were of superb stone construction. There was a street full of businesses including a tavern, an inn, an armorer, a tailor, and a flower shop.

Some of the roofs were covered in tiles, and some buildings had sculptures of fantastical creatures that served as gutters, their mouths open, waiting for rain.

Farther overhead, several massive guard towers stood against the canopy of darkness. The castle, perhaps.

All this and no sense of any person anywhere. Incontrovertible proof that this place was dead.

"Do you know the story of the ghost ship?" the elf asked. He was using his know-it-all tone, but at some point, he'd pulled out his dart gun and looked prepared to fire if necessary. "They say it always looks as if there were people there until just a moment before, and yet it's always empty."

"Seems simple enough. There was a fire or a storm or something, and all hands abandoned ship," Young Warrior said. He'd heard that story, too, or one like it.

Normally, he would have expected the dwarf girl to snap at the elf over a comment like that. He'd only spoken up because she hadn't. Instead, she was staring at the towers, looking equally horrified and reverent. Their teacher stood beside her, and he sounded even more serious than usual as he said, "This is most strange."

"You see it, too, Teach?"

"I do." He nodded.

The silver-haired girl cocked her head. "I don't. What's so strange?"

"The roofs," their dwarf scout replied. "I mean… Not exactly the roofs. The gutters. The towers. The walls. All of it!" As she went on, she seemed to be talking more and more to herself. Her agitation, like her muttering, was not directed at any of the others.

"???" The silver-haired girl looked more perplexed than ever.

"Think about it! It doesn't rain underground!" the dwarf shouted. "There's not even any subterranean water here! Everything about this city is *wrong*!"

The place was clearly not the work of a people who ordinarily lived underground. The towers were meaningless. The walls, pointless. The roads, to no purpose. Everything pointed to just one fact.

Overnight, this city...

"Sank underground..."

"Hoh...," the wizard breathed, perhaps a sigh, perhaps a sound of amazement.

Young Warrior looked at him. Even his teacher, who had lived so much longer than he and knew so much more, couldn't believe what he was seeing. Young Warrior was discovering that this person he'd felt knew everything in fact didn't, and he wasn't sure what to do with that revelation. His parents had only ever yelled at him at moments like this.

"I've heard of such legends. There was even a rumor once that such a place had been discovered, but this..."

Therefore, Young Warrior was relieved when his teacher humbly admitted his own ignorance.

Young Warrior—or maybe it was the silver-haired girl—asked as if begging to be instructed, "Legends?"

"Stories of an empire destroyed by a demon in a single night, such that now not even its name remains to posterity."

"I have heard such legends as well," the elf said. "The way my elders put it is—" Then he began to speak, or rather almost sing, in words they couldn't understand yet which were nonetheless immensely beautiful to hear. It was the ancient language of the elves, and even the dwarf girl refrained from asking, *Is now really the time to speak of such things?*

"A most ancient and most holy protection prevents the city from being destroyed even today, or so they say," the elf added. How old must that protection be for even the elves to call it ancient? Young Warrior couldn't imagine. Nor could the silver-haired girl. Could anyone?

"So that's this place?" Young Warrior asked, looking around, still overwhelmed. He felt no profound emotion, no excitement. Only astonishment—he couldn't believe what he was seeing. Or perhaps more accurately, it didn't feel real. He thought of the adventures he'd dreamed of when he was a boy…

How's this compare?

He thought of the legend of the lone adventurer who had braved the ancient city in the sky, a place thought to have been lost. Young Warrior had been so taken with the story. He'd wanted to be just like that adventurer. He'd even bragged that he would have done it better.

Well, here was his chance. And the only thought in his mind was: *I don't believe it.* Nothing more.

He hadn't come here seeking these ruins. He'd just been looking for a way out. There was nothing dramatic in it—there was nothing at all. He'd only gotten himself swallowed by a fissure in the ground. He hadn't planned to face an adventure in a place like this, wasn't psychologically ready for it.

"Wow… This is amazing."

Thus, he was deeply grateful for the earnest, honest whisper from the silver-haired girl beside him.

"Yeah," he said, forcing himself to nod, then to smile. "I feel bad for the other guys, though."

"It's his own fault for collapsing before the adventure began," the dwarf girl said with a snort, recovering from her amazement.

"Such are Fate and Chance. All things are at the leisure of the gods' dice. Or perhaps… No. It is not yet time," Elf Cleric murmured importantly with one of his annoying gestures.

"Spit it out!" Dwarf Scout practically jumped on him, causing the silver-haired girl to panic—all just as usual.

"Now, where did I put my notebook…? I have to record what we're seeing here!" Their canid teacher didn't bother to reprimand them for fighting but only searched in his pack.

Guess I can't blame him. He'd become an adventurer exactly to see sights like this. The thought brought a smile to Young Warrior's face.

A thought crossed his mind, unbidden: If the half-elf girl were here, how would she have reacted to all this? Young Warrior was sorry that she and the others weren't here. But he didn't feel that rush of loneliness. He had other party members now, lively and noisy, even if their ability to cooperate remained something of an open question. And although he didn't really feel it in his bones yet, it seemed he was effectively their leader. In which case…

"All right, you know what they say. You can't slay a dragon without going into a dragon's den. Let's press on."

"And then you don't get the dragon's egg!" the silver-haired girl chirped, her eyes shining. "We learned that one the other day!"

"You don't seem worried about the possibility of, you know, a dragon," Dwarf Scout said with a laugh. Then she moved to the front to do what a scout did best. As soon as she got there she snapped, "Everyone stop."

The party members reacted instantaneously. Young Warrior drew his sword, the silver-haired martial artist took up a fighting stance, the elf readied his dart gun and the canid his staff.

What's going on? Young Warrior didn't say the words aloud, but his lips moved. Maybe that didn't mean anything.

"Footsteps," Dwarf Scout whispered. "Thought it might be a dark elf assassin or something."

They all knew she was joking. Dark elf assassins never made a sound.

"Urgh…" The silver-haired girl stuck out her tongue. "I don't like assassins. They don't fight fair."

"No one likes assassins," Elf Cleric quipped with a shrug.

"Quiet," the canid wizard warned them.

The next time the footsteps sounded, Young Warrior heard them, too. Someone—or something—was coming closer.

Do we attack?

They could take the initiative. No. Bad idea. They still didn't know what they were dealing with. If it was someone friendly, attacking would be a critical mistake.

"Do we do it?" asked the silver-haired girl, who looked ready to launch a flying kick right then and there.

"No," the warrior replied with a shake of his head. "We see who it is; we give them a nice, friendly greeting; if that doesn't work, we do it."

"Good idea. People who don't return a friendly greeting are so rude!" The silver-haired girl snorted and nodded. Very heartening to know she agreed with him.

The footsteps continued to approach as they talked, a heavy, powerful sound. Their owner moved decisively, without hesitation or question. These were the footsteps of someone who was confident that no matter what stood in their way, they could trample it with their own strength.

Frightening, Young Warrior thought, feeling sweat creep down his brow. He was nervous. He couldn't resist a smile: This was ridiculous. His excitement at exploring unknown ruins was outweighed by the sense of responsibility he felt toward his party members as they faced down this possible enemy together. That had to be a sign of personal growth, right? He just hoped he had the skills to back it up.

Then finally…

"So! There were a few more of you stragglers, eh?"

A warrior appeared, looming large, his whole great body covered in the blood of his enemies. What shocked Young Warrior the most, though, wasn't his hulking frame or the massive sword he carried.

It was the glint of gold from the man's neck.

A rank tag from the Adventurers Guild.

Shingo Adachi

CHAPTER 3

The Enemy Is...Goblins!

I feel like I've been here before.

That was the first thought Goblin Slayer had as he stepped into the village. He worked his not particularly sharp mind, trying to remember, but he had no recollection of having come here in the past.

It was a perfectly ordinary village, the kind you might find anywhere well off the main thoroughfares. The villagers lived diligent, dedicated lives, and adventurers rarely went there. Goblin Slayer felt the suspicious looks of the farmers in the fields like physical blows.

The sun was getting lower in the sky, and dusk was coming on. Anyone would be vigilant about adventurers arriving at that hour. There was no proof that they weren't bandits or robbers. When he thought about it now, he saw that his sister had been right to warn him to stay away from the adventurers.

"Is something the matter?" Examiner asked primly from where she stood behind him.

Goblin Slayer shook his head. "No. We didn't accept a quest, so I was thinking about who we should talk to."

"Good point. An Obsidian or Porcelain who washes up solo in a village is hardly different from your average barroom brawler," said the woman who was in a position to approve or deny the very rank she referred to. She made it sound so obvious.

Goblin Slayer wondered: If he relied on her to do the work here, would that influence his examination? Then again, considering everything he had done to this point, he might well have failed the test long ago.

No, he thought.

"Can I ask for your help?" he said.

"Very good," Examiner replied with a nod, and to his surprise, her lovely face was even graced with a small smile. She walked toward one of the people doing farmwork, as proper and collected as she was in the halls of the Guild. "Excuse me," she said. "I am terribly sorry to bother you when you are busy, but might I trouble you with a question?"

"Er… Yes, o' course," the farmer replied, looking nervous—probably intimidated by the woman's beauty or her flawless etiquette or both.

"My apologies for not introducing myself properly." Examiner offered another smile. "I am an employee of the Adventurers Guild." Having established her credentials, the discussion went far smoother than it ever would have for Goblin Slayer. Examiner didn't hesitate to crouch down so she was eye to eye with these people, though they were so much more lowly than a certified public official. When she spoke to them from that position, the farmers could hardly get angry; instead, they opened up to her.

"You'd be lookin' for the headman's house. It'll be that one over there." The farmer pointed to a building not much bigger than an average house, although on the large side by the standards of this village. A light could be seen flickering in the window against the encroaching dark, and the smoke puffing from the chimney suggested someone was cooking dinner.

Goblin Slayer was taken for a second by a vision he'd thought he would never see again. In an effort to shake it off, he turned his helmeted head toward Examiner. "There's no problem, then?"

"None at all," she answered—however it was that she had interpreted his question. "Knights, nobles, and clerics, among others, frequently engender trust regardless of rank. Letting them do the talking is one viable strategy."

"I see."

Trust was something that seemed far from him. He nodded. Now was not the time to worry about it. There was one thing he had to do. Goblin Slayer turned toward the headman's house and started walking.

At that moment, he heard the voices of children playing in the distance. Then someone calling them inside. Not from one particular house—from every house. Every house. Every house he passed.

Goblin Slayer walked by the voices, shaking off the stares and scowls that seemed to cling to him as he went by. Examiner walked breezily behind him. "What do you plan to do?" she asked.

"The same thing I always do." He didn't know what answer Examiner was looking for. There was only a limited range of things he did know. And so without hesitation, Goblin Slayer pounded the answer home: "The only question is whether I'll kill the goblins."

§

"Goblins aren't frightening," said the headman, who seemed awfully young for his station. He sat in his chair, looking relaxed.

Of course, his youthful looks were only on the surface—he wasn't an elf or anything. He was probably, in fact, just a bit past the age of majority, Goblin Slayer guessed. He was slim but well-built enough that his muscles pressed at his shirt.

There were plenty of such people among village youth. Sometimes they turned up wanting to be adventurers or soldiers. This young man sitting calmly in his chair, however, possessed a composure beyond his years. That was clear even from the way he had gladly welcomed the two visitors despite the fact that they were imposing on his dinner. He retained that composure despite being greeted with a brusque "There are goblins."

Now Goblin Slayer and Examiner were seated at the headman's table, and still he seemed calm and collected. Maybe that was only superficial—but even being able to put on a mask of composure was achievement enough.

"Nor are they unusual," the man continued. "One or two show up near a village, make some mischief. We chase them away. If that's all this is—"

He stopped abruptly.

"Here. For you." A pleasant woman—his wife—had made tea, which she offered to them with a quiet smile.

"Thank you," the headman replied, while Examiner said, "My thanks," and each took their tea. Goblin Slayer remained silent and simply drained his cup through the slats of his visor in a single swig. The tea was hot. The wife's eyes widened, and the headman smiled wryly, but neither of them commented. They knew it was better, at this moment, to continue the conversation.

"If that's what's going on, then a will-o'-the-wisp is more frightening," the headman said. "However..."

"..." Examiner lifted an eyebrow ever so slightly. Neither the headman nor his wife appeared to notice. Goblin Slayer's gaze shifted behind his visor, though it didn't seem to him that he should say anything at that moment.

"What *would* be frightening is if their thoughtless mischief were to lead to some greater danger."

"I agree," Goblin Slayer said, nodding with utmost solemnity. The headman was exactly right. He clearly understood the situation his small village was in. He picked up a cane resting against his armchair and leaned on it as he got unsteadily to his feet. His wife went to help him, looking both urgent and accustomed to this, but he forestalled her with a smile.

"I lied about my age, you see. Went to war with my friends."

"Hoh," breathed Examiner. "So that limp is a wound of honor."

"Something like that. I took an arrow to the knee." His tone lay somewhere between serious and joking.

"Come now," his wife chided, but perhaps because there was company, she let it go at a glare.

The headman gave her a friendly smile and continued, "I'm not sure whether to curse my lack of military prowess or feel blessed by it."

Goblin Slayer had a suspicion, just a feeling, that this was what had led to the young man becoming headman of this village. In these days, it was hardly unusual for soldiers to return from war and assume such positions. Then again, it was hardly unusual for them to return from war and find their villages burned and their families dead.

In the endless conflict between Order and Chaos, villages appeared, disappeared, and appeared again. To do brave deeds against that backdrop and in reward to be made headman of the village…

That's one path one could take.

Wasn't it? The thought crossed Goblin Slayer's mind, although it was no more than that—a thought. A possibility with no chance of becoming reality was nothing but a fantasy.

"I knew there was a goblin nest near the village," the headman said. "I knew we'd have to deal with it someday."

Then he whispered, "Someday…" If it was just ten goblins or so, then they hardly seemed to warrant attention immediately. But…

"You're telling me more goblins are gathering?" the headman asked.

"That's right." Goblin Slayer nodded without a hint of hesitation. "Goblins riding on…something or other—some sort of dogs—have been making the rounds of this area. We followed them here."

"We presume they are runners," Examiner broke in smoothly. "They must be taking goblins from this nest to other places. Although we cannot be certain."

"Whatever it is, I guess we can assume it's not good," the headman said with a low sigh. His wife looked uneasy, and he gave her a wave as if to tell her not to worry about it. Supporting himself with his cane, he went over to the small window of the little house and looked outside. The sun was low over the horizon, and the gloom of night was upon them, held at bay only by the sun's last rays.

Out there, amid the encroaching darkness, fires could be seen glinting, surrounded by people eating their dinner after a day's work.

"I've fought goblins in pitched battle before. Although only their foot soldiers."

"I won't fight a pitched battle," Goblin Slayer growled. "Never again."

"You and me both." The headman turned back toward them, rested against the window frame, and nodded at him. It was the gesture of a man who knew whereof he spoke. "We've got hotheaded youngsters in this village, like most villages, but even they aren't too eager to get into a proper battle with goblins."

Although the headman's perspective shared something in common with Goblin Slayer's, they weren't quite the same. But Goblin Slayer didn't care to pursue the matter.

"Now, then," Examiner started, and she glanced at Goblin Slayer's filthy armor in a way that suggested she wanted to say much more than she did. "This adventurer intends to hunt the goblins regardless of whether a quest is offered." She sounded like she was dutifully reciting the facts.

"Of course," Goblin Slayer replied brusquely. "There are goblins. That's the only issue."

"It is not," Examiner snapped. Then she sighed quietly and turned to the headman. "As a representative of the Adventurers Guild, I must ask your opinion."

"You mean, what we intend to do about this situation?"

Examiner nodded: exactly. The headman adopted a thoughtful air.

His wife spoke up. "You'll need these, I suppose?" She took a portable candlestick and a sand tray she had gotten out and placed them carefully on the table.

Ah yes. In light of what they were about to discuss, these would be most useful.

"You are a most thoughtful person," Examiner said.

"Yes—when there's company!" The headman laughed. "You should see her the moment you walk out the door!"

Hey, you. His wife's lips moved, but she didn't chastise him out loud. The headman returned to the table, this time making no pretense of doing so without his wife's support.

With that, their council of war began.

Granted, that makes the scale sound grander than it was. This council consisted of one adventurer, one employee of the Adventurers Guild, and one soldier back from the wars who had become a village headman. And they were strategizing against some goblins.

The goal of this discussion, however, was very much that of a council of war. Only the ignorant would suggest sending the villagers to fight or trying to summon the army. The three gathered here, at least, each had more knowledge, more experience than that.

"Roughly how many goblins would you say there are?" Examiner lit off the discussion (a turn of phrase that had become popular with the advent of firearms). "Or perhaps I should ask: How many have the villagers been able to confirm?"

"We think it's about ten of them… Erm, not that we've spotted that many." The headman worked a quill in the sand tray, his tone grim. "Just a few of them skulking about on the outskirts of the village. No significant damage. That's why we think ten at most."

"Then I believe we should assume their numbers have grown beyond that," Examiner said, evidently taking the headman at his word.

Whatever else, the headman could be seen to write numbers and letters in the sand tray. An education like that was ample evidence of knowledge and intelligence. Such was hardly the full measure of a man, of course, but it was one tangible achievement. And Goblin Slayer knew that the measuring device had now turned to him.

"I have read your reports, boy. You have dealt with nests of this size before, yes?"

She seemed to mean: *So come up with a plan.* Was this another test?

He didn't know. Because he didn't know, he was cautious and chose his words carefully. "We could possibly draw them into the village, cut off their escape route, and face them here."

"Out of the question." She was ruthless. "That would mean exposing to direct danger the village we are supposed to protect, and what purpose would that serve?"

"There was a time when doing so was my only option," Goblin Slayer said, but it sounded like an excuse.

No.

There was always a better plan. He just hadn't been able to think of it. It was as simple as that.

"…At that time," he added slowly.

"*This* time is different."

"Hrm…" He grunted softly. What argument could he offer? Instead, he repeated, "Regardless, I don't intend to meet them on the open field." Then he added brusquely, "I believe I was told that even opinions that would be opposed should be voiced."

"Well!" Examiner's one visible eye widened, then she blinked. Then the look in that almond-shaped eye softened. "Yes, that is true. You are exactly right, boy."

He didn't respond to that. He didn't even think to glance at Examiner's smile. He was angry, however—at himself for letting each of her little tweaks get to him.

There are more important things to focus on right now, he told himself for what felt like the umpteenth time since the promotion exam had begun.

There were no actual goblins in front of him at that moment. This was a village, not a goblin nest. Which meant...

"If we don't know their precise numbers and location, we can do no good," Goblin Slayer said.

"You seem to have some idea where the nest is located, sir," Examiner noted.

"There's a forest near the village—it's in there," the headman told them. "I've warned everyone not to go near it, but we know where it is." In the sand tray, the headman sketched the positions of the village and the woods. He wrote the distance between them, then nodded. "It's what I guess you would call a limestone cavern. It's a maze—if you get lost in there, you might not come out."

"Very good. Looks like we will get to test your mapping skills as well."

"..."

Goblin Slayer couldn't tell if Examiner was joking. He supposed she was treating him like a child. It was not a very good feeling. Especially because it was obvious to him that the most childish thing of all was to be annoyed by it.

Then did he want her to treat him like a full-fledged adventurer? He wasn't sure.

"You're saying it's large?" he asked the headman.

"I think quite a good number could be hiding in there," the headman replied with a serious nod. "Certainly enough to make a pitched battle unrealistic. Maybe impossible."

"I agree." Goblin Slayer nodded back. He understood it well. "That would be a great deal of trouble."

"Yeah. Ugly stuff." The headman sank into his chair and let his eyes drift shut. He seemed to be less calling on buried knowledge than remembering some hideous nightmare from the past. "Meat shields, magic, knights. In the end, it was just about throwing human waves against them..."

"Human waves," Goblin Slayer repeated in a murmur. To him, the words sounded almost like a spell.

Meat shields, magic, knights. Magic and knights—those he knew about. But there were many words he did not know.

He tilted his helmet down just slightly. Examiner looked at him. "Throwing your soldiers against the enemy one after another has a heroic ring to it, but it simply means you have split up your force." Of course, there were times when that was effective. She made it all sound so natural.

I see. So that's what that means.

Goblin Slayer could not fathom why Examiner hadn't chosen to point out his ignorance. He grasped, at least, that she had not embarrassed him—and also that this could not be the end of the matter. He would trample his own ignorance.

"What is a meat shield?" he asked the headman.

"I suppose you could say...a hostage. They tied their hostages to boards usually used to soak up arrows."

"Hostages," he echoed. That, too, was a word he knew.

The headman shrugged. "Only a barbarian would say you should just go ahead and kill those poor people. What arrogance!"

"I agree." Goblin Slayer nodded. He had never once imagined himself as so far above anyone. It was only thanks to the pips of the dice that he wasn't rotting in some goblin nest himself.

It always would be.

"The Guild would be most grateful if you would go beyond agreeing and actually work to rescue them," Examiner said, closing her eyes and sighing. The Guild very much wanted him to rescue them.

Was Examiner—or perhaps even the headman—testing him? Goblin Slayer considered the possibility for a moment, then decided he didn't care either way. He knew what he had to do. "I'm going to the nest, then."

"..."

He got up from the chair with a clatter.

Night was already falling upon the four corners of the board, but in fact, that made this the perfect moment to head for the goblins' cave. He would arrive around morning—a better time to attack than high noon, he thought.

He noticed that Examiner seemed to want to say something. "What?" he asked.

How did she take his question? What he meant was, *What's the matter?* For a moment, she stared at him as if she couldn't believe what she was looking at, then she sighed again.

"...First things first," she said. As if by magic, she produced from her item pouch a sheet of parchment, a brush, and a pot of ink. They looked as new and as neat as if she had pulled them from a drawer at the Guild.

She put them on the table beside the sand tray. She placed the paper facing the headman and gestured at it with a practiced motion. The parchment bore the Guild's standard boilerplate, written in small, neat letters.

"I recommend that you convey what you have just told me to the Guild in the form of a formal quest offer," she said.

"Suppose that means we'll have to come up with a reward." The headman didn't object. He'd known they would have to offer a quest sooner or later. This was just sooner.

Goblin Slayer looked at the paper, the handwriting on which was far finer than his own, and muttered, "Is this necessary?"

"But of course." Examiner probably took the question in a somewhat different sense than Goblin Slayer had intended it. Regardless, she answered his doubts in a professional tone. "Disciples of the Trade God sometimes describe coin as the world's lifeblood—but in a bureaucratic office, the vital humor is not money but paperwork." She held up a finger and waved it elegantly as if expounding on the very truth of this world. "Things simply do not order themselves without anyone's intervention, you see."

So that's what's going on.

Well, it made sense, Goblin Slayer thought. It seemed very obvious now. If things simply put themselves in good order without anyone doing anything, he wouldn't be here at this moment. When he thought of it that way, his doubts vanished. He was sure she was right.

"As I'm sure you realize, we don't use a lot of silver coins out here in the villages." Even as Goblin Slayer was thinking, the paperwork was done up and the headman was handing it back to Examiner.

"Yes, but rules are rules," she said emotionlessly and shrugged. "They must be observed."

Few were those who could live by eating mist—fewer still among adventurers, let alone state organizations. Even Examiner's remark about the Trade God might have been intended to forestall any objections from the headman.

Examiner glanced over the paper, then muttered, "Very good," and signed her name at the bottom with a flick of her brush. Goblin Slayer noticed the quill emerge from her sleeve and saw it disappear there again, but despite having seen this twice now, he still had no idea how she did it. The only thing he knew was that it wasn't something an amateur like him could figure out just from witnessing it a few times.

"I have affixed my signature, which should expedite processing if you take this to the nearest Guild," she said.

"Appreciate it."

The headman would have to gather money, give it to a trustworthy messenger, quiet the anxieties and dissatisfaction of the villagers, then wait for adventurers...

There were so many things to do—things that must be done—and after all that, the goblins still waited.

The headman, with all this on his shoulders, fiddled with his cane and looked at Goblin Slayer. More precisely, he looked at both Goblin Slayer and Examiner, who had risen silently from her chair. "May I ask you both one thing?"

"What?"

"Yes? What is it?"

"How does it happen that an adventurer and an employee of the Adventurers Guild are hunting goblins together?"

Goblin Slayer was silent. He looked to Examiner as if for an answer.

She met his eyes past his visor. Then the two of them turned to the headman.

"A promotion exam," they answered in unison, though slightly out of step as one of them began with "It's" and the other "It is."

For the first time, the headman was left speechless.

§

He was forever being reminded that the accumulation of fatigue and a lack of sleep could cause all manner of undesirable outcomes. His head weighed even heavier than his helmet, yet he felt strangely agitated. His body seemed too hot, his breath fast and shallow.

Still, if he put one foot in front of the other, he would move forward. He could continue to be aware of his surroundings as well. Goblin Slayer grasped all this as if walking a step behind himself and observing his own situation. He hadn't reached the point of having to tell himself to be careful, so there was no problem yet.

The darkness was like ink around them; they seemed to swim through it, advancing through forest underbrush not even the animals frequented.

The one thing he didn't understand was…

"…"

…Examiner, who trailed behind him. They were in the middle of a forced march. The two of them had done the same things for the same amount of time, she as much as he. And yet she betrayed not the slightest hint of exertion. Perhaps there was a speck of dust on her outfit, but if she brushed it off, she would have looked ready to step up to a Guild reception counter and speak to a customer. That was how she appeared to Goblin Slayer anyway.

There wasn't a drop of sweat on her neat, angular features. Not a wrinkle in her clothes. She'd closed her eyes for just a few minutes and now seemed perfectly ready to press on.

A most startling ability.

Was it something inborn in her or some secret she had learned? Whichever, Goblin Slayer didn't imagine for a second that he could learn to do it.

"Why?" she asked.

"..."

Was the delay in answering because he was thinking or because he was tired? Or did he get lost in thought *because* he was tired?

"Why what?" His voice worked its way out of his mouth, drawn and dry. He took out his water pouch, judged roughly how much he had left from the weight, then took a gulp. It was lukewarm and unpleasant.

"Why are you so bent on reconnoitering them first thing in the morning that you would even engage in a forced march?"

"Experience," he replied.

He heard the faintest rustle as Examiner worked her way through some brushed behind him, then an exhalation of "hoh."

"They sleep during the day and are awake at night. Meaning that day is night for them, and night is day."

"I see, I see."

"In which case it is best to come at either dusk or dawn, when their guards are most tired."

"Very logical."

Goblin Slayer realized that he was not much for explaining. When his thoughts did manage to work their way past his throat, they always seemed to crumble as they sat upon his tongue.

Maybe it was the fatigue. Nerves? He didn't think he was nervous. Most likely.

He didn't have to turn around to know Examiner was watching him like a hawk. As ever, she followed him without making so much as a footstep, but her voice pierced him. "You seem to have given this more thought than I gave you credit for. I am glad to know it."

"I see."

I think she's praising me.

Praising him? Why would he think she was doing that?

Still unsure of the answer, Goblin Slayer consulted the map in his head, considering the time and direction of travel.

They should be there soon.

"GROORGB!"

"GB! GORGBB!!"

There.

The entrance to the cave sat yawning in the middle of the forest. Nearby were two goblin sentries holding crude spears. Beside the entrance was a mountain of filth, while on the other side was a bizarre tower made of mysterious junk.

He was not interested in goblins' diets nor in their philosophies. What mattered to Goblin Slayer was that he spotted human bones in both of the piles.

I shouldn't be surprised.

There were goblins in this goblin nest. No surprise at all.

What? Had he expected them to be remarking, *Oh! That village is so wonderful!*

Or had he thought they might be planning, *Since that village is so wonderful, let's attack somewhere else?*

Or perhaps he had supposed they might be reconsidering their lives: *Let's stop doing all these awful things and live in harmony with everyone else!*

Ridiculous. Impossible.

This was a goblin nest, and those were goblins. No more and no less. Even if such a thing as a good goblin were to appear in the Four-Cornered World, he would have to be smart enough not to show himself in civilized society. If he could say, *I'm a good goblin! I've changed my ways! Let's all live in harmony!* without a pang of conscience, well—it would only prove what a goblin he was.

Such was the nature of goblins.

"This is more than we expected—but it is not a surprise," Examiner whispered. He could almost hear her scowling.

"True," Goblin Slayer replied, nodding. He didn't worry about the spite in her voice.

The quantity of filth, the number of footprints crisscrossing this way and that, and how the entrance had clearly been dug out and enlarged: These facts together suggested that this nest was far more than ten goblins. It would be *at least* ten, but there was no upper limit. Such was the situation.

He thought about how this would be a great deal of trouble, but he felt no special emotion about it. That was a good thing. It showed that even this dull boy had progressed in the space of five years. A very good thing, indeed.

"We should go back to the village," Examiner said. "It would be best to get some rest before we attack. And there is a hard limit to how much rest we can get camping in the field."

It was a logical suggestion. A way of protecting against any twists they hadn't factored in. But Goblin Slayer was loath to give them any more time than he had to. There wasn't one single reason to let the goblins live.

"I," he said, his voice terribly dry and rasping, "can sleep with one eye open."

"I would not call that getting rest, boy." Examiner exhaled sharply, somewhere between rebuke and exasperation. "Granted, we do need caution. I will stand the first wa—"

The way she broke off mid-word alerted Goblin Slayer. If he had been alone… Well, no point in that thought. It was less important than what was right in front of him.

"GOGGRGBB!!"

Namely, a goblin.

A massive goblin, great and fat, who had loped out of the cavern and now stood in the entrance.

He was more than just obese, though. In his hand, he proudly held a huge ax.

"GOBGB?!"

"GOROG! GBBGB!!"

Under his glare, the grunt goblins bowed their heads, a mixture of jealousy and obsequious flattery in their eyes. Whoever this creature was, he obviously ruled over the other goblins. That was clear from the way he kicked the other creatures around and yet no one fought back.

He was huge. At least a head taller than the others and as wide as any two goblins. He wasn't muscular, but he clearly wasn't weak.

He didn't seem to have any special business at the cave entrance. He was simply there to strut around and lash out.

He jabbered something angrily at the other goblins, who didn't jabber back.

"That's no hob," Goblin Slayer mused.

A hobgoblin—a particularly large goblin. This was smaller than one of those, but it was still larger than the other goblins he had encountered up to this point. The creature wore a ring of red-rusted metal around its largely empty head.

"A lord," murmured Examiner.

Goblin Slayer was silent for several seconds, then he shifted his gaze behind his visor and stared at her. "You mean a king?" he groaned. "A *goblin* king?"

"Nothing says they cannot have them. Even if they are only imitating the kings they see in our world."

"I see…," Goblin Slayer murmured to himself, then looked forward again at this ridiculous thing, a goblin lord.

It wasn't precisely unexpected. If someone had told him that such things existed, he would have believed them—it would not be the first time the subject had come up for him.

That wizard, he thought. What had she said? *That perhaps goblin hordes have hierarchies as well.* Yes, she'd said something of the sort, almost talking to herself. *He's probably newly assumed the "throne."*

Wanderers would kidnap women, looking to expand the size of their nest. As the nest got bigger so did their egos, and in the second stage, they would have the audacity to attack villages. So she had speculated, counting the stages on crooked fingers.

"And then they would arrive at step three…"

"Destroying the village."

"This means the horde has grown to quite a substantial size already."

Goblin Slayer found his awareness snapped back to reality. It must have been the fatigue. Not a good sign. He would need rest. Hours of it.

"There are more here than we can handle on our own, boy. We must secure the village's defenses and wait for reinforcements."

"Do you think I care?" Goblin Slayer broke off, thinking about how tired he was. It wasn't worth contemplating. "I'll wait for evening; then I'll go in."

It didn't matter to him if he was facing one goblin, or ten, or a hundred, or a king, or whoever. His choices remained the same: Do or do not. And he had made his choice.

Examiner looked at him as if she couldn't believe what she was seeing. "What?" she asked.

"They put out a quest, haven't they?"

For the first time, it seemed he had succeeded in surprising her.

Goblin Slayer ignored the faint burst of satisfaction he felt at that. He conquered it with composure as he said, "Therefore, if I die, it's not a problem."

"…Please do not forget you are in a party," she managed. She seemed to mean that his actions could affect the survival of his entire group. Or perhaps she was saying she would come with him. Goblin Slayer couldn't decide. But it seemed to him that he didn't need to.

"That has nothing to do with my life or death," he said.

This time Examiner was simply lost for words.

"Right, then. Is there a stage four?" He heard the woman chuckling in his memory. *"I've never heard of a nest getting big enough to reach that level."*

A goblin kingdom, she had said, almost humming the words to herself.

"They're opportunistic, violent little devils. Even if they had a king, I'm sure his kingdom would fracture immediately… Or he'd be assassinated."

"There are adventurers, too." He seemed to recall that had been his response. *"Most of the time."*

Yes, most of the time: Five years ago, there had been none.

Even here, at this moment, there were no adventurers.

There was only him.

Goblin Slayer.

In which case…

"I am going to kill all the goblins."

INTERLUDE

Battle in the Underground Empire

"A dog got me," the barbarian man said, unimpressed. He bit off a piece of meat as he sat before the crackling fire. His remark was prompted by the silver-haired girl, who had looked at the scar on his chest and said innocently, "That's amazing!"

The Gold-ranked adventurer's smoldering anger seemed to wipe out every sound but the crackling of the fire. He himself hardly seemed to notice; he gave the canid wizard a leer, then smiled as if baring his fangs. "No relation of yours, I'm sure."

"I appreciate your avoiding discriminatory broad brushing," the canid teacher answered. He actually seemed quite pleased. The barbarian, for his part, hardly seemed to know what the word *discriminatory* meant. He just took another mouthful of meat.

The dwarf girl looked less happy than their teacher. She snorted, almost laughing, and said, "You talk like a real winner for someone who came out the worst."

"Worst, nothing. It got away, but it'll die someday," the barbarian replied, unfazed. "If I'm still alive when that happens, then I win." He made it sound as simple as the fact that the sun would rise in the morning.

The dwarf fell silent. It would have been easy, if pointless, to continue arguing, but she didn't. Would it be fair, then, to say that she had been overawed?

When Elf Cleric saw the state of his sparring partner, he spoke up himself, choosing his words carefully. "Why, with the things he says, I could almost mistake this guy for a lizardman."

"So I should go around looking beaten for the rest of my life because I lost one fight? Show me someone who believes that, and I'll show you a fool who's never been in battle."

It was a harsh thing to say to an elf. Elf Cleric looked nonplussed, and the silver-haired girl's eyes flitted back and forth between him and the barbarian.

Young Warrior didn't say anything but only watched the barbarian closely. *This guy is incredible*, he thought—only that. He rippled with muscles; he looked like he had been hewn from the very stone. The picture of a warrior. Combined with the cruel blade he carried, he looked, to Young Warrior's eyes, like the quintessence of what any man would hope to be.

Not like me.

The barbarian was the opposite of Young Warrior in every possible way. Surely, he had never watched his cherished party members die before his eyes.

Young Warrior felt in his bones that he would never be like this man. He could never make his body a sculpted specimen like this. Long ago, he'd heard stories of warriors like this man in the far north. *They must have been true*, he thought.

"I must agree," Young Warrior's teacher said, interrupting his reverie.

"Hoh," breathed the barbarian, impressed to hear that from the academic-looking dog-man. "Good to know we're on the same page. Here I thought all you scholarly types had a few screws loose."

"Meaning?"

"Meaning you always march around like your shit don't stink, babbling on about who gives a rat's ass."

"Ah. I suspect you think that because you are seeing only a snippet of a much longer journey. A much longer story." He let that remark hang in the air for a second, the same way he did when he was teaching Young Warrior or the silver-haired girl. Then he said, "My good warrior, if you swing your sword you can kill the foe, yes?"

"Damn right I can."

"And how many training swings did it take you to learn to deliver that fatal blow?"

"More than I could count." The barbarian shook his head. "Only a fool would even try."

"What, then, if someone saw you practicing your swing and said, 'He's not attacking the enemy—only the empty air! He must be mad!' What would you do?"

"I'd kill 'em," Young Warrior snapped. There was no hesitation, no hint of humor. He was simply stating a fact. "So that's what you're getting at."

"That's what I'm getting at." Teacher clapped his floofy hands together approvingly. "Scholarship is a path by which we train ourselves in the way of the sword, so that we can cut at something in the great, vast emptiness."

"*Something.* Real specific," the barbarian said and groaned in a way that sounded like a growling wolf. "I feel like we're trying to grab empty air here."

"Indeed," the wizard said with a smile. "This discussion of ours is precisely to grasp at the air."

"Makes no goddamn sense," the barbarian grumbled, but then he smiled, showing his teeth like a shark. "I get one thing, though—you're up against something bigger than I can imagine!"

"I sincerely appreciate your understanding."

Just because you have learning, or can read and write, or can speak a language doesn't mean you'll always make yourself understood. There are plenty of people out there who ignore things they don't want to see and try to force everyone to accept their own way of thinking. Nor does it always take a whisper from an evil god to make people assume that it's always someone else who is wrong.

In such a world—ah, what a beautiful thing it is when understanding is achieved!

Not that mutual understanding necessarily means we won't end up trying to kill one another.

Peace was far more difficult than that; it required ceaseless effort and compromise.

Even as all this passed through his head, the canid wizard wagged his tail, pleased to have reached some measure of understanding.

"...So, uh."

The moment he spoke, Young Warrior felt every eye on him. He'd figured that if he was going to break into the conversation, this was the only place. But now that he'd done so, what should he do? He had no answer. The elf-dwarf pair looked at him expectantly, wondering what he would say. His canid teacher mumbled, "Well," not so much surprised as happy. He gave Young Warrior a smile.

Directly across from Young Warrior, the barbarian man watched him, his craggy features unreadable. Young Warrior felt like if he made a single misstep with what he said, the barbarian would cut him down on the spot and throw away the corpse.

He suddenly noticed one of his wrists felt heavy. The silver-haired girl was squeezing it very hard.

Young Warrior took a breath in, then let it out. To grasp at the empty air. To speak of the grasping.

"Do you think you could tell us what the situation is in there?" he said.

"Thought you'd never ask."

Passing marks for him, it seemed. The barbarian nodded at him as if at a fellow leader.

Then he gave them the story.

"My quest is to see what that Chaos lot is up to," he said.

It had been five years since the great battle. The forces of the Demon Lord said to have ruled the Dungeon of the Dead were broken. They had not, however, been annihilated down to the last creature. Just as the forces of Order had been replenishing and reestablishing themselves over the last five years, so too the enemy had been husbanding its power. There were mysterious incidents and accidents all across the land. People disappeared or were killed; monsters appeared and every manner of strange and weird creature.

It transpired that the root of one of these dark schemes lay deep beneath the earth...

"And that led me here."

"...So the local governor was kidnapping people and sending them down here?" Young Warrior muttered, scratching his chin. He didn't mean it as a doubtful gesture. A situation like this was well above his rank.

Man... Politics.

He thought of the black carriage that had come to the Guild. He couldn't imagine himself being involved in such things.

"Could that really happen? I mean, we're talking about the governor, right? Isn't he supposed to be important?" The silver-haired girl appeared flatly disbelieving—or perhaps terrified. She had to know there was evil in the hearts of people, but still she resisted this.

"Those of the four corners believe that what has come into their hand is theirs to destroy. They shall not leave one person for anyone else," Elf Cleric said, almost as if reciting a poem. The silver-haired girl flinched. "There was a governor in these parts who killed every human in the area, up to and including his own wife and child. I don't remember how long ago that was now..."

"For an elf to forget, it must have been well before *our* times." There was a dull *thump*, and Elf Cleric writhed, unable to make a sound. The dwarf had an iron elbow.

"Yeah, I hear you. That whiny little prick at the Guild didn't believe, either," the barbarian said, paying no heed to the elf and dwarf. Instead, he looked at the vast, dead city that towered over them. He almost seemed admiring, but maybe he was just calculating how much loot there must be in this place. "Turns out he was as big a liar as he was a whiner. The city's here and a mountain of old bones and monsters."

"...Now that you mention it, you were covered in blood," the silver-haired girl mumbled, curling into herself like a small, frightened animal. She seemed to think he might eat her otherwise. She had, however, let go of Young Warrior's sleeve.

"Yes, I was," said the barbarian, seeming to enjoy the girl's discomfort. "I encountered dark elves, giant spiders, and sacrificial victims. And that's before we even mention the gruesome, indescribable statue monster."

Just then, Young Warrior thought he heard a rustle; he felt like the darkness puffed up around them. By the time he grabbed his sword and got to his feet, the barbarian already had his greatsword out and ready.

Despite the gentle haze coming from the city and the adventurers' campfire, there was still a darkness beyond. And in that darkness…

Something's there.

Young Warrior felt sweat on his palms.

"Wha—wha—wha—?" The silver-haired girl jumped up, fists at the ready, in something of a panic, and the rest of the party followed her. Elf Cleric had his beloved dart gun out, while Dwarf Scout had drawn her short sword and held it in a reverse grip.

The canid wizard was the last to his feet, but he held his staff and whispered sharply, "Form a circle!" as he looked around.

"…You mentioned dark elves?" Young Warrior asked. He didn't want to frown; he forced himself to smile instead.

"And giant spiders," the barbarian said, the sharklike grin on his face once more. He was genuinely enjoying this. "And don't forget the monstrous statue!"

The adventurers formed a circle, keeping their spell caster and their campfire behind them as they faced the darkness.

The next moment, dark elves riding on giant spiders burst from the heart of the underground empire.

CHAPTER 4
Massed Combat

They must be idiots to build a village there! the goblins thought, snickering to themselves.

The idiots built a village in a big open spot, then they started storing crops. There were even women. They were practically *begging* to have their stuff stolen. They'd brought this on themselves.

If the goblins attacked them, why, that was only natural. They couldn't be blamed for it. Not when they were so much smarter, so much more logical than foolish humans who would build a village right out in the open like that.

The goblins, they would have done a smarterer job. A better job. Because they were better. Better than those humans.

No—not *they*. Each of the goblins assumed *he* was better, smarter, stronger than the idiots around him. It was simply how they thought.

They had no idea what it took to cultivate a field nor to defend a village. They never thought that humans had achieved these things by trial and error—it never even occurred to them. Not even after one who dared to call himself king emerged among them.

Ah yes, this king did seem to have some sort of plan up his goblin sleeve. They would attack the village *en masse*, impregnate the women to increase their numbers—certainly something they looked forward to—and then move on to the next place.

He seemed to have planned that far ahead. But in the end, even he would be only someone else's errand boy.

But that's fine for now.

Let him wave his weapon around and pretend to be king. Soon he'd know who was truly a greater king—far greater even than those who stood behind him.

Before that, why not enjoy the village to get in the mood?

It was all that trash was good for.

§

Goblin Slayer's eyes fluttered open as he heard a rustling.

The angle of the sun hadn't changed, but it was already a dark red. His mind had been dormant for only a short while, then.

Disgusting.

He'd thought he was made of slightly sterner stuff than that. His teacher must have overestimated him.

He should never think so highly of himself.

"I have returned," said Examiner, who stood in front of Goblin Slayer where he sat on the ground. She brushed off her clothes.

Goblin Slayer raised his strangely heavy head and forced himself to focus his hazy vision on her. With the evening sun shining behind her, the expression on her face was a shadow, and he couldn't make it out.

"You've returned?" he asked, his voice terribly hoarse. His throat felt like he was speaking for the first time in ten years.

Examiner didn't answer his question but said, "I see you are tired." She reached into a small pouch she kept at her hip and tossed something to him. The air whistled faintly as it dropped toward him; Goblin Slayer caught it reflexively.

In the palm of his gloved hand, he found a bottle. Some kind of liquid sloshed inside.

"I have some of these myself," he said.

"Perhaps, but at the moment, I am not tired. Therefore..." She shrugged and stared fixedly toward the goblin nest. It was obvious she didn't intend to argue any further.

Goblin Slayer followed her gaze toward the cavern entrance, the little bottle still in his hand. The scene was the same as it had been before, a listless goblin standing guard outside. The king had appeared several more times, and occasionally another goblin, either on foot or wolfback, would arrive at the nest and join the horde.

There was no time. Not until sunset, not until the goblin lord set forth with his army.

Time was always limitless and always in short supply.

Goblin Slayer grunted, then he pulled the stopper and drank the potion in a single gulp.

Delicious.

He recognized the flavor of the stamina potion by now, at once sweet and bitter, promising to restore his strength. With that gulp, the lead that seemed to weigh on his head vanished as if it had never been there.

"If...," Examiner began quietly. She stood as still as the tree whose trunk she was by; her eyes never moved from the entrance to the goblin-infested cave. "...you think you cannot stop because this is a test, I can suspend the examination at my own discretion."

"———?"

Goblin Slayer blinked under his helmet, utterly failing to comprehend what she meant. "No. It hadn't even occurred to me."

"I see," she said, and the faintest breath escaped her. A sigh? Or a sound of annoyance? "There are not very many paragraphs we can go to from this point."

Goblin Slayer nodded, pouring the dregs of the potion down his throat without a word, waiting for her to continue.

"First, we charge into the nest and try our luck." That, she added, was what they were already doing. Then she continued, businesslike, "If things go well, we will be able to kill the goblin lord and put the horde into disarray."

"..."

"If things go poorly, we will be overwhelmed by the goblins, and both of us will go to fourteen."

"Fourteen?"

"Dead as coffin nails, unable to tell anyone about the gravity of the situation."

Examiner sounded moderately embarrassed to have been caught using slang; she covered by explaining the unfamiliar expression brusquely.

As a woman, likely a far worse fate would await her…

But mine will not be much better.

He thought of the husband and wife in the house next door. He thought of his sister. The other villagers. The captives he had encountered in other caverns. The corpses. Anyone who could judge which of them was the better off must have been sitting in a very fine chair, indeed.

"If we do not wish to try our luck, then we must retreat to the Guild with all haste and summon reinforcements."

That would be the logical thing. Even Goblin Slayer understood that much.

"You and I are an adventuring party that has accepted a quest. But the two of us are unlikely to be able to defend the village. We could call reinforcements—"

"During which time the village would be destroyed," Goblin Slayer said. This was his answer. It was enough. It was everything.

He rose from the bushes, careful not to make a sound, still clutching the empty potion bottle. What she thought or did had no relation to what he thought or did. If they twiddled their thumbs, the village would certainly be annihilated. He already knew from experience how difficult it was to defend a village all by himself.

I will not be drawn into another pitched battle with goblins.

Even if they called for reinforcements, they wouldn't get more than one party. This was a goblin hunt. Novice work. Of this, he was sure. Whether that one party would be enough to achieve victory, Goblin Slayer neither knew nor cared. They might be destroyed; they might be triumphant. It depended on the dice of Fate and Chance.

Anyone who thought too much of goblins must surely have been asleep at the time of that battle five years ago. Goblins were not capable of great victories. They would be defeated eventually, scattered.

And then they would attack a village somewhere. Before the world was destroyed.

He did not feel that one village was a small price to pay for the world's salvation. At the same time, neither did he feel the world should be sacrificed to save a single village. That would just be reckless philosophizing. Did he think he was the only one who had suffered?

Do or do not: That was everything. He reminded himself of that yet again.

As he had time and time again over the last five years.

"...Well, I know I have a decent idea of your character," Examiner said and looked at Goblin Slayer—or no. Goblin Slayer looked at her. She was smiling. In the gathering darkness, an eye seemed visible behind her black hair, shining like the first star in the ultramarine sky. "I took word, boy," she said before whispering, "to the village." She then pulled herself away from the tree trunk with a movement so crisp it looked like she might leap into action even then. "This is a dangerous situation, and they had to be alerted."

I would never have guessed. She looked exactly as she had before; nothing to betray that she had done such a thing.

"It was not like I was conveying word of our victory. I did not push so hard as to risk my life."

So she said, but even at a rush, the round trip from here to the village would take...

No.

Was this another facet of the footwork she'd demonstrated on their march? Goblin Slayer couldn't fathom.

There were so many people in the Four-Cornered World who knew things he didn't. Far more than the opposite.

"You're saying," he began slowly, thoughtfully, "that there is no need to worry about what will happen after this."

"There is every reason to worry, which is why we must do all we can."

"Hrm..."

The smile had already vanished from Examiner's face. As night deepened, the first stars appeared in the blackness, then vanished as if in a haze. There was a sense of gathering darkness. Goblin Slayer looked up at the sky, still clutching the empty bottle.

He felt like he was in the palm of her hand. But so what?

Were there not goblins in front of him?

"GOROOGGBB…?!"

The sleepy goblin never got to be relieved from guard duty. He died first.

Goblins could see in the dark, but they couldn't dodge a projectile they never expected. The empty bottle impacted against his skull, but it didn't break; it just buried itself in his forehead.

"GORG?!"

The second goblin finally realized something was wrong when his companion tumbled over backward.

"That's two…!"

"GOOBBOOGRBBG?!?!"

The creature managed only a gurgling death cry, a blade buried in his windpipe. Then it was over.

That was noisier than I'd hoped, but…

But good enough. No goblin was diligent enough to stand guard duty without jabbering now and then.

Goblin Slayer appeared from the bushes and heaved a sigh as he walked over to the corpses.

Examiner followed him with a "hmm." She put a hand to her chin, and as if continuing the examination, she asked, "You can throw with both hands?"

"I've practiced."

"There is something to be said for a bow and arrow, you know," she remarked. "Or perhaps a party member who can use them."

"I know how to use a bow," Goblin Slayer said succinctly. Then he braced a foot on the corpse and pulled out his dagger. He flicked it to get the blood off, then checked the blade. Once he was convinced he could still use it, he put it back in his scabbard. "I'm going in."

"Not so fast."

He could see that Examiner's chain was already in her hand; she had been ready in case he failed as she emerged from the undergrowth. This wasn't "working with him" in the strict sense—she was preparing to clean up his mess.

That's fine with me.

"We should take out the relief guards as well. That will buy us more time."

"Hrm," he said and thought for several seconds. She was right. "Let's do that."

In that case, they would have to proceed carefully. They couldn't let the next pair of guards get away—that would undo all their plans.

Goblin Slayer looked at the goblin corpses, then at the towering pile of filth. Then without so much as flinching, he took his dagger and held it in a reverse grip. "We'll need to erase our scents," he said.

"No, I do not believe I shall."

"…I see."

§

A moment from the past flickered in her memory. A small thing—it felt like just the other day, though it was now some time ago.

"Don't you think we should be pushing forward?"

They couldn't spend their whole lives earning pocket change. They were adventurers! If they were only in it for the money, there were plenty of better ways to earn. They should be pressing on. Ever onward, ever forward, ever inward, ever deeper. That was their calling.

"I can handle more than just goblins with my martial arts, and you have your spells."

"Yeah, I do, but…" She'd smiled, still uneasy. *"But only the basics really. It's tough! I don't know if I could pull it off."*

"If you don't try, you'll never know. Besides, whatever happens…"

It'll be fine. That's what that stupid girl had said before tromping straight down into the depths of the Death. What had happened to her?

The slightest sigh escaped Examiner's lips.

"What is it?" asked the adventurer inspecting the goblin corpses. He was much younger than his equipment would suggest. Who had been the better, him or that girl? They had much in common. Gods. She had hardly changed at all.

"Nothing," the woman said with a gentle shake of her head.

"I see," the boy muttered, and then he walked into the dark. Examiner was about to follow him, but she hesitated at that first step. Why did she hesitate? She didn't know.

Should she stop him? Simply watch him? Or follow? Her choices were three. She chose the third.

"...I suppose it means I understand how you feel," she mumbled so quietly that only she could hear—or maybe there was someone else. She took that step.

This was no big deal. That lightless space spreading before her was a goblin nest.

It could not go down nearly so far as the Death, at least.

§

How easy things would have been if he could simply push forward, thinking nothing, just killing goblins.

That was the thought in Goblin Slayer's mind as he clapped a hand over a goblin's mouth from behind. The creature had been quite at his ease, expecting nothing.

"GORG?!" The goblin's eyes went wide, but Goblin Slayer had no intention of giving his foe time to comprehend what was happening. He was already holding his dagger, and with it, he slashed the creature across the throat. "GORG?! GOORGB?!"

The goblin died choking on his own blood. If the blood loss didn't get him, the suffocation would.

It's important to do a thorough job.

His thoughts felt slow. He shook the blood off the blade and returned it to its sheath, then dug through his belongings. Yes, his mind wasn't working fast enough. Just thinking felt like too much effort. He breathed in, then out. The smell of garbage.

"This cave is larger than I might have expected."

Examiner's voice seemed too crisp, too clear, for a sound in a goblin nest; it gave him the shivers. She ran her hand along the wall, catching a bit of dirt that shook loose and crushing it dispassionately between her fingers.

"It is crude, but they appear to have enlarged this cavern themselves. There is a hobgoblin about, boy."

"A goblin is a goblin," he spat, shoving the corpse behind a convenient stalagmite with his foot.

That made—how many? The guards at the entrance, the relief guards—that was four. Then counting the goblins they had encountered since entering the cave…

"Thirteen?" he said.

"…I cannot say I see the necessity of counting." Examiner watched the dirt fall from her hand, almost sounding annoyed. "If you believe that experience points are based purely on the number of monsters you have killed, you are mistaken."

"I've never wanted experience points."

The number of corpses already exceeded the number of goblins he'd expected. The twisting labyrinth of caves seemed to go on forever. How many of these creatures were there? Did the goblins themselves know the full extent of the cave system?

If so, they are smarter than me, he thought. There beneath his helmet, he felt his mouth tighten. *And they are* not *smarter than me.*

They'd simply found a hole and started digging, and by happenstance had connected one path to another. They wouldn't have been thinking about the most efficient way to make those connections nor what would be most likely to confuse an enemy.

Goblins were stupid, but they were not fools. *Yes. Stupid—not fools.* Even if they didn't remember the complete layout of their own caves, they would know the routes they used most frequently. And that had to mean…

"As long as we are encountering goblins, we are on the right path," Examiner said.

"Agreed." Goblin Slayer nodded. She was right. And that was good. They were going the right way.

"Let us go, then." With that, Examiner strode off, virtually ignoring Goblin Slayer. She was the one who took—who said she would take—the job of looking for enemies, checking ahead. In other words, of being their scout.

Indeed, her scouting proved to be exemplary. She found the goblins' childish traps, of course, but she also caught footsteps coming from afar. She was very perceptive. She could tell the goblins were coming before they even spotted the adventurers' torch. Then they would douse the torch and set an ambush for the goblins, a powerful tactic.

The many ways she had of killing goblins, amply demonstrated in these halls, were likewise helpful. Perhaps he should try to learn some of them, even if he couldn't pick up the unique way she walked.

"How do you do that?" he asked.

"Huh?" she said, glancing back at him and sounding so surprised it was almost comical.

Just for a moment, it was as if he had heard her true self—relaxed, soft, unguarded. Of course, that impression might have been his imagination, mistaken like a ripple on a pond, and even if it was there, it swiftly disappeared.

"Qi, I suppose… An aura might be the simplest way to explain it." She coughed, trying to sound particularly nonchalant in order to cover for her lapse. "It means honing the intellect. Paying attention to sounds; smells; the particularities of wind, colors, or the trees. Footprints…"

"Honing the intellect," he repeated.

"If you train your intuition day in and day out, it will begin to work passively, and then you come to notice these things."

"I see."

He would have to train his intuition in that case. His master had told him that intuition was merely experience put to work. He would have to accumulate more experience, then.

One must constantly think, *In such and such a case, this is what happens.* One must constantly remember, learn, and internalize. With enough time and sheer guts, even he could do that. That pleased Goblin Slayer. There was a skill that even a talentless person like him could learn. He was grateful for that.

"Stop," Examiner said, and Goblin Slayer was so caught up in his thoughts that he didn't react immediately. After a beat, however, he sank down into a vigilant stance, his hand on the weapon at his hip. He looked around, scanning for anything out of the ordinary.

From the darkness, he could smell something rotten. He heard his own breath echoing around inside his helmet. There was something around the next corner. His voice was faint as he spoke: "Goblins."

"What else?" Examiner muttered with the slightest of smiles.

"True, there might be something else. If you think only of goblins, you will die, boy."

Boy. With that whisper in his ears, Goblin Slayer approached a fork in the caves. The deeper he went, the more acutely all five of his senses picked up signs of goblins, the hints thick in the air. They'd been burned into his mind since that day five years ago. He knew the moment he detected them.

The problem might be the distance at which I detect them.

Practice, that was the only answer. Go by trial and error until something more was possible.

But whatever might come later, right now the priority was the door in front of him.

It was rough-hewn and didn't even appear to have a lock, let alone a trap set on it. Even from this distance, he could hear something striking flesh within and the hideous laughter of goblins.

Under his helmet, Goblin Slayer took in a breath, then let it out again. Nauseating air filled his lungs and was expelled once more.

He crouched down and was about to approach the door slowly, carefully, but Examiner held up a hand to stop him. "Hrm..."

Before he could say anything, she pulled the chain from her sleeve and sent it dancing through the air. It wrapped itself around the door like a thing alive and pulled it open just slightly, without a sound.

"The proverb holds that there may be a corpse-eater under any door," she said.

In other words, open doors carefully seemed to be the point. Goblin Slayer didn't really understand what she meant.

More important to him was the scene on the other side of the door.

"Ahhh...?!" a woman cried weakly, accompanied once more by the pounding of flesh. It was a young woman, held against a rotten wood board. Perhaps she'd been an adventurer or a villager; it was impossible to tell at this juncture. Rusty nails had been pounded mercilessly through her pale, now-bloodless hands, pinning her to the board. The intermittent sounds of the hammer were probably explained by the goblins' perverse pleasures: They were enjoying watching her squirm, and anyway, they didn't want to give her a chance to get used to the pain.

"GOBR! GOOG!!"

"GOROG! GBB!"

In spite of all this, Goblin Slayer didn't act immediately.

It's a cramped space.

And it held a great many goblins. More than he could take out in a surprise attack. If he went in there, he would be taking them on head-to-head—he would be at a disadvantage against an enemy who relied on their numbers.

"......"

Despite the danger, not going in was never an option.

Do or do not.

He repeated the words to himself. They were everything he needed. You could not accomplish what you didn't do. *Because* you did something, you achieved it.

And yet Goblin Slayer still couldn't act immediately. Or perhaps he simply didn't.

He found himself pierced by a gaze—Examiner's beautiful eye, cold as ice, holding him in place.

Goblin Slayer searched for words in the empty air. "What...," he managed to squeeze out, his voice rasping, "...do you think?"

"I think the hostage complicates things. And I think there are a lot of them." Her answer was immediate, and just as quickly, her chain was in her hand, and she knelt near Goblin Slayer. "However, it is also true that they cannot kill the hostage if they wish for her to continue being of use to them."

"...These are goblins," he reminded her.

"Yes, meaning they are not smart enough to realize they can kill the hostage as a form of political attack against us."

She was right about that. Although they might kill the hostage just before they themselves died as a tiny form of triumph.

"What we will have to be careful of is letting them interrupt our momentum. That and the risk of an attack that may seek to sacrifice the hostage."

She pointed out that in a cloistered space like this one, the advantage of their numbers was distinctly lessened. They would have to avoid friendly fire, but he and she could strike almost at will and expect to hit an enemy. Moreover, she said, it would be a lot of trouble to use the hostage as a shield. "Analyze the battlefield situation step-by-step, boy. Where are you at a disadvantage? Consider those factors one at a time and neutralize them."

"..."

"They may be monsters, but they stand on the ground and walk; they have ears and eyes and a nose; and they breathe. There is a way."

Much as she might wish they had some spells...

Her whisper never even reached Goblin Slayer's ears. He was reaching into his item pouch, which he was finally getting used to having at his hip. He felt like he could hear the whistling of a snowstorm. And amid it, his master's chortling laughter.

Who knows? Might be a birthday present in there!

"...I should not have to say this, but just to be clear," Examiner began, reminding Goblin Slayer that he was not in the snowy cavern in which he had spent all those years. There was an edge to her voice; his silence seemed to pique her suspicion—or perhaps she simply assumed the worst. "Only ruffians and rogues would think it was acceptable to kill the hostage in a situation like this."

"I know," Goblin Slayer said, not pushing back even though this was the second time Examiner had pointed this out.

He considered explaining what he was about to do—but another scream from the woman convinced him to abandon the idea.

Faster to show her.

"I have a plan. Here I go."

Without waiting for an answer, he launched into action. From behind him came first a belated *tsk*, then the clank of the slithering chain.

"GOROOGB?!"

"GOROG! GBBB?!"

The door flew open with a *slam*, and something on the order of ten goblins—more goblins than a person would ever want to see in his life—turned toward the sound.

"Hmph!" Even as he burned the image into his memory, Goblin Slayer flung the egg he'd pulled out of his item pouch.

"GOOROGGBB?!?!"

"GBBOR?!?!"

A cloud of red-black powder filled the air, and the goblins started screaming. They'd dismissed it as a stone that didn't even hurt if it hit them, but that moment of contempt would cost them their lives.

Goblin Slayer held his breath, squeezed his eyes shut, and plunged into the cloud, counting on his mental image of the goblins' locations to tell him where to direct his dagger.

"GORGGB?!"

"One…!"

The first goblin was clawing at his face, and when Goblin Slayer was done with him, a geyser of blood spouted from his windpipe. Goblin Slayer relied on the sound to know he'd done his job. He gave the mortally wounded goblin a violent kick out of the way. Next came…

"GORGB?!"

"Two!"

This goblin lunged at him despite the tears streaming down his face; Goblin Slayer backhanded the creature with his shield. Lightening it had given it that much more momentum, and the force of the impact broke the goblin's nose and almost made his arm go numb. He didn't care.

Goblin Slayer continued the motion, smashing the goblin's head against the wall, then stabbing it through the eyes with his dagger.

The bone behind the eyes is thin. When Goblin Slayer gouged into its brain, the monster jumped like a fish on a line. Goblin Slayer resisted the sickly spasms and judged the distance to the woman on the board.

"GBBGR?!"

"Three…"

No, not yet!

Goblin Slayer had pulled his sword out and flung it at a goblin behind him, only to watch it bounce off the creature's skull.

Maybe he was tired. Or perhaps it was a problem of skill. Whichever, there was an instant's opening.

"Shaaaa!"

From shadow to shadow, she entered, a mysterious movement, almost impossible to follow with the naked eye. Her spiked chain danced through the air, wrapping itself around the hilt of the sword like a living snake and bringing it down on the goblin.

"GORG?!"

And that *makes three!*

He heard the scream behind him; he picked up the club the goblin had dropped and advanced forward.

"GOROGGB?!"

"GBBG?! GGOROGB?!"

Four, five. He swung the blunt instrument right, then left, trusting to luck to break goblin bones and crush goblin sinews. Ahh, what a thing it was to be able to kill goblins without even having to think about it.

He had advanced only a few feet, yet how many goblins had he killed?

A scream. The sound of the club impacting flesh. A groan. Much like those that had filled this chamber until moments ago—and yet decisively different.

During those ten seconds or so, was *that* goblin fortunate or not? Only the dice knew. If nothing else, he'd been some distance from his companions, allowing him to promptly escape the cloud of tear gas. That gave him freedom of movement, and though he didn't think it through to speak of, he acted quickly.

"GGBROG!!"

"Nngghh!"

He dragged the woman up, ripping her off the board and the inexpertly driven nails. Blood flowed, flesh tore, but what did he care? This was what she was here for—he might as well use her.

Privately scoffing at his idiot companions who didn't even understand that much, the goblin shifted his grip on the woman, a limp, dead weight.

"GOROOOGGGB…!"

He saw Goblin Slayer in front of him and grinned, baring his crooked, yellowed teeth.

Goblin Slayer figured the creature thought he had won. These foolish monsters believed the hostage made them untouchable. This one, at least, would be saved—or so he thought.

No doubt they also believed they would be able to have their sport with Examiner, who stood behind Goblin Slayer. It was obvious from the goblin's hideous expression what he was thinking as he pressed a rusty nail to the woman's neck.

"Hmph." Goblin Slayer ignored the goblin's yammering; he took a single, unhesitating step forward.

"GOROGGBB?!?!"

Then he kicked—lower than the woman's crotch, the goblin's crotch.

I knew they didn't understand how to use shields.

There was a most unpleasant feeling against the tips of his toes. The goblin let the woman go and fell to the ground, writhing; Goblin Slayer tried to get the nasty sensation out of his toes by grinding the creature underfoot. It didn't help much. "Hrm," Goblin Slayer grunted again, then raised his club.

The handful of goblins left behind him were already succumbing to Examiner's fists and chain; they wouldn't live long.

"That's six."

It was like smashing a pumpkin.

Which was a wonderful feeling.

"...I feel slightly relieved," Examiner murmured from very close to him. She caught the woman the goblin had let go, crouching between the former hostage and her dead captor. The woman was unconscious, whether from the effect of the tear gas grenade or from sheer relief at being rescued. Examiner saw her chest move gently up and down, however, and gave a quick nod. "As I said in the village, we do not need those who would kill hostages."

"I'm here to kill goblins," Goblin Slayer said briefly, brusquely. There had definitely been a bit too much powder in the tear gas bomb. If it was enough to incapacitate him when he dove in, then it provided no tactical advantage.

He popped the club out of the goblin's skull, trailing brains.

"That should be enough," he added.

"...It is. For now."

He never did see the expression on Examiner's face as she said this, for suddenly there was a sound like sizzling meat and a powerful impact hit him from behind.

Goblin Slayer was knocked unconscious.

§

"GROGGBB…!"

"GBB! GROBBGB!!"

The first thing he noticed was that his head felt strangely light. Then there was the dull ache all over his body. He didn't even know what hurt; everything seemed stiff and uncomfortable.

His head pounded with every beat of his heart, and then he realized he wasn't stiff.

I'm tied down.

Goblin Slayer discovered that he was sitting in a crude rotting chair.

"GRBB! GBOROGBB!!"

His helmet and the padding underneath had been pulled off his head. He was still wearing his armor. Maybe it had been more than they could do to get it off him.

How many years had it been since he'd seen goblins without the slats of his visor between him and them? Five years maybe.

Cruel, hideous laughter echoed around his head.

My head.

He was sure they must have burst through the wall behind him. He'd been hit on the head by a tumbling rock, or some earth, or a goblin club. His helmet had saved his life, but it had also kept him from realizing what was happening.

Meaning it's not all-powerful.

He had to look around. Listen closely. Sniff and see what he could smell.

Despite being in a goblin den, he didn't see any women nor hear screaming nor smell burnt flesh.

That's good, then.

He was quite satisfied with that, in fact. This wasn't bad at all.

"GRRB!!"

There was a *thud*, and his vision reeled. He understood that he'd been hit in the head with a club.

He felt something warm and damp dribble down his cheek. His forehead must have split. He was still conscious, though.

He forced his muscles to tense, moving his eyes, trying to tell how many goblins were in the room with him. Five. As far as he could see.

"GRG! GOOGB!!"

"GOOGBB!!"

Next, a lightning bolt of pain shot down his arm, which was leashed to the chair. Struck with a club from above, he felt the pain lance straight to the marrow of his bones. The goblins showed no restraint—of course they didn't. At least he was wearing his gauntlets; that saved his arm from breaking.

"________"

Still, he gritted his teeth and managed not to scream, only looking at the goblins.

"GBBB!"

"GOBOGB!!"

The goblins didn't appear to appreciate his attitude.

Of course not.

He'd known how goblins treated their captives since he was ten years old. In short, as their toys. They weren't looking for revenge. They weren't even angry. That was his reasoning anyway.

What they were doing might best be described as torture—but they weren't looking for any particular information from him. Goblins simply assumed whatever information was most congenial to them at any given moment.

Take this adventurer: They were sure their idiot comrades had simply missed him, let him escape.

They, for their part, would beat him, hurt him, make him scream and writhe. They would grind him into the dust and laugh at him, the lowly worm.

Only by doing this could goblins satisfy themselves.

Why should he feel any pity for them? They were disgusting creatures.

"________"

So he sucked in the next breath and refused to scream. Refused to react. He pushed it all down to boil in his belly.

"GRGB!"

The goblins started jabbering. So he was right: There was such a thing as goblinese.

He suspected it was something like: *We're taking all the time and trouble to beat him, but he doesn't scream! The insolence! He doesn't know his place. We'll show him.* That sort of thing.

"GBBOOGRG!!"

The next blow was particularly vicious, a club slammed full force into his hand. He lost all feeling below his wrist; then there was a burning numbness that forced ragged breaths out of his mouth.

It was all he could do not to make a sound. The pain was almost enough to drag a groan from him. But what did the goblins care?

They beat him. They hit his head, struck his arm, punched his cheek, jabbed his stomach so hard that vomit came out like breath.

Goblin laughter rang out around him, his ears buzzed, and his vision narrowed.

There was nothing particularly notable about any of this. He felt almost at ease, in fact, as if he had been here for the last five years.

The more time he could buy, the better for him and his companions. At least Examiner and the former captive were probably safe. Goblins didn't know the word *self-control.* If the women had been taken, none of them would be here. If they were passing the time with him, then that was to his advantage. Let them stay here forever, indulging in their stupidity.

Goblin Slayer observed all this as if from a step removed, while the goblins continued to laugh and jeer.

Yes. Of course.

He remembered a frozen cavern. His master's cackling as it echoed off the walls. It was such a familiar sound it almost brought a smile to his face.

Yes, this hurts. But that's all.

He exhaled, breathing out the fire that smoldered in his belly. He'd endured. He always had. Now the time was ripe.

If they wanted to laugh, let them laugh. It was impossible to teach goblins a lesson anyway. Goblins always believed they and they alone were the victims, and everyone else was at fault. They would just wait for their next chance. It was simply how they were. And so...

It's do or do not.

"GOROGGBB!!"

"Hoo!"

At the same moment the goblin raised his club, Goblin Slayer twisted forcefully. The rotten chair creaked and cracked and fell backward, and then it took the blow from the goblin's club full force.

There was a *crack*. An impact. Splinters of wood flew everywhere. And in the middle of it all, his hand grabbed the legs of the chair.

Their mistake, not nailing me down.

"GROGB?!"

"Hrroh!"

A goblin yammered and came lunging at him; Goblin Slayer met him with a kick, thrusting out with his feet even as he rolled along the ground. He found the goblin's small body, slamming it into the rock wall behind.

"GOROGB?!"

"GRGB! GGOORRGBB!!"

The goblins spent one precious instant mocking their comrade, wasted it pouring contempt on him.

"Ahhh!" Goblin Slayer heaved himself up off the earth, lifted his arm. It was a wild blow, no more precise or measured than if he were swinging a sandbag attached to his shoulder, but it was enough to crush a goblin skull.

"GBBRG?!"

"That...makes...*one*!"

He pounded the broken chair leg into the goblin's face, then stepped on the twitching body. He couldn't even tell if the dark blood everywhere was his or the goblin's.

Four...more...!

"GOB! GROGB!"

"GRRRGBB!"

There was no time to think about it. The goblins were already coming at him from behind.

"Rraah!" So Goblin Slayer literally gave it no thought but only lashed out with his improvised club. He didn't worry about striking with a sharp point or hitting a vital area. He ignored everything and simply pounded his opponent.

"GORRR!!"

"Hhhf…!"

Abruptly, there was a dull *clang*, and something intercepted his club.

The goblin in front of him leered at him, triumphant. Between them, between the goblin and his club, he saw a round shield.

Goblin Slayer reacted immediately. "Yah—yaaaah!" He rammed into the goblin, trusting not to his strength but to the sheer difference in body size, putting all the force he had left into the shove.

"GORGB?!"

The club pressed forward into the shield. The goblin was too small to push back effectively. The creature must've stripped it off him when he was captured. The straps were in tatters.

The polished edge of the shield began to bite into the goblin's throat…

"Yaaaah!"

"GROGBB?!?!"

It sliced through the thin, fragile windpipe. The goblin's breath began to escape the hole, whistling, and soon he would be dead. Goblin Slayer didn't let up, though, until the corpse began to twitch listlessly.

That's four…

Yes, four.

"GRBB!!"

"…Hngh?!"

The first goblin, the one he'd kicked into the wall, was up and about again. Goblin Slayer felt a sharp blow to the back of his head, and his vision swam. A fist or a rock, he realized, but although his awareness tracked the blow, his body failed to react.

He was slammed to the ground amid the blood and filth. He scrabbled with his hands, his feet, seeking some way to rise back up.

He had to stand or at least roll out of the way. He had to get back to a fighting posture. Or else…

Time seemed to slow down, threatening to stagnate. To his surprise, he felt no fear, nor even regret. There was only the certainty of what would come. There could be nothing else, nothing more.

"Hrr…rraaahhh!"

"GROGB! GROGBBB?!"

So he thrust out his arms and legs mechanically and bucked the weight off his back.

There was no hope to speak of; the startled goblin, thrown clear of him, was soon back on his feet.

The club was gone from Goblin Slayer's hand—when had he lost it?

What did he care? He forced strength into his frozen fingers, pulling the shield from the dead goblin's windpipe.

What do I care?

Let the goblin come.

"Everyone, whoever they be, owes a life."

Yes, no hope, not to speak of. Ahead of him, in the darkness, was no hope—only goblins.

He did, however, see a flash of silver light.

"Shaaaa!"

A piercing yell split the darkness and a spiked chain of silver raced through the air. It wrapped itself around the goblin without a sound, dragging him upward.

"GROGBB?!"

The creature was pulled into the air almost before he could scream. He kicked helplessly at the empty air, and then—

"——?!?!"

Snap. There was a sound like a dry branch breaking, and the goblin died.

"Haah…" Goblin Slayer slumped to his knees before the corpse even hit the ground. Someone—he thought it sounded like his sister—called out and ran over to him. He heard the footsteps.

That makes five...

That was Goblin Slayer's last thought before he slipped into darkness, unconscious.

§

His awareness seemed to fade in and out, the world changing in nonsensical ways each time. He was in a goblin nest, in the snowy cavern, under the floorboards of his house, on the outskirts of the village soaked with rain, and then again back in a goblin nest.

As he finally began to focus, he found himself in a cavern somewhere, the air dank and filthy. A stone ceiling spread out wide above him, and there seemed to be a campfire burning nearby.

He was lying on the thinnest excuse for a mat. He turned his head and saw a brass lantern glowing faintly. There was an untidy collection of boxes all over, some containing digging tools, others with all manner of other items. This would be the goblin storehouse, then.

Examiner was there, too, almost buried among all the stuff. She'd placed her jacket over the hostage girl like a blanket and was sitting with her legs thrust out easily. Her clothes seemed unruffled, and she appeared unhurt. Her eyes were closed, the only sound her deep breathing. In through her nose, out through her mouth. Then again and again, until at length she began breathing through her nose only.

Her chest drifted gently up and down—she had taught him that this was the rhythm of meditation.

For a moment, he simply watched her. Under that black hair was her other eye, the one she kept hidden. The one covered by a burn.

Abruptly, her good eye snapped open and fixed Goblin Slayer with a stare. "You are awake, boy?"

"The goblins—"

"Are not here."

Yes, not *here*, at least. Her brief addendum produced an "I see" from Goblin Slayer.

He looked up at the ceiling. The space was rough-hewn, the rock shaved and broken away. The various objects the goblins had brought here seemed out of place. Could there be someone behind them? Or was the goblin lord really intelligent enough to have them gather things like this?

He couldn't be sure.

"Where are we?" he asked.

"Still in the goblin nest—in their storehouse, I would imagine." Examiner patted a wooden chest nearby, and it rattled, the sound of glass bottles bumping against one another. "Maybe they attacked a workshop somewhere or perhaps a passing carriage. They have digging implements and even fire powder here."

"Hmm..."

"I could not plunge into a horde of goblins with a rescued captive in tow," she explained. It was clear that she was not offering an excuse but simply stating an incontrovertible fact. Therefore, Goblin Slayer didn't press the issue but only nodded acceptance. Should he tell Examiner to prioritize him over and above a poor captive, or the village, or even her own safety? He would never be so brazen.

He hadn't been anticipating rescue. Of course not. But as it happened, he *had* been rescued. In which case:

"That was a help," he said.

"..."

Examiner blinked in surprise. She didn't seem to have expected him to thank her.

She sighed deeply, looked down as if to hide her face, and finally murmured, "Not at all. We are a party for the time being. A mercenary might have acted differently, but an adventurer... Any adventurer would do the same."

"I see."

He had not expected it, this thing that any adventurer would have done. That only went to show that he was no adventurer.

If our positions had been reversed...

What would he have done? Whatever, he would not have done it as well as she had, of that he was sure.

Perhaps his thoughtful silence stirred something in Examiner, for when she spoke again, the edge in her words was softer. "Do you regret it?"

"No," he said, groping about for his helmet and the padding that went under it. Examiner glanced at him, then held them out to him. He pulled them over his head; they scraped his cheeks and lips very painfully. "I was thinking it would've been easier if we possessed some sort of magic that would make them go to sleep. Or perhaps a spell that could eliminate sound."

He suspected it was all the noise the goblins had made that had attracted reinforcements—the ones who had burst through the wall. Gaining such spells all by himself would be very difficult, however. In which case, he would simply have to figure out how to kill goblins silently and then practice it diligently.

So long as he was alive, there would be a next time. If one did not let experience feed one's understanding, there was no point.

"With a new place in life comes a new perspective… I see now." The words sounded exasperated almost to the point of scorn; Examiner seemed to be talking to herself. Then she said, "Long ago, you know, I could not do what I did."

"What do you mean?"

"Striking a bit of empty air from a hundred paces as if striking the stars in a well." She recited the words almost like a song and balled up her right fist loosely in demonstration. "That is why they call it the Well-Style Fist."

Ah. Goblin Slayer nodded. He remembered how the empty air had caused the leaves on the trees to dance.

An exhalation left Examiner's lips, and she looked away, perhaps self-deprecating or slightly ashamed. "I still cannot use it in a real fight to speak of."

"I didn't realize anyone could do such a thing at all."

"Once a girl too confident in herself believed she could manage it and prevailed upon her party member to go deep into the dungeon."

So of course they found themselves with their backs to the wall. And what then?

Goblin Slayer didn't have to ask the question; Examiner smiled slightly and lifted her bangs. "The girl insisted her companion use a spell—or perhaps I should say, her companion was good enough to use a spell for her. And this is the result."

Maybe it was friendly fire or an explosion. No one knew which way the dice of Fate and Chance would go, not even the gods—and yet it seemed as if Examiner knew.

"To this day, I do not feel there was any call to help me, but now I see how one finds oneself wanting to help."

Goblin Slayer simply repeated, "I see." He didn't believe Examiner was really looking for a response from him. Whatever he might say would only be something she had grasped already long ago. So instead, he put her question back to her: "Do you regret it?"

"No, I do not," she said with a shake of her head, although she thought for a moment first. "She and I chose that adventure. Other people may have their clever quibbles, but as for me, I have not one shred of regret."

"I see."

That was good, then, he supposed.

Goblin Slayer reached for his item pouch and *tsk*'ed when he discovered it wasn't there. He looked out past the slats of his visor and saw his equipment in a pile. Examiner must have retrieved it for him. He took his item pouch from the pile and fished out a potion with unsteady fingers. He clutched it in his hand, undid the stopper.

"What do you plan to do now?" Examiner asked.

"Kill the goblins," he replied without hesitation. That was why he was here. He wanted to become a machine for that purpose. But he had failed. He lacked the capability, lacked the skill—so the most he could do was think as hard as he could. To go without a plan would mean more failure.

He took a mouthful of the potion. It would dull the pain and restore some of his strength, but it wouldn't immediately heal his wounds. Of course not.

"They know we're here. This place isn't safe. And even if we escape, they'll still attack the village."

"You are saying that the only way to truly survive this is to kill the goblins. Yes, on that point, I agree with you." Examiner studied him, then brushed the cheek of the former captive. "The question is how to do it."

The exhausted young woman was finally sleeping peacefully. They had to get her home safely.

Goblin Slayer wished intelligence would well up like a geyser. He downed the rest of the potion, then grunted thoughtfully at the empty bottle. What could he do as he was now? What did he *have* in this place?

He gazed at the lantern, which continued to crackle and burn, and asked:

"You said something about fire powder?"

§

The goblin lord was listening to the trash—as he referred to his subjects—deliver a report that he didn't like at all.

They were in the innermost sanctum of his castle, where he sat upon a throne assembled from cast-off junk. Needless to say, it was not to his satisfaction. He believed he deserved a bigger, more sumptuous throne.

Displeasure—yes, that was the only thing he felt. If it wasn't the dark elves yammering self-importantly from above him, it was the trash grumbling from below, despite the fact that they never did any work.

And that wasn't even to mention the humans, who had stupidly built a village right next to his castle, like they could do whatever they wanted. One day he would trample all of them underfoot and make them give him what was rightfully his.

But first, to deal with the matter at hand.

The goblin lord at least possessed the reason and intelligence to focus on that.

"GROGB! GOROGGBB!!"

They told him that two miserable adventurers, two little rats, had infiltrated his castle and were going around killing the trash.

What could be more displeasing?

How was it that this trash couldn't even stop two measly adventurers? Worse, how could they be so stupid that instead of doing something about it, they ran to tell *him*? Why couldn't they simply kill or capture the intruders without bothering him about it?

"GOROGB!"

"GBBR?!"

The goblin lord roared an imprecation and sent the unfortunate messenger flying with a vicious kick. The creature glared at him, but he mercilessly kicked the monster again.

"GRBBBB..."

The goblin lord bellowed, summoning the lazy trash to him. The throne room (as he had dubbed it) was in the deepest part of the caverns. And they were large caverns. The perfect place to collect more troops than could be counted with a goblin's intelligence.

The goblins, who had been gathered from many different places, now shuffled to the lord, full of displeasure themselves. They shuffled, and plodded, and came with no motivation and minimal morale.

The goblin lord did not like what he was seeing, not at all. Simultaneously, he knew it was only natural for the likes of these to follow him. It was he who gave them prey and food and toys and a place to live. So yes, it was only natural that they should labor like workhorses—not that goblins knew what those were—for him.

"GROB! GROGB!!"

The goblin lord leered a terrible leer as he imagined himself ruler over the whole Four-Cornered World.

Needless to say, the Four-Cornered World as he knew it extended no farther than a few of the villages in this area. But for him, this was the entire world, and as such, he was more important than anyone in it. More important than the goblins in this nest. More important than the dark elves who had set him up as king. More important than the Demon Lord—he stood above them all.

"GROGGBBB!!"

Goblins.

Goblins!

At all times and at every moment, they believed they themselves knew the Truth, whatever contrivances of logic it took for them to think so. It was always others who were wrong, and so it was others who were stupid, and foolish, and below them.

And this conviction that they were and must be the center of the world turned itself around when someone meddled with them. Then they could not believe that they had met such a pitiful, such a sad, such a tragic fate, and they would not abide it.

The goblins were always right, always great, always the victims…

Which is just another way of saying that goblins were always goblins.

"…GBB."

When the worthless trash had at last finished filtering into the cave, the goblin lord hefted himself from his seat. He would give them orders to hunt down the two adventurers—such simple orders to give and yet so troublesome.

They said one of them was a female…

In that case, the lord would enjoy her first; that was his right. Naturally, each of the other goblins was thinking the same thing about himself, but the king paid this no mind. The lord's mind was already full of the image of himself dominating this faceless female adventurer. She'd had the temerity to kill goblins, and he would punish her for it.

But in order to do that…

He would have to light a fire under the asses of these layabouts. They were stupid, worthless trash. He should pick one to make an example of. Any one would do.

The goblin lord looked slowly around the throne room, and he decided—how about that one? The goblin who had come shuffling in last of all, nearly falling over himself, almost tumbling along the ground?

The goblin lord opened his mouth to upbraid the hapless fool.

Indeed, his plan was to mock the creature, hold him up to ridicule, humiliate him, and then punish him.

He was about to unleash the first words of his tirade.

Then he saw the burning bottle stuffed in the mouth of the goblin who had flopped onto the floor.

"GROGRB?!"

Someone shouted, and someone jumped back; the goblin lord didn't know who. A great wallop of fire assaulted the throne room, and chunks of flesh fell like rain.

§

They're coming.

There was an explosion and goblin flesh flew everywhere, a beautiful sight if ever there was one. Somewhere beyond, he could hear the frenzied shouting of goblins. They wouldn't let the adventurers lurking in the tunnels of the cave system—as he had begun to think of it—escape.

"GOROOGB! GOOBBGR!!"

Green lumps rushed at him, howling, waving their arms. There were so many of them he could barely count, but they were all headed for the same narrow entrance.

Two people stood against them. Outnumbered by far. If the two tried to take the many head-on, they would be destroyed.

But Goblin Slayer did not panic.

I simply won't engage them in a straight fight.

He held a bottle in his hand with a burning wick made of twisted paper. He flung it as hard as he could.

His wounded hands ached, and his arms threatened to cramp, but what of it? He didn't need to throw accurately.

He could follow the flame as it described a wide arc, glittering red orange as it flew, then landed among the goblins.

"GOBBR?!"

"GOORGB?! GOROGGB?!"

There was an explosion. A crimson conflagration blew goblins everywhere, filling the air with chunks of flesh once again. A far, far quicker way to kill them than with a sword or a club.

"Next," he said. He held one hand behind his back toward Examiner, who stood near the former captive. Still exuding that indescribable calm beauty, she took another bottle from her sleeve. In a single fluid motion, she cracked her spiked chain, producing a spark that lit the bottle, which she then handed to him.

"This is not what my ability to conceal weapons was intended for," she said.

"I don't care," Goblin Slayer replied. "This is how I use it."

"GOROOGGGB?!"

"GOROGG! GORGGB!!"

The goblins were cowed by the explosion, but they were equally goaded forward by the rage of the goblin lord behind them. Morale, however, was in short supply.

The explosives being lobbed at them were bad enough, but then they heard a *thud, thud* coming from elsewhere. They couldn't know when or where they might be blown up.

"Next."

"But of course," Examiner said, handing him another bottle. She glanced up. "I am not sure this place will hold up to this."

Goblin Slayer didn't say anything but only flung the next bottle. There was another explosion. He had noticed the shock waves coming intermittently from all over the nest; bits of earth fell from the ceiling and scattered over his head.

Finally, he replied, "At least all the goblins will die."

Examiner could only sigh.

"Also," Goblin Slayer added, "I've been wanting to try attacking them with fire."

Flames. Shock waves. Shards of the glass bottle became projectiles, shredding through goblins who escaped the initial blast. Even with all this, it was obviously not a comprehensive form of attack.

The first wave of goblins who had managed to evade the series of explosions would soon break upon their attackers.

"GOROGGB!!"

"GGB! GORGGBB!!"

"GBOR! GOROGGBB!!"

"Hmph."

He assumed they were shouting things like, *Kill him! Violate her! She's mine!* and so on. He knew exactly what the goblins must be imagining when they saw Examiner. He could picture every moment of what they intended to do. He didn't have to look at the former captive to see it; he'd learned it all five years before.

There is no point learning goblinese.

What could they possibly say to him if he did? Maybe they would beg for their lives.

That might be fun to hear.

"Continue throwing the bombs at intervals," Goblin Slayer told Examiner, saying only what was absolutely necessary. Then he pulled out the sword at his hip. The entrance to the cavern was narrow, and the walls to either side were thick. There would be no bursting through them this time.

He only had to focus on what was in front of him. He'd learned this in the tower. It was better than an open battlefield, like in the village.

The potion was the only thing holding him together; he was moving his body through sheer force of will, yet he did not feel he was going to lose this fight.

Why should I worry? There's not even a hundred of them.

"...I will watch your back," Examiner intoned, although she sighed as she said it. Goblin Slayer dropped into a deep stance.

"GROGB!!"

"...One!"

The first goblin was stupid enough to come at him head-on, and he simply stabbed him with his sword. The weapon pierced the monster's windpipe, lifting the creature off the ground. Goblin Slayer begrudged even the time to pull the sword out. He simply let it go. Instead, he kicked up the hand ax the goblin dropped, swiping it out of the air.

"GOROGB?!"

"GBB! GOROGB?!"

"Two...!"

He slammed the ax forward, splitting a skull. That had to be fatal.

He pulled the ax out and immediately slung it, catching a third goblin who had attempted to use his companion as a diversion at point-blank range.

"GOBBG?!"

"Three!"

Weapons came rolling to his feet, as many as he could want. He picked up one of the stones that had come raining down and flung it. Four.

The hob, that was what he had to watch out for. And any wolves. Or was that wargs?

I don't care.

They were just goblins. They could act big, they could carry equipment, but they were still goblins.

"GOROGBBGOROGGBB!!"

"GORO! GOBBG!!"

A high-pitched voice reached him over the explosions, an unfamiliar one that uttered a malediction. So they had a shaman or some other kind of spell caster. Most troublesome.

He already had his hands full with the enemies in front of him, but he had to communicate what was necessary.

"To the right, farther in. Destroy the spell caster!" he said.

"…I must say, your throwing arm is one thing about you I rate very highly." She added that he should realize not everyone was such a fine throw. Then she lobbed a burning bottle, which flew lazily over the goblins. Unwilling to wait for it to hit the ground, Goblin Slayer flung a stone, then thrust a hand into his item pouch. He was out of tear gas bombs. He would have to make two or three extras. If he had another chance.

"Eggshells *are* better." He pulled the stopper out of the bottle he had taken out, so that it scattered its contents among the horde of goblins when he threw it. It flew harder and faster than the explosive bottle, scattering a powder of crushed poisonous bugs of every kind he'd been able to find.

"GOBOGRB?!"

"GBRR?! GORBBG?!"

The goblins choked and coughed. The incantation stopped, and the next instant the fire powder erupted.

"GBBGB?!?!"

Goblins went flying. Arms, legs, innards, and the occasional head tumbled everywhere.

Seems none of them have the guts to pick it up and throw it back at me.

He grunted something that passed for a laugh. It amused him terribly. Although he wouldn't have wanted the girl, his childhood friend, to see this.

"GOOROOOROGBB!!!!"

"Hrm…!"

The thought, however, didn't cause him to let down his guard. He heard the frenzied howling. And the sound of claws on the earth.

They must have arrived via the other tunnels: Goblins on wargs came charging.

Goblin Slayer was lost for how to respond. If he had to grapple with them, it would be hard to protect the rest of his group. It would take time.

"The answer to riders is polearms!" Examiner produced something from her sleeve—not her chain this time but a Far Eastern–style long spear.

Without a word, Goblin Slayer took it from her and planted the butt in the ground. Not from experience—he'd simply heard about it. An old man in his village, someone who'd been in the wars, had told him.

Or had it been his sister? She might have said that when their father was facing a bear, he would wait for it to stand up and then drive a spear into its belly to kill it.

Whichever, it was a hazy memory from his younger days, but his body moved automatically.

"GROGBB!"

"Hrr...raahh!"

The oncoming warg almost seemed to plant itself on the spear, skewering itself. Goblin Slayer braced himself, supporting the lance, and turned his glare on the next rider, when—

"Shaaa!"

—he saw the chain like a living snake whipping past, catching the rider's mount by the legs and sending its occupant tumbling to the ground.

A true professional would have understood how foolish it was to get just within range of a spiked chain. They would have seen the potential danger of that attack of opportunity and come up with another plan, a different strategy.

But these two were facing goblins. They imagined nothing but what they already knew.

"Good!" Goblin Slayer grabbed the pitchfork the goblin had been carrying in lieu of a rider's lance, flipped it around in his hands, and drove it into the goblins on the ground, killing them.

"GOBOGB?!"

"GOROGBBB!!!"

The goblin lord finally seemed to grasp what was happening. He shouted what must have been a proper strategy, because from among the goblins milling in the distance appeared several drawing crude, creaky bows.

"Hrm..."

None of their archers, however, was ever likely to fire straight enough to hit a target standing in a narrow tunnel entranceway—especially not with dead wargs providing an additional obstacle to shoot around. Goblin Slayer could make this work.

As arrows pelted around him, he focused exclusively on what was directly ahead. He deflected arrows that got too close with his round shield, and they hit the ground with little clicks. Then there were the goblins, who saw the archery attack as an opportunity.

Goblin Slayer let go of the pitchfork, which was still stuck in a goblin, and picked up an arrow by his feet.

"Hrm."

The arrowheads were dripping with something. Some sort of poison. Well, if they never touched him, it didn't matter.

"GBOG! GOROGBB?!"

"Hraah!"

Regardless, shooting an arrow wasn't the only way to hit something with it.

He took the bolt in his hand and drove it through a goblin's eyeball, sending the creature reeling. He had no idea how effective goblin poison was but applying it directly to the brain was probably fatal.

"They are coming from behind as well...!" Examiner cautioned.

While he had been busy, some of the goblins had tried to go around through another tunnel—an obvious scheme. They were poorly coordinated, however, and this sad excuse for a pincer attack hardly passed for tactics.

The goblins who began to appear irregularly from the tunnel died.

"GOBOG?!"

"GROOGB!!"

Some were hit by a chain, some by fingers; all left this world spewing blood from every hole they had, uttering unearthly screams.

Examiner and her martial arts would never let the likes of goblins get anywhere near the rescued captive with her.

"Yaaah!"

The explosions ceased while Examiner was busy dealing with the goblins behind. Goblin Slayer took up the slack, deflecting the attacks of the goblins in front of him, sometimes responding barehanded, taking their weapons, and then killing them.

The goblin bodies piled up, forming an obstacle for would-be attackers. When one did get past the corpses, Goblin Slayer simply killed them and added another body to his pile.

The ground was slick with blood and vomit. Well, cavern floors were always slippery. There was no problem.

There was another blast wave, and another collection of body parts went flying past. He spotted some larger limbs among them. The hob was dead. Excellent.

He was not doing anything unique or special. He simply worked his weapon, aiming for vital spots, again and again. That was all.

He killed the goblins. He took their weapons. Then the next goblin came at him, and he killed that one, too. It felt like as long as his strength and willpower held out and there was a steady supply of goblins, this would never end. It would go on and on for the rest of his life.

I knew it.

Goblins were weak enemies. No matter how many of them you brought together, the most you could hope to do was assault a village or two. He didn't mean to make light of that fact—but it remained the reality that goblins were pitiful and always would be. They were a threat, yes. But a small one. They might destroy a village. But they would never destroy the world.

What would you call someone who accumulated the corpses of—not demons, not dragons, but only goblins?

I knew I was not an adventurer.

At that moment, an unusual blank space opened in the battle. He heard no more sound of explosions, and the death cries of the goblins faded away; there was only the adventurer's harsh breathing in his helmet.

None of the goblins wished to rush to their doom, and neither did Goblin Slayer desire to relinquish the field.

So the two forces squared off, staring each other down. Until…

§

This wasn't how it was supposed to go!

The goblin lord, seated upon his throne, gnashed his teeth.

He had made no mistakes, not one. It was all because of the trash and those adventurers. *He* had done everything right. His trash had screwed up and gotten in the way, and that was how they had ended up in this mess.

The only thing to do was cut them loose. Leave them behind and start again. As long as he was around, that would be enough—so he didn't care about anything else.

"GORO! GBB!!"

The goblin lord patted his throne fondly, then howled orders to his trash.

Everyone was to attack!

Most goblins didn't know how to conduct a battle, except to charge in. They were convinced that if they charged at the enemy, they would be victorious. So when the lord ordered them to charge, that was what they would do.

"GOROOGGBB!!"

As the goblins went pounding away, shouting furiously…

"GOBBGB…"

…their king dashed like a fleeing rabbit, making for the very back of the nest.

§

It was Examiner who noticed first. Even as she kept up the barrage of bombs, she spotted the goblin lord on the move.

"He is running away!"

"Pfah…!"

Goblin Slayer couldn't react immediately. He was busy deflecting a club with his left hand and burying a short spear in a goblin with his right. Now that the goblin lord had given the order for a general assault, dealing with the encroaching horde had become his top priority.

Weapons.

They were around. But he didn't have time to collect them. In the turn it took to do so, the goblin king would escape and be beyond his reach. If Goblin Slayer stayed safe behind these obstacles, the goblin leader would get away before he could cut through this army.

Instead, he acted almost on instinct. He grabbed his shield with his right hand and tore it off his left arm—the straps were nearly lost anyway. The edge was so sharp it hurt his fingers through his glove, but he didn't care. The beating earlier had left him without much sensation.

A goblin leaped at him, jeering at the stupid thing he was doing; Goblin Slayer smashed it with his free left hand, then he swung to his right.

He took a step forward, stomping on the downed goblin as he went. The distance? It would be okay. Farther than the frog at the festival. But not a problem.

"Hi...yah!"

He gave a great sweep of his right arm and let the shield fly. It whistled through the air, spinning as it went, soaring over the heads of the goblin horde.

"GBBGOBG?!"

With a dull *thump*, it buried itself in the goblin lord's shoulder.

"Shit!" Goblin Slayer hissed.

§

"GBBGOBG?!"

The goblin lord's shout was at once one of mockery, of pleasure, even of ridicule. It was hard to ignore the burning pain spreading through his shoulder, but—

He missed!

That thought brought a smile to the lord's face. He missed, he missed, he missed! The foolish adventurer had failed!

What had he thrown? His shield? A shield was for protecting

oneself! What idiot would throw it away? That stupid adventurer obviously didn't know how to use a shield. The goblin lord wished he could clap and point.

He didn't, though. He was too smart for that—smarter than anyone in these caves. Instead, he ran, covering the ground as fast as he could. He had to get away. He had to keep going.

He shoved other goblins aside, kicked them out of his way, demanded to know what the hell they were doing when they should be attacking the adventurers…

"GORG!!"

He felt something plunge into his knee: a rusty dagger.

"GOBOGRRG?!"

He stumbled, fell. The crown tumbled from his head and clattered across the ground. What was this? What was going on? What had they done to him?!

"GOROGB…!"

He looked to find the goblin he'd pushed out of the way standing there. The creature cackled and picked up the crown.

The goblin lord did not realize that this goblin was the one who had come to report earlier. He didn't care.

He sat up, shaking his fist and jabbering as he pulled out the dagger: *What are you doing? I am your king!*

But the other goblin didn't run away. He didn't even look scared. He looked…contemptuous!

"GBBGR! GOOOGB!!"

The goblin only leered at him, the crown upon his head. This was wrong. He wasn't the king!

"GOGB?! GBBBOGBR!!"

The goblin lord—or perhaps former lord—stared in disbelief. What was he saying? Was he an idiot?

The lord was the king! As long as he lived, there was hope of victory. The rest of them, they were no use at all.

"GOR! GGOGB!!"

The other goblin, the new king, only kicked him and laughed.

You're wrong. I am the one who can turn this situation around. We lost because of you. But I *am different. I will do better!*

The two goblins—the king who had lost his crown and the king who had gained one—stared at each other. They traded curses.

They could not know how precious was the turn they wasted in mocking each other.

At that moment, a great and terrible shout rent the air: "*Ba'yeshayahe!* O great power, I summon you!"

§

It is not a matter of can or cannot—but do or do not.

Maybe, she reflected, she was unduly influenced by the words she'd heard the boy muttering to himself.

Like a bird flying through the sky or a fish swimming in a river.

Simply *be* as you *are.*

She took a lungful of the nauseating air and felt her chest expand.

The sounds around her grew distant; objects took on an indistinct, hazy appearance, like blobs of paint. She was focused on something much, much farther away. The noon star reflected in the bottom of the well.

She took a deep breath and felt her blood flow throughout her body. Her hands and feet began to shiver, almost tingling.

She took a step forward. She pulled in both fists, placing them by her hips, tensing, every muscle as taut as a bowstring.

And then, impelled by an overwhelming force, she let the arrow fly.

"*Ba'yeshayahe!* O great power, I summon you!"

Her fist struck the air, accompanied by her great and terrible shout.

This time, she heard it: the cry of her fist tearing the air.

The blow became a wind unknown, ruffling the tassel on the helmet of the boy who called himself Goblin Slayer, passing him by. She could tell that, under his helmet, he watched it go past. She felt a small smile cross her lips.

The distance? Exactly a hundred paces. The wind would strike everything between her and that point.

"GOOGBB?!"

This—this *is what we call the Sacred Hundred-Pace Fist.*

Soundlessly, the head of the goblin who had taken the boy's shield in his shoulder burst like an overripe fruit.

"GBBG?!"

Next, the head of the jeering goblin who had put on the crown was split like firewood by a sword that came flying at him.

"That's... How many? I lost count." The two bodies collapsed with a *thump* that sounded inordinately loud. "I'm almost certain it's not yet a hundred..."

The boy was breathing hard but seemed calm; Examiner chose to act the same. She straightened her collar, tightened her tie, and affected to feel nothing, not agitation or excitement or happiness or relief. "I should imagine you have!"

At least, she thought, *my skills are enough to work on goblins!*

Then she said, "Very good," and smiled.

§

Of course...

"GROBG?!"

"GBB! GORGBB!!"

The goblins were not about to surrender simply because their leader had been brutally murdered. Maybe they were each arguing that they should be the next king or perhaps that only they could get everyone out of here alive.

"GOROGB!! GORBBB!!!"

Or perhaps they weren't thinking anything. They shouted furiously and surged toward the adventurers. Not quite all of them—a few small groups broke off and tried to sneak away. Frankly, that was more trouble than the ones who came charging.

"I would say it is time."

"Yes," was all Goblin Slayer said. He tried to heft the former captive onto his back, but Examiner stopped him. "What?" he asked.

"Which of us runs faster?"

"..." He grunted, then nodded slowly. "You do."

"Then it is decided." Examiner lifted the girl onto her back as easily as an empty sack, and then she set off running like the wind.

Goblin Slayer followed—but at the first step he took, he felt his knees go weak and he began to pitch forward. He forced himself to stay standing with the second step, then took the next, and the next, almost falling at every moment as he ran along.

What about it? He remembered his master shouting at him over a snowy gale. *People don't run—they're just constantly falling!*

What were humans but living machines with springs of muscle and cogs of bone? Get their parts moving, and they would go forever. Drawing breath, chest rising, feet moving forward, ever forward.

"GBBOOB!!"

"GOB! GROOGB!!!"

Goblins pressed in behind him. He wished he had something he could fling backward at them.

"Feh…"

If he did that, though, he wouldn't be able to resupply his weapons. For now, escape was the only concern.

I should have set up a rope or something on the way in.

His brain was dull with fatigue and starving for oxygen, but he still managed that frustrated thought.

He was able to run through the lightless caverns without hesitation and without getting lost because Examiner ran ahead of him. He heard her footsteps, her steady breathing guiding him forward. When he thought about it… Yes. On reflection, that was how this goblin hunt had gone from beginning to end.

Realizing he had failed his promotion exam, he smiled under his helmet. He discovered that he felt nothing about that realization. This goblin nest was the perfect place for him. If he could just keep fighting and killing goblins, that would be best, he was sure.

"Are you still with me?!"

"_____"

Taken by these thoughts, there was a second when he didn't understand what he had been asked. Somewhere ahead, he saw a light beyond his visor. Examiner was looking back at him, haloed by the glow. Her one eye watched him, but he didn't understand the emotion he saw there.

"I don't believe there's any problem," he said nonchalantly.

Goblins were approaching from behind. There was no time to rest. But he thought—distantly, the idea half-formed—this was necessary. If he was asked a question, he should answer. For he had been treated as an adventurer who had formed a party, even if only temporarily. "No goblin is intelligent enough to ask where an explosion is coming from, even if it happens in front of his face."

§

In fact, the goblins themselves had completely forgotten. Or perhaps more accurately, they had never cared. Why should they? That storehouse had neither amusements nor victuals.

It was full of stuff they had left there because they didn't really understand how to use it. In one corner, among all the other flotsam, was a box still packed with powder even after many bottles' worth had been removed. And there, a hazy light could be seen: a shattered lantern lying right next to the mountain of powder in the wooden box.

The lantern's wick crackled and burned down—it was nearly gone.

The time it had taken to burn was exactly as they had predicted.

And when it reached its end, it would certainly ignite the oil that had dripped from the lantern.

It would take the twinkling of an eye.

The fire lapped at the oil spread across the ground, racing forward.

We need hardly describe where that oil led or what would happen when the fire raced to its end.

Was it an uncertain method? Certainly. It could have been stopped. It wouldn't work everywhere.

But these were goblins they were dealing with.

The dice of Fate and Chance would determine the outcome, along with their vitality, skill, and luck.

So we also need hardly describe what that result ultimately was.

We need only one word.

§

Explosion.

§

The two of them burst out of the cave at almost the same moment as they heard the blast.

"Eek…?!" Examiner gave an involuntary girlish cry at the earsplitting force. In her younger days, she might have even tumbled forward. But not now. Now she held fast to the rescued girl clinging to her back and made sure the boy was still behind her.

She quickly lowered the former captive to the ground and turned, placing herself between the young woman and the cave.

"__________"

Dawn was breaking. She hadn't realized so much time had passed since they'd entered the cavern at dusk. A pale purple light filled the sky, along with smoke drifting lazily upward.

Fire, wind, smoke, shock waves. That was the entirety of what she could feel, and strangely, the whole world seemed quiet and calm. No noises reached Examiner's ears—not the cries of goblins, not the blast of the fire powder.

"_____"

Against the backdrop of this quiet, elemental world, Goblin Slayer slumped to his knees.

"Boy," Examiner called, but to her surprise, she couldn't even hear her own voice. Instead, she walked over to him and put a hand on his shoulder, which seemed at once large and rough and younger than she would ever have expected.

The filthy armor flinched. She could see an eye blinking in the darkness behind the visor.

"Are you all right?" she asked, speaking slowly, enunciating each syllable. She didn't know whether he could hear her, but the helmet nodded.

Finally, Examiner felt like she could breathe again.

This is an awfully theatrical way of killing goblins.

Just as she had the thought, there was a *thump*—it seemed sound was coming back to her—and she heard the cave start to collapse as if at a great distance. The entrance of the cavern belched smoke and flame, and the place fell in upon itself, unable to withstand the shocks.

This part didn't surprise her so much: They'd scattered the fire powder well into the cave network and made sure it would all be set off.

Gods. She would probably never see that much fire powder again in her entire life.

And we used it all to kill some goblins.

"If we had brought it back instead, it would have fetched quite a price."

"I'm not interested," Goblin Slayer growled. To Examiner, it sounded like sheer stubbornness, and she chose not to reprimand him for it.

"Ah well. Fireball and Firebolt are both more powerful—and more versatile."

That wasn't just an excuse; it was true. Fire powder needed accuracy; the conditions couldn't be too humid; Weathering and Deflect Missile and a dozen other spells could hinder it. It was hardly the most convenient stuff around, hardly the best. In the Four-Cornered World, it was swords and sorcery that did the talking—and adventure.

Adventure, eh?

Examiner watched the boy get unsteadily to his feet. He wore a cheap-looking metal helmet and filthy leather armor, he had no weapon worthy of the name, and didn't even have his shield on his arm; he had torn it away. Could she call this an adventure? Could she call *him* an adventurer?

"...I have to wonder," she said, choosing not to pursue the thought. "Who in the world decided to give goblins fire powder?"

"I don't know," Goblin Slayer replied, and his voice was that of someone exhausted, someone who didn't think of his victory as a true victory—who had only done what he had to do. To her, it didn't sound at all like the voice of a boy who had recently become an adventurer. "Whoever they are, they'll meet a fitting end eventually."

INTERLUDE

A Preliminary Skirmish, or Buying Time

"So yeh pursued the dark elves and discovered them in the middle of a ritual to resurrect the Demon Lord right here in the underground empire—and it *failed*, and things went all to hell?!"

"Don't make me repeat myself."

"Think I could go on home now?!"

"Hell no."

"Argh! This is just not my day."

As the dwarf shieldbreaker traded barbs with the barbarian, he hacked at a zombie in front of him with his hand ax, then smashed it with his hammer. On military orders, he'd tracked the dark elves, discovered the source of the earthquakes, then delved deep underground…

"And what'd it get me? A horde of zombies! That doesn't even make sense!"

"Less whining, more chopping, Gramps!"

"I won't take that from a beardless whippersnapper, do you hear me, young lady?!"

Kids these days! That wayward, magic-mad nephew of his was no different.

The dwarf girl who normally served as a scout was working her dagger, preventing the undead from crowding any closer. It had been damned good luck that he'd found allies like this when he jumped into

this underground battle. When he'd followed the rumblings in the dark, he sure as hell hadn't expected to find a bunch of adventurers engaged with a horde of zombies.

The dwarf shieldbreaker gave thanks to the Smithy God for having met these adventurers with whom he had now been sucked into battle. He also absolutely cursed the Smithy God for having thrown him into this place. That deity bestowed courage and not much more. Courage was all that he needed here—but it really was a hell of a thing.

Yes, these adventurers could be as courageous as they liked, but their resistance would be fleeting. They'd formed a circle in the middle of the abandoned city, but the undead were pressing in upon them and would soon overwhelm them.

These weren't dark elves they were facing. They weren't even spiders! They were an endless supply of zombies and the king who ruled them.

"It would seem that palace was not here to protect this city after all!" called the canid wizard, firing off a Spider Web spell from where he stood in the middle of the circle with the others protecting him. The webbing flew through the air, trailing from his fingers, expanding to become a net that trapped several zombies. Ten of them maybe, certainly not twenty. The creatures, stuck in a lump together, helpfully became a blockage that slowed the advance of the others.

But then…

"GHOOOOOOULLLLL…"

"ZZZZZZZOOOMMBBBIIIEEEEE…"

The undead surged forward, even as their limbs broke and their skin peeled off, even as their flesh tore away with a dry, crackling sound. They didn't care if they trampled on their companions. They didn't care if their own bodies were destroyed. Consuming the living was their only imperative.

The elf cleric fired his dart gun into the advancing horde, doing something to keep them at bay. It had only the merest effect, but it was an accumulation of such tiny acts of defiance that was keeping the party alive.

"What in the gods' names is it, then?!" the dwarf shieldbreaker shouted back.

"The *city* is here to contain the palace—or more properly, the one who rules there!"

The dark elves, the forces of Chaos, had failed in their attempt to resurrect the Demon Lord—and not because their vanguard, the goblin king and his forces, had failed to follow instructions. Perhaps their mistake had been in trying to harness the foul energies generated by the massacre perpetrated by this ancient ruler.

Behold the black shimmer welling up upon the wall far above them. What could burn so dark? It is morning for the zombies, dawn for the undead.

The high priest of the dark elves had been there, intoning his spells at the top of his voice.

The massacre perpetrated at the whim of a mad king. Even the dark elves might fathom such madness, logical though they were.

But logic was not enough. They thought they grasped it—but by the time they realized they were wrong, the high priest's head was already flying through the air.

"Ahhh... Is there no one? No one whom I might kill this night?"

The graveyard's mysterious ward still endured—that was why the king had not yet awakened but only dreamed blood-colored dreams amid a sparkling purple snow.

He killed simply to kill. He had become king so he could kill more. Why should death stop him?

He had slept long and had not died; in the course of this monstrous eternity, he would see even the end of death itself.

Truly, this was none other than the return of the Army of Darkness.

"O God! O Gygax!" The barbarian was put back on his heels by the evil spell but only for an instant; even now the breath of the Smithy God was hot in his nostrils. The strength to hack through the horde of evil beings at a stroke would be overwhelming in the extreme. But that alone would not be enough to achieve victory, not by far.

The Smithy God bestows only courage, not victory.

"At this rate"—the silver-haired girl crunched a zombie's jaw with a kick—"we'll never make it out of here!"

"I know that!" Young Warrior shouted, but he saw no way to turn this situation around.

When that king makes his move…

Then it would all be over. The thought was hardly fully formed, but he could feel it. The king of darkness stood atop the wall with a look of ecstasy on his face—or so it seemed, even though his face was only a dry skull.

They had to do something about him, and they had to do it before he went into action.

"GHOOOO… GGGGGGOOOULLLLLL"

"ZOOOMM… BBIEEEEE…"

If they were going to deal with the king, though, they would have to get through the masses of undead first. If they didn't try *something*, they would be finished even if the king never lifted a finger.

They had to find a way to break through—but how?

"It's undead, isn't it?!" the warrior shouted to his cleric. "So it should be weak to Dispel!"

"Don't be silly! I doubt there's been an undead that powerful since the Dungeon of the Dead!"

Not happening at his skill level, in other words. The warrior couldn't help grinning at the elf's stubborn refusal to just say so.

There were many rumors about the Dungeon of the Dead, but if it was a hell worse than this…

…then I guess the world's not in danger just yet.

Well, that was a comforting thought. Why worry, then?

"Hoh," said the barbarian man. "I like the look on your face."

"Hey, not the first time I've stared death in the eye!"

Even as he spoke, Young Warrior worked his sword relentlessly. He had no idea if zombies had vital points. He just hacked off their legs, broke their arms—the best he could do was to render them immobile.

"Urrghh…!"

Then there was the silver-haired girl, kicking and smashing the zombies with tears brimming in her eyes. He didn't want to leave her to a cruel death, so he fought on. The girl struggled mightily to survive, kicking free of the goop that clung to her feet.

One could be engulfed by the undead, her innards consumed while she was still alive, weeping and crying until the moment of her death.

Or one could be swallowed headfirst by a massive worm, chewed to pieces before she knew what was happening.

One fate was not better than the other. Young Warrior wanted to avoid them both.

"Tell me you've got some kind of plan, Teach!" he shouted.

"I'm afraid killing those who are already dead is outside my expertise—personally, I would love for us each to take a turn to run away!"

But they couldn't leave these monsters here. The canid's eyes narrowed, and he was clearly thinking hard.

So these were zombies. Dead people. Until this moment, they'd been sleeping in this abandoned city.

That had to mean…

"If we simply bury them again, that should stop them for the time being!"

"Cave in the ceiling? I like the way you think!" the barbarian said, his sword buried in the corpse of an unidentifiable giant. "That would solve all our problems!"

"Alas, I haven't yet learned the Fireball spell." The canid wizard shrugged and bared his lower fangs in an expression of genuine regret. "I hope, should this ever happen again, that I will know it by then."

"You want more earthquakes? Fine!" the dwarf girl said as she sliced off a ghoul's claws, then jumped out of the way to give the elf cleric a clear shot. "But those were coming from that ritual, right? I think you're out of luck getting another shot at this!" A bolt went flying past her and impaled the goal—the two of them had actually gotten to where they made a pretty good team.

Unfortunately, being a good team isn't going to be enough.

That alone wouldn't secure victory. They had no spells they could use, and the ritual was over. What else was there?

"If that lot had a base, that might be another story," the dwarf shieldbreaker growled as he hacked up another zombie with his ax.

Like the barbarian, his movements were refined, powerful, and came utterly naturally to him. "I don't think those dark elves know about the Dungeon of the Dead, and I don't think they were at the battle."

If they'd known, they would never have been so brazen as to believe that they could control death itself.

That implied they weren't skilled explorers of labyrinths. Which could mean…

"The underground might be their turf, but they must have their *stuff* somewhere around here!"

"Guarded by something like goblins, knowing them!" The canid wizard smacked a zombie with his staff, presumably in an effort to conserve his magic. The dwarf girl jumped on the stunned creature and quickly broke both its legs to keep it from moving.

"You think they might have fire powder or something around here?!" she said.

"A stick or two of it wouldn't even match the power of Fireball," the wizard replied.

"So what, a box or two, then?" The elf shrugged. "That would be worth a fortune if—"

He broke off; the barbarian looked up faster than any of them, followed by the shieldbreaker, and then by the elf, each of them appearing more surprised than the last. Someone, one of them, shouted that it was going to collapse.

The others might have heard them—or might not. Because at that moment, a massive explosion rocked the cavern in which the city lay. The ceiling began to shake and shiver; they could hear little stones clicking as they fell—and then it gave way.

A landslide of debris fell like rain, dust pouring everywhere. The buildings hardly flinched; they had lasted this long and seemed they would last longer yet.

"GHOOULLLLL…"

"ZOM…BBIEE…"

The undead proved less durable. The rotten corpses, the mummies, the ghouls were crushed and destroyed one after another by huge stones.

And of course, the adventurers were equally at risk of falling victim to this abrupt turn of events.

"Shit!" the dwarf girl yelled, loud enough that even Young Warrior could hear her. "Get inside, fast!"

"Right...!" He scrambled to pull his helmet up over his head from where he had stashed it on his back, even as he urged his companions to start running.

When he looked around to make sure everyone was there and safe, though, every other thought vanished from his head.

"——"

The silver-haired girl stood trembling. In spite of the shivers, she had both feet planted firmly on the ground, holding up knees that looked ready to collapse. She stared firmly upward.

Upward toward the place where the crumbling debris had begun to pile up.

On top of the wall...

"Help me out here!" she shouted and started running. The words weren't enough for Young Warrior to grasp everything—but he had a faint memory of that stance, of the way she ran with her fists clenched.

The moment he realized, he exclaimed, "Yeah!" and he started running, too.

"Hey, do you wanna die?!" the dwarf girl cried.

"Don't listen to her! Go!" the barbarian warrior howled, like a wolf bearing its fangs. He stood smack in the center of the raging storm of death, slicing this way and that with his great blade. "O, great Gygax, what a day this is!"

The undead might not care that they were being crushed by a cavalcade of debris, but even they couldn't stand before his mighty steel.

One of them turned its attention to the running adventurers, but a great crash of weaponry sent it tumbling to the earth, its back broken.

"Argh! This is why I hate working with mortals!"

It was the doing of the experienced dwarf, the shieldbreaker: Ax and hammer stood side by side in his hands. He'd met this barbarian warrior only a short time ago, yet they fought in perfect synchronicity. He had the man's back, and any undead lucky enough to escape the barbarian's blade found itself laid low by the dwarf's ax, forced to bow its head before the Smithy God.

"I swear I'm not moving from this spot…!" the cleric yelped.

No one, of course, expected such feats of courage from an elf. From an elf, one expected only a skill with arrows that bordered on the magical.

Elf Cleric had ducked into a building with his preternatural agility and was sniping from the window with his dart gun. He had his right hand on the trigger while his left worked the spring, the mechanical *chak-chak-chak* truly the sound of the Smithy God's blessing.

"Arrgh! Dammit! I'm so over this! What am I supposed to do?!" Beside him, Dwarf Scout stuck fast by the window, her eyes pinned on her two party members as they raced forward. She didn't have the courage to run out among the falling debris, but she lacked any means to attack the undead from here. So it went sometimes—everyone had their role. "Hey, Teach!"

She might as well have cried: *Do something already!*

"There's always something greater. Something higher," the canid wizard said, lashing out with his staff even as he gazed up at the shadow of the Death upon the wall. "That is a cruel and immutable principle of our world."

The king, terrible and unmourned, had drawn a fearsome enchanted blade, which he would point at the two youngsters running past the debris toward him. Its awful curse could wither a rose in the bloom of summer.

"But not all death has mythic meaning or brings eternal glory!" the wizard howled, unleashing the magic power he had marshaled, reconfiguring the very logic of the four corners. It was not, of course, anything like enough to have a serious effect on the king of darkness.

"*Terra…ubiquitous…restringuitur!* Undo the bonds of earth!"

The wall upon which the king stood, however, was another matter.

"———?!"

Perhaps it was only a collective delusion on the party's part that the undead king showed even the slightest hint of surprise. His regal posture faltered. His body, composed of only bones and skin and battle garments, sank down under its own weight.

Of course it did. When the ground beneath one's feet is turned to quicksand, any who can't fly will sink.

The king leaned, then he sank—and then he tumbled through thin air.

The silver-haired girl fixed her eyes on the undead ruler plummeting toward the ground. She was like an arrow loosed from a bow.

"Work with me!" She exhaled hard, then filled her chest with air and shouted, "Please!"

"Y-y-yeah, you got it!"

So he didn't hesitate. He gripped his sword firmly with both hands, then twisted his body as if cutting in a circle. It looked silly and slow, nothing like the elf warrior spoken of in the legends—but he gave it his all, and he was fast.

With all the momentum of his swing, he brought the blade around and let it fly—straight toward the silver-haired girl.

"——"

Just for a second, he thought he saw the girl smile, but then her hair whipped in front of her face and hid it from view.

Thmp. She landed lightly on the flat of his sword, her slim legs pushing off the weapon. Riding the combined momentum of them both…

"Hiyaaaaaaaaaaaaah!"

…the girl flew.

In the blink of an eye, she let loose three strikes against the king of darkness as he tumbled through the void. She threw in a knee, slammed him with her elbow, and finally planted her fist in his jaw.

There was a dry sound like cracking firewood, and his skull went flying through the air.

"I did it…!"

For one glorious second, the girl was triumphant—but everything that rises has only one fate.

Having exhausted all her force, having uncoiled every spring in her body, she hung in space for an instant—and then she fell.

"Nooooo!" she cried.

Debris. The tumbling king of darkness. The skull chattering with laughter. Rushing in. Catching her. Something soft.

Young Warrior held her tight, making certain not to drop her. And then—and then…

§

What happened after that, even Young Warrior didn't remember so clearly.

He remembered throwing his sword, catching the girl, and then running as fast as he could. He remembered the dwarf girl giving him grief while the barbarian and the dwarf shieldbreaker helped him flee inside a building. Then for a long time, he wandered lost in the darkness.

Where had he walked to? What had he talked about with his companions? He didn't really know.

When he'd come to, he was looking up at the morning sun, clambering out of some hole in the ground. Only then did it finally sink in that he had escaped with his life.

"We're alive…aren't we?" he mumbled.

"Alive and kicking! Now *that's* what I call a victory." The barbarian warrior pounded him on the back. *That* let him know he was alive. Young Warrior stumbled a couple steps, blinking as he came out into the sun. It was painfully bright, making tears bead up in his eyes. "Curse that dog. Myths and legends, my ass! It was all true!" the barbarian said from beside Young Warrior, cursing someone somewhere. Then he laughed. It was the sound of his triumph, and it was already full of anticipation for his next adventure.

"I can only feel sorry for scholarship… I so would have liked to make more notes about that city."

"I'd like to know how the hell we got out of there! I couldn't tell you which way we went if my life depended on it."

Young Warrior turned back to see the canid wizard emerging with Dwarf Scout, both of them looking exhausted.

"Gods! You adventurers must be *crazy*. Why would you put yourselves through all this?"

"Heh-heh-heh. The time to speak of such things is not yet come, Shieldbreaker."

The dwarf shieldbreaker looked unimpressed by Elf Cleric. Young Warrior contemplated letting it slip that the elf had become an adventurer to pay off his debts.

Come to think of it, that old dwarf never told us why he *was down there.*

Investigating the cause of some earthquakes turned into an encounter with dark elves, the work of an evil cult, kidnappings, murders. An abandoned city. The king of darkness.

Gods, but this had turned into some adventure. Would the Guild even believe him when he made his report? For that matter, *should* he report this?

"——"

Finally, Young Warrior paused and looked at the silver-haired girl, who stood silently by the cavern entrance. She was a sorry sight, muddy, exhausted, sniffly and weeping. Yet the hint of a rosy hue in her cheeks—was that the doing of the morning sunlight?—made him think that, in spite of all of it, she was beautiful.

He went over to her, careful to walk quietly, and just like that, her shoulders started quaking.

"Are we…are we home?" she asked.

"Not yet," Young Warrior said with a smile. He almost gave her a pat on the head, but then he thought better of it. She didn't notice; her hands were clenched into fists in front of her knees, and she was looking straight at the ground.

"I really thought we were gonna die…"

"Believe me—so did I."

There was no response. Instead, he heard only a quiet moan, followed by sniffling.

She must have been completely lost in the moment. When she'd jumped up there, it must have been terrifying.

What she'd done, that technique? It wasn't one of those "secret finishers" you hear so much about in the stories. Just something someone had described to her once. Her little attempt to mimic what she had heard.

How much courage must it have taken to try to bring something like that to a real battle?

Young Warrior gazed at the sun, pretending he didn't hear the crying. He rubbed her back gently.

The rest of the party pretended not to notice the girl or him. He was grateful for that.

"Did we," the girl managed to choke out, "save the world?"

"For now. Although I don't think it's really over," Young Warrior said softly. He wasn't trying to dismiss the girl's wish. It was just that the abandoned city hadn't been destroyed. The mysterious ward endured. The king who had died would still dream of death.

A little fire powder and a cave-in wouldn't be enough to hold back magic, true power.

Yet still uncertain himself, he smiled. He shared her wish that it would be true.

"I don't think this is nearly enough to destroy the world," he said.

"Right," came back a small voice, like a promise. For Young Warrior, that was enough.

Their wish was not wrong—and just as certainly, not correct.

The cult's foul plans had been foiled but only for the time being.

This was certainly no threat to the world.

The true threat would come when the Demon Lord was resurrected—five years from now.

EPILOGUE

What Good Is Glory?

Goblin Slayer took an entire day to rest at the village. He simply didn't have the strength to walk directly back to the frontier town. He slept like the dead, made his report to the village headman, took a warm meal, and then set off on the way home.

He looked back only once—as he went by the meager fence that passed for the village's defenses—and he saw the farmers working in the fields. He knew very well that, at least, *he* had not been victorious.

"...Strictly speaking, I do *not* acknowledge you."

It was only at this stage that he learned he had not failed his promotion test. But it seemed he had not precisely passed, either.

"I see," he replied. He only nodded brusquely at Examiner, who stood with him looking at the village. If she said so, then he was sure it was true. She'd seen many more adventurers than he had, after all.

"I shall return directly to the capital. You may take this." She handed Goblin Slayer an envelope that was fancier and of finer quality than any he had seen before. It was sealed in red wax with the sigil of the Adventurers Guild, showing that it was official correspondence.

He looked at it for a moment, turned it over, then back the other way. Then he closely inspected it again before delicately placing it in his item pouch.

"You won't travel back with me?" he asked.

"I have much business to attend to, boy."

So he mumbled only, "I see." He heard Examiner let out a small sigh.

She looked at him with her one eye, right at his visor. He found it very uncomfortable. "You should never welcome those who have naught but fulsome praise for you. That merely goes to show that they cannot see the true value of things." Her words were piercing, perfectly chosen. "Your methods are not those of an adventurer. *You* are not an adventurer."

"..."

Her words did not set him back on his heels; he didn't get angry or upset. It was simply that as naturally as the blowing breeze, he knew she was right. It was exactly what he thought about himself.

"No," he said. "I am Goblin Slayer."

That was what people called him, and that, as far as he was concerned, was enough.

"However, at the present time there is no evidence that you are doing anything specifically in contravention of the regulations of the Adventurers Guild."

Examiner actually smiled at him, this boy of a mere fifteen years of age. Her businesslike pronouncement *did* give him pause.

No.

He understood the reason, even if it would have been immensely painful to voice it.

"...Boy. Try rolling the dice sometime." She struggled to come up with something that might get through to him. She hoped and prayed that her words of advice at least might penetrate that helmet. "Because that is the essence of adventure."

Even if the outcome was death. They were all of them adventurers because they went on adventures. Only brainless munchkins lusted after battles they were certain to win, safe fights and easy victories. The likes of them were not adventurers—and she didn't want this boy to become one of them.

"...Why do you say that?" he asked, clearly puzzled.

"Three reasons," she replied and held up a neatly manicured pointer finger. "First, because we cannot have other adventurers going around thinking it is enough just to kill goblins."

Next, a slim, pale middle finger joined the fray.

"Second, because there are never enough talented scouts. I would like to see you party up with other adventurers at your skill level."

The boy didn't say anything. Within his helmet he fell silent, except for a thoughtful grumble. At length, he asked, "And the third reason?"

Examiner raised her ring finger and smiled. "A woman's intuition."

She could see the boy was exhausted. Barely standing. He seemed to exist only to kill goblins. Under his steel helmet, he was mumbling something. The excitement she'd felt on delving the depths of the Dungeon of the Dead? The sense of youth that stood alongside the death and ashes? Of these there was none.

If there were any person who praised this way of life, who affirmed it, that person would be…

…tremendously cruel.

For they would be condemning this boy to a life of killing goblins, a life in which he would never know adventure and would die in some goblin hole.

"…"

Examiner didn't know whether her words had reached him. But that's how it goes. No one can control if or how others receive what they say. No matter how diligently you explain, you won't reach someone who's set on not hearing you.

Being a clerk at the Adventurers Guild had made that abundantly, inescapably clear to her.

Even a wayward young woman from the nobility who ran off to learn martial arts figured out that much. That is growth.

"What happens next?"

"To you? Give them that letter, and that should be the end of it. You need not worry."

So she imagined—she hoped—that the son of a hunter and a medicine woman could learn at least as much.

"As for me, I am going to go back to the capital and…apologize to my friend. Yes, I think I will do that."

Maybe it was about time she submitted her resignation and went back to adventuring. The thought filled her mind as she looked up at the sky, where a few clouds drifted. They were hardly more than mist,

©Shingo Adac

like a child had smeared white paint across the blue. Sunlight drifted down through every little gap in the clouds, a golden belt thrown from the heavens to illuminate the squares of the Four-Cornered World.

"I *do* like this sky," she said and smiled. A happy sound escaped her. She'd almost forgotten how it felt to laugh like this. "I like it best of all."

The boy grunted quietly, then mumbled, "So do I."

With that, their conversation was over. They traveled the road back toward town wordlessly, and at length, they came to a fork. One path went toward the capital, the other toward the frontier city. This was where their roads diverged.

"..."

The boy stood silently, appearing deeply unsure what to say. Examiner stood equally silent and waited for him.

"...See you," he finally managed. Examiner's eye widened, and she smiled.

Ahhh. Gods' sakes.

"You too, boy."

What did she mean by "you too"? Even she hadn't been sure what to say.

She found it deeply humorous, although she tried not to show it as she walked away.

Whatever thoughts, feelings, and emotions the boy had put into those words he'd spoken—whatever they were—

You too, boy.

—one thing remained unchanged: her hope that wherever they ended up, she and he would both find adventure.

§

"Hey! What happened to the quest about searching for a dark-elf caravan?!"

"I'm sorry. I believe that quest has already been completed..."

The clerk's unflappable calm only made the warlock angrier as she stood there, drenched from head to toe in filthy water.

It wasn't such an unusual sight there at the reception desk of the

Adventurers Guild. Low ranks and recent registrants were generally limited in the quests they could take. So as one went about doing whatever sundry tasks were available to raise their rank, the quests that one had one's eye on naturally disappeared.

Situations and circumstances were ever-changing.

Quests that continued to wait in spite of the world's ever-shifting nature were either exceptionally difficult—or involved goblin hunting or maybe the sewers.

"Argh! Fine!"

The warlock knew that shouting wouldn't bring the quest back. Instead, she turned on her heel and stalked away, grumbling. Not that she had anywhere to go. She made sure to stomp with the fur-lined boots she'd found in the mine, making her displeasure obvious.

I can't believe this! What a rip-off!

She had to join up with the Adventurers Guild, they said! She couldn't just go adventuring all on her own, they said!

Of course, it was also thanks to the Guild that she, an unknown factor from a far place, had been received with something resembling courtesy. She had no complaints about that. No, no complaints, but she still just wanted to lash out!

I know whose fault this is. It's the government types who let those dark elves steal their spell book to begin with!

She began chewing on her thumbnail, which was not only bad manners but a little disgusting since her fingers were still filthy. She paid the fact no mind. It wasn't just her hand that was covered in muck, either. It was in her hair, on her face, her skin—all of her. It had even soaked through her clothes to make her shirt cling to her skin; she shivered at the chill.

She was used to this by now, sure, but that didn't mean she had to like it.

Sensing eyes upon her, she pulled up the hood of her cloak and made sure it covered her face. The last thing she wanted was to be found out for a girl from some far-off location who didn't know her right from her left. At least around here, the owner of the general store wasn't in cahoots with the local bandits, the way they had been back home.

You know, now that I think about it, home was a heck of a place.

Okay, so it was better than her hometown. That also didn't mean she had to like it.

Besides, how could she come all this way and find out they *still* had Slime Eaters in their sewers?! The rats and giant bugs were bad enough. She couldn't stand it. She couldn't *stand* it!

"This is why I hate the sewers!"

One day she was going to fry them all with Fireball. Hmm... Maybe a pair of nose plugs was in order first?

No, no. Not the point. If those dark elves had been wiped out, then so had her chance of finding any clues. She was back to square one. Ugh! It just made her head hurt!

"Hey, uh, were you asking about the spell book?" someone said.

"What about it?" she snarled, wheeling on the source of the voice with a glare.

She found herself face-to-face with a man who couldn't have been called friendly looking even in flattery; a wood-handled ax hung from his hip. A warrior, then. Warriors always started with a sword or at least a weapon of some kind.

"So you must be a wizard, right?" the warrior asked.

"...Pretty much," the warlock said guardedly. She reached for the sword at her own hip, just to be sure. She wanted to think he wasn't here to try to get her drunk and then sell her into slavery, but you could never be too careful.

"Cool! How about—?"

She had no way of knowing that this was and had always been how parties started.

§

"I've gotta go! Right *now*!"

Heavy Warrior crashed down the stairs, shouting so loudly that he interrupted the conversation between the ax-wielding warrior and the suspicious warlock. His color still wasn't very good, and he was wearing only simple clothing, but he had his huge sword at his hip.

A boy and girl followed him down the stairs, practically clinging to him, looking like they would burst into tears—in fact, the tears were already in their eyes. They were helpless to stop Heavy Warrior, who pressed on, almost dragging them with him.

"Why'd you tell him about *that* quest?!"

"I don't know! I just thought a nice, easy goblin hunt might be the perfect thing to get him back on his feet!"

The kids must have been relieved when Half-Elf Light Warrior and Female Knight came down the stairs behind them. Scout Boy and Druid Girl couldn't slow him down, but those two would be able to talk some sense into their leader.

Female Knight did indeed grab Heavy Warrior by the shoulder. "What kind of an idiot do you have to be to go running off like that? What's wrong with you?"

Whether because he was weakened by his illness or because Female Knight was just that strong, Heavy Warrior came to a sudden halt.

"I'm sure glad I decided to take this opportunity to send your armor out for repair," Female Knight said. "What were you planning to do with nothing but your sword?"

"It's more than enough to chop up some goblins!"

This was from the guy who had caught his greatsword on the walls of a cavern on his first quest.

Female Knight forced Heavy Warrior to turn around and look at her—but she had never seen the expression on his face before.

"______"

She stood, lost for words, her heart pounding. What could she say to him?

"...Is there some kind of story here we should know about?" she finally squeezed out. An obvious question. A dumb thing to say. What would she do if he shot back, *Can't you tell?*

He'd been agonizing over their promotion. She'd known it, but she hadn't done anything for him until he'd collapsed. So when she heard that a modestly challenging goblin hunt had come up, she'd brought it to him.

That was obviously a mistake, she thought. Why couldn't everything in the world be dealt with just by swinging your sword at it? She'd known since she was a girl that you couldn't do that, but moments like this always made her feel like crying anyway. She sure didn't need anyone else to tell her that she'd been careless and screwed up.

In the end, she could never say the right thing. She always seemed to bungle it.

Now that I think about it…

After the commotion with the kids and their ages, they had all talked to one another about their respective motivations, but this was the first time she'd tried to go any deeper than that. She never would have imagined she would broach the subject in this way, at a moment like this.

"……My buddy's there," Heavy Warrior said.

That was all. Female Knight, mostly just relieved that he had answered, let out a breath. "Your buddy. Like a friend?"

"Yeah," Heavy Warrior replied, sullen. "Him and his wife. They're about to have a kid—maybe already have. Should be anytime now."

"I…"

She could see. She could see how that would make you want to go help at any cost.

Goblins were coming. They might not do *much* damage in the grand scheme of things, but they would do enough.

There was no real reason to hesitate over a goblin hunt. They were the weakest monsters, after all. She herself had killed one on her first quest. She wasn't going to clutch her pearls and shriek about the danger. One good adventuring party was more than enough to destroy a goblin nest.

And yet…

Was a party led by a maddened, still-recovering Heavy Warrior a good one? As much as she wanted to help that village, she equally didn't want to see her party member get hurt.

It's always times like this.

These were the times when she wished she knew what to do, but the Supreme God never seemed to give any guidance. That deity, august as they were, was loath to interfere with people's free will.

To ignore her party member's safety and go to the village—or to prioritize her companion's health at the village's expense? It was not the gods who decided which of those things was right. The ability to deem either to be the appropriate choice was a blessing—one that weighed very heavily.

Female Knight fell silent, unable to say anything at all, and Heavy Warrior shook off her hand.

"Oh…," she mumbled.

"The point is, I'm going! I'm not about to let a bunch of goblins—"

"You said goblins?"

The voice was quiet, indifferent, almost inhuman, like a wind blowing through the depths of the earth. No one had noticed this adventurer come into the Guild; no one knew when he had gotten there. Female Knight couldn't blame Heavy Warrior for staring openly.

An adventurer stood in the entrance to the Guild, looking scruffy at best. He wore filthy leather armor, a cheap-looking metal helmet, and at his hip was a sword of a strange length. A peculiar stench wafted from him, and his feet appeared to be covered in mud. If someone had claimed he was a Living Armor, everyone would have believed them.

It took a moment for everyone to realize this was the adventurer they called Goblin Slayer.

"…Yeah? So what if I did?"

"In which village?"

"Whazzat?" Heavy Warrior frowned as if he didn't quite follow.

"Which village?" The question came again, evidently alluding to the goblin hunt Heavy Warrior was fixated on.

What, is he gonna go?

Blood rushed to Heavy Warrior's head with anger; it felt like his brain was going to fry. He was going to trust his friend's life to a guy like this?

Nonetheless, he gave Goblin Slayer the name—and the filthy helmet nodded.

"I already killed them."

"Wha…? Wha—?"

This time, he flat-out didn't understand.

"If that's the village you're worried about," came the voice from inside the helmet, businesslike, "I killed all the goblins."

Then Goblin Slayer strode off, walking right past Heavy Warrior and toward the reception desk. His footsteps were amazingly quiet for such a violent gait.

Heavy Warrior stood with his mouth open, watching Goblin Slayer go, absolutely deflated. The expression on Female Knight's face must have been similar—but she soon recovered.

"..."

Then she sighed, reached out the hand he had shoved away, and took Heavy Warrior's arm. She would brook no argument this time.

"H-hey, what are you doing?!"

"Taking you back upstairs, where you're going to sleep!"

The goblin problem, it seemed, had been solved. The only thing left was to get this guy some rest.

The Four-Cornered World could be a confusing place, but as long as you focused only on what you had to do, things were nice and simple.

She began to drag Heavy Warrior back up the stairs. He resisted but feebly, and it was easy enough to pull him along. "Come on, shrimps! Help me!" Female Knight barked. "No, I mean, go make up the bed! I'll haul this guy up and fling him in it!"

"*Fling* me? Now, just a minute!"

"We're on it!" the boy and girl said, dashing up the stairs. Half-Elf Light Warrior merely grinned and shrugged. His smile seemed to say he understood everything.

"Quiet, you," Female Knight growled, trying to sound extra fearsome in order to cover for herself. She pulled on Heavy Warrior's arm, which was bigger and stronger than she had expected. "And when you're better, you're gonna answer a few questions for me!"

Maybe over a drink at the bar!

Somehow, the thought made her footsteps lighter and hastened her trip up the stairs.

§

"Oh, Goblin Slayer!" Guild Girl exclaimed, her face aglow. Her colleague in the next seat gave her a tremendous *look*, to which Guild Girl replied with a kick in the shin under the desk.

She'd heard a couple of adventuring parties yammering at each other by the door, but there didn't seem to be any real trouble. More important to her was the return of this adventurer, for whom she had waited so long.

Okay, so when she noticed the mud all over him and then the smell, her smile might have faltered a little…

But there's always next time! We can always improve!

He was back home safely, and that was what mattered. That put the smile right back on her face. One thing did bother her, though…

"My senior colleague… I mean, are you alone?" Guild Girl asked.

"Yes," he said.

They had set out as two but returned as one. Horrible visions began to bubble up in her mind.

He, however, continued brusquely, businesslike, "She said she would go directly back to the capital."

"Oh… I see." For a second, Guild Girl wasn't sure how to react. She was happy that her colleague was all right but disappointed that she didn't get to so much as say good-bye.

That's very in character for her, though!

The thought caused her to naturally settle on an expression of relief. She didn't know if he heard her mumble, "Thank goodness."

Now, that having been settled, there remained an outstanding matter that consumed her attention. She was as nervous to ask as if it were her own test. She looked at him, almost peeking furtively, but she couldn't see anything deep behind that visor.

"Your test… Did it go well?" she asked.

"I don't know," was his brusque reply. Well, that didn't help.

But then again…

During this brief exchange, she found that he was actually talking. Look, at that moment he was even digging in his item pouch, from which he extracted an envelope.

"She said to give this to you."

"If I may, then."

Guild Girl took the envelope, sealed with the sigil of the Adventurers Guild, her heart pounding. She took a letter opener from a drawer and gently broke the seal. Inside the envelope was a folded piece of parchment covered with writing in her senior colleague's familiar, delicate hand.

Guild Girl read the letter through from beginning to end, then did it again. And then…

"Congratulations!"

"Hrm…?" He almost sounded like he didn't know what to make of this, but as for her, a smile of relief came over her face like an opening blossom.

"*Ahem.* This still needs to be officially vetted, but your examination is safely complete."

He's passed his tests with flying colors.

From Porcelain to Obsidian, then from Obsidian to Steel. He had completed brilliant adventures and was becoming a brilliant adventurer.

She could hardly help but feel a rush of pride—she'd recommended him, after all.

Just the same…

Just the same, she felt joy well up in her heart, as if she herself had passed the test.

"I think you can consider yourself promoted!"

"…"

From him, no answer came immediately. Maybe it didn't seem real to him, or maybe he couldn't quite believe it, or maybe he simply wasn't interested. Whatever the case, he stood there vacantly. After a long moment, he said only, in a quiet voice, "I see." Then he asked, "So this is the end?"

"Oh! No, um, please hold on for a second!"

Guild Girl clapped her hands and began rifling through desk drawers. She also privately vowed to steal her friend's tea, since the other woman had spent the entire time smirking at her.

At length, she came up with a bundle of parchment. She gave herself a mental smack on the cheeks to invigorate herself.

"All right! If you could give me your report on this adventure, please!"

"My report?"

Guild Girl nodded. *Yep!*

©Shingo Adachi

He was back home. Her senior colleague was safe. His promotion had been approved. And the enemies had been goblins.

I guess some might say there's not much point in asking for the details of an adventure like that, she thought. Yet nonetheless she wanted to hear them, wanted to write them down for posterity. She looked at the metal helmet expectantly.

She was following procedure, indulging the bureaucracy, yes—but it was so much more than that.

"...Very well." He grunted, and then in quick, short words, he began to relate the story of his adventure. "There were goblins."

She nodded again, smiling, and dipped her quill pen in the ink.

She was sure she would have many more conversations like this with him. Finding the adventures behind those brusque, cold words and keeping adventure logs.

That was fun. It made her happy. It would be crass to ask why.

Besides, on this adventure, he'd been promoted. Yes, slaying the goblins was helpful, but that wasn't all there was to this. He was moving ahead, going forward steadily—on his way, she was certain, to becoming a great adventurer. And she got to see it from close-up.

It would be her special privilege to be the first—at least until he formed a party—to know about his adventures. Who knew? Maybe, just maybe, one day he would come back and tell her he'd slain a dragon.

I'd sure like to hear that tale! she thought, letting her pen dance across the page.

If the story looked like it would be a long one today, maybe she would make him some tea...

§

Two full cups of tea later, he set off out of town, still full of doubts.

He'd never believed for a moment that he would be promoted. Now he didn't know how he should feel about it.

There was surprise—but no happiness. No excitement—but also no pride. There was only a sense, a feeling: *The Guild has acknowledged me.*

The sun was hot, the sky vast and dizzyingly blue. It seemed a tremendous effort just to put one foot in front of the other and work his way through the hubbub of town.

He wondered if the roadway would grow sticky and take his footprints, but he pressed on. People stared and muttered, but he ignored them. He was thinking about goblins and about how to kill goblins.

In the end...

From start to finish, the battle had been like that Guild employee was pulling him along. He'd made many screwups, many miscalculations, and he'd done hardly anything worthy of the name of success. He could barely stand to think about it.

He'd lost or damaged a substantial amount of equipment. Used more tear gas bombs than necessary and damaged his shield beyond repair.

The Guild receptionist's eyes had widened at the story, and she had said something about increasing his reward, but still.

I will do better next time.

So that he didn't give her too much trouble.

So that he didn't give *her* too much worry.

Those thoughts welled up within him and then subsided again, like bubbles rising and bursting.

This is ridiculous.

She was not his older sister. Similar, yes, but not the same. The very idea was disrespectful to both his sister and Examiner.

Who would he be repaying if he did that?

What he was doing was hunting goblins.

It was not adventuring.

"Oh!"

The voice came unexpectedly. It was his old friend with the red hair, leaning against the fence and watching him approach. He realized he could see the farm in the distance, the town gate already far behind him.

I didn't realize I had walked so far.

Another mistake. If this had been a goblin's nest, it could have cost him his life.

"Welcome home! Did you just get back?"

She sounded like she'd been in the middle of work. She dusted off her hands and hopped over the fence in a way that made it seem clear, to him at least, that she had in fact been waiting there for quite some time.

"Yes."

To think she had been waiting for *him*, though—that would have been the height of vanity. He continued walking toward the farm, slowing just slightly as she jogged up beside him.

"S-so how'd it go…?" She looked at him anxiously.

Was I always…?

So much taller than her?

He didn't know. The Four-Cornered World seemed to be entirely things he didn't know.

He had a vague feeling that she might even have been taller than him five years ago.

"…I passed," he said quietly—and then, because he didn't quite believe it, he added, "it seems."

"Yes…!" She leaped into the air, her red hair rippling. She grabbed his muddy glove and shook it vigorously and bounced up and down almost like she was dancing. "That's great! That's amazing! Congratulations! You did it!"

"…I see." He hated that this was the only thing he could come up with.

Was it really amazing? Perhaps it was. There were adventurers who died as Porcelains or Obsidians. People who died when they threw themselves at things other than goblins.

He could not and did not think that he, who killed only goblins, was better than them. There must be as many adventurers more amazing than he as there were stars in the sky.

Nonetheless, as he watched his old friend jump up and down, he stayed silent and let her celebrate. He'd shot her down once when she was joyous, five years ago. That was more than enough for him.

Instead he said, "Your hair," as it rippled red in front of him when she waved his arm around. "It's grown."

"Huh? Oh—oh!" She suddenly seemed to realize what a scene she'd been making, because she let go of his hand and veritably jumped backward. Flushing with embarrassment, she ran the fingers of both hands through her hair. "Uh, y-yeah. A little, I mean. Yeah. A little. I guess it has grown a little."

To that he said only yes and nodded.

It was longer than five years before. But shorter than when they had been reunited.

Did he think it looked good like that? Yes, he did. Although he thought any length of hair would suit her.

So when she suggested timidly, "Maybe… Maybe I should cut it?" he fell silent.

"…"

For him, it was an impenetrable riddle. Was it right for him to say something that would dictate her appearance?

Even though he only really knew her as she had been five years before?

When the only thing he really knew how to do was kill goblins?

"……It's not bad the way it is now," he replied finally, choosing his words carefully. "But perhaps it would be good to cut it just a little bit."

"…I will!" she chirped.

I guess I wasn't mistaken. The young woman was beaming as brightly as when he'd told her he had passed his test.

She walked alongside him again, nodding to herself in affirmation, playing with her hair the way you would with a toy ring you won at a festival. Then she looked at him. "Hey…"

"What?"

"I saw when you took off your helmet before you left. Speaking of growing!"

He didn't know whether she meant he had grown taller or if she meant his hair. He didn't know, but on this last adventure, he had learned what to do when you did not know.

"…Is that so?"

"Yep. It sure is."

"I see."

"Uh-huh."

You simply asked, and the answer would come.

If you needed something, you simply had to speak of it.

The thought that there was something he could do besides goblin slaying made his heart ever so slightly lighter.

"I'll cut it for you," she said.

"...I see," he replied.

So the conversation went, meandering but steady.

They spoke of repairing the fence. Piling the rocks back up in the wall. How he would help when he had the chance.

They spoke of the animals. Of the earthquakes. Of the dwarf who had come looking to buy provisions.

They spoke of how the weather had changed day to day while he was out hunting goblins.

It's the same while I'm away killing goblins.

The world went on unchanged. It was simple, it was obvious—but, he thought, it was good. At least, if he killed goblins, the world would not change.

"All right! I'll bet you're hungry!" the girl said, twirling toward him as they reached the main house, her smile as bright as the sun. "I'll have food on the table in a jiffy— Oh, or you could wash up a little first, if you want."

"Yes."

"That doesn't tell me which one you want!" She giggled as she went into the kitchen.

Yes... At the very least...

The goblins were dead.

Goblin Slayer took a modicum of satisfaction in that fact as he pulled the door shut.

The *clack* as it closed seemed inordinately loud.

AFTERWORD

Hullo, Kumo Kagyu here!

Thanks for your patience with *Year One*, Volume 3. Thankfully, it's here now. *Phew!* I had the draft, but it just so happens that drafts don't turn themselves into books overnight.

Anyway, at least the book is in your hands, so that's a relief for me.

My thanks go out to Kento Sakaeda, who's handling the manga version, and Shingo Adachi, who did the illustrations for this volume.

I put my all into writing this book, so I would be overjoyed if you had fun with it.

So in this story, there were goblins, and Goblin Slayer had to slay them. The problem is, that's not the only thing going on in the world. There are lots of people doing lots of things, and there are many things that need to be done. That's how life is.

It's not easy to find people who will have hopes for you, who will help you and teach you. When you meet some, it's only natural to want to do well for them, even if you complain and moan and have to drag yourself every step of the way.

This book only made it to you with the aid of many, many people—including my readers and the support they've given me. They always have my thanks.

* * *

Speaking of!

Tens of thousands of years ago, the land lay in darkness after the sinking of the continent of Atlantis. This was before the revenge of Conan, hero of the Cimmerians, was complete.

Thulsa, later the great king and the object of Conan's vendetta, was still nothing more than one of the prominent priests of a powerful snake cult.

Conan, who had been traveling in quest of his vengeance, sneaked into the dark fortress on the occasion of a solar eclipse.

In the fortress, two warriors are engaged in a duel to the death in an effort to offer an immortal body to the king. At the moment the two great priests complete the ritual to transfer the king's heart into a new body:

"O Crom!"

The Cimmerian leaps forth with a bellow, his sword striking down one of the priests.

The king rises, his heart racing, and he lashes out with his crimson sword, seeking to destroy the barbarian. But Crom's steel and Conan's courage are not to be defeated by evil.

The king's sword shatters, his heart is struck through, and the whole deep chamber is plunged into darkness.

The other priest escapes, but what need is there to chase down an insect like him?

The castle crumbles away as the sun peeks out once more from behind the eclipse, and the song of Conan's victory rolls across the plains.

It will be fifty thousand years, in fact, before the king's heart is resurrected once again. And the name of the cult with the snake as its crest will be Gorgom…

That's the story I'd love to tell. What? I can't? Oh, all right.

Now that you've learned the truth of this terrifying myth, please make a sanity check.

If you succeed, you lose one point; if you fail, you lose 1d3 points. Schwarzenegger could do it!

Actually, I've always wanted to do a story about a rampaging lizardman barbarian. Smarts and courage and strength! Kicking monster ass, loving beautiful women, proud and badass and *let's go!*

Who knows? With enough support from all of you, maybe I'll get the chance someday. Certainly, everything else I'm doing now is thanks to all my supporters.

I've still got lots more books to send your way, starting with *Moscow 2160*. Plus, I think I might find time to watch *PANZER WORLD GALIENT: The Iron Crest*. Or maybe I'll check out *Ninja Assassin*, or *Troy*, or *Gunhed*! Maybe I'll even go catch the revival screening of *Gothicmade*.

Maybe I'll geek out over the new edition of *The Complete Conan the Barbarian* and Yoshihisa Tagami's *Fedayeen*.

Maybe I'll play the eerie fifth-edition RPG *Call of Cthulhu*.

Maybe I'll think about how much I love fantasy, and sagas, and robots, and fairy tales.

Listen, *Gunhed* is really good. I must've seen it dozens of times since I was a kid. The VHS version is great, and so is the DVD, the Blu-ray, the manga, the novel, the game books, the plastic models, and the fan guides. The point is, *Gunhed* is one of the greatest movies in my personal history. You should all see it.

You should also read Yoshihisa Tagami's work. And Conan.

Ninja Assassin is pretty good, too! The Wachowskis really know how to film some cinematic murder.

Hideyuki Furuhashi's *Black Rod* is something else I'm looking forward to—that's coming out in a new edition. Fwoo—boom!

So getting back on topic. *Just forget about all that.*

In Volume 4, I plan to do a story where goblins appear, and Goblin Slayer has to slay them. I'll put my all into writing it, so I would be thrilled if you kept reading!

See you next time!

HAVE YOU BEEN TURNED ON TO LIGHT NOVELS YET?

86—EIGHTY-SIX, VOL. 1–12

In truth, there is no such thing as a bloodless war. Beyond the fortified walls protecting the eighty-five Republic Sectors lies the "nonexistent" Eighty-Sixth Sector. The young men and women of this forsaken land are branded the Eighty-Six and, stripped of their humanity, pilot "unmanned" weapons into battle...

Manga adaptation available now!

WOLF & PARCHMENT, VOL. 1–7

The young man Col dreams of one day joining the holy clergy and departs on a journey from the bathhouse, Spice and Wolf. Winfiel Kingdom's prince has invited him to help correct the sins of the Church. But as his travels begin, Col discovers in his luggage a young girl with a wolf's ears and tail named Myuri, who stowed away for the ride!

Manga adaptation available now!

SOLO LEVELING, VOL. 1–8

E-rank hunter Jinwoo Sung has no money, no talent, and no prospects to speak of—and apparently, no luck, either! When he enters a hidden double dungeon one fateful day, he's abandoned by his party and left to die at the hands of some of the most horrific monsters he's ever encountered.

Comic adaptation available now!

THE SAGA OF TANYA THE EVIL, VOL. 1–12

Reborn as a destitute orphaned girl with nothing to her name but memories of a previous life, Tanya will do whatever it takes to survive, even if it means living life behind the barrel of a gun!

Manga adaptation available now!

SO I'M A SPIDER, SO WHAT?, VOL. 1–16

I used to be a normal high school girl, but in the blink of an eye, I woke up in a place I've never seen before and—and I was reborn as a spider?!

Manga adaptation available now!

OVERLORD, VOL. 1–16

When Momonga logs in one last time just to be there when the servers go dark, something happens—and suddenly, fantasy is reality. A rogues' gallery of fanatically devoted NPCs is ready to obey his every order, but the world Momonga now inhabits is not the one he remembers.

Manga adaptation available now!

VISIT YENPRESS.COM TO CHECK OUT ALL OUR TITLES AND. . .

GET YOUR YEN ON!